PORTAL TO LIBERTY

Printed in Australia

Cover design by Jessica Chaplin
Typeset by Mikayla Cairney

First printed July 2022
This edition first printed 2024

Paperback ISBN - 978-1-7637872-0-9
Ebook ISBN - 978-1-7637872-2-3

A catalogue record for this
book is available from the
National Library of Australia

ENTER PORTAL 1:

PORTAL TO LIBERTY

A. J. ELKSNIS

For Andrew and Dianne

Synopsis

The leader of the freedom fighters, Luke Palmer, has disappeared after a failed attempt to find his sister, Emma, who has been taken by slavers and sold to the Corporation.

Rachel Navara is a soldier. She and her brother, Rowan, were sent from Earth to Silica, to aid Luke and those resisting the militant group known as Sabre Company. In Luke's absence, Rachel must lead. And to her horror, she finds out what happened to those who could not escape the tyranny of corporate rule.

Lana is Professor Peter O'Conner's Augmented Human creation. While she was being rapidly grown, Lana was taught everything she needed to know through O'Conner's special neural connection program.

Once Lana reaches the developmental maturity of a twenty-four-year-old woman, her purpose is revealed. Professor O'Conner wants her to brave the unknown and venture into alternate realities. However, he knows Lana may want to go her own way and live a normal life.

But there is no time for Lana to take either path. Due to Professor O'Conner's involvement in aiding the forces led by Captain Henry Drake and his crew, Lana's home—everything and everybody she has ever known—is now under threat.

Four years after the liberation of Silica and its capital, Liberty, the escaped militant criminals known as Sabre Company have returned to exact retribution upon Rachel Navara and the Universal Community, who fought for freedom.

What begins as a game of cat-and-mouse soon becomes one of intrigue, as the identities of Sabre Company's infamous General Dennis Conroy and his informant within the Universal Community's Council are discovered. When Fiona Parker, Junior Council member and former freedom fighter, who served during the liberation of Silica, acts on her suspicions and finds those responsible for the death of her parents and countless others, she is captured. Her husband, Rowan, will do anything to bring her back.

Using her ability to dream of memories that are not her own, Rachel discovers the location of the hidden Sabre Company base and their plans to regain control.

Lana and Rachel join Captain Drake's team of Autonomous Machine soldiers to fight back before Sabre Company's plans kill millions of innocent people. Using grit, intelligence and Lana's ability to alter people's thoughts, they successfully foil Sabre Company's plans and capture its General, before he wreaks havoc on the entire galaxy.

Cast of Characters

IN ORDER OF APPEARANCE:

Rachel Navara – Rowan's sister; Sam's partner; long-time member of Hank's team of peace-keepers.

Luke Palmer – Liberty underground leader.

Rowan Navara – Rachel's brother; Fiona's partner; aspiring security advisor for the Universal Community Council.

Fiona Parker – Rowan's partner; she becomes a Junior Council member after surviving the nightmare that was Sabre Company occupation.

Captain Henry "Hank" Drake – Lex's father; Captain of the Black Bird.

Jolie – Medical Officer; Automated Machine.

Lincoln – High ranking leader among combat assigned Automated Machines.

Lana – Professor O'Conner's Augmented Human; the **future**—he hopes—of safe realm travel, and the pursuit of knowledge and insight from alternate realities.

Professor Peter O'Conner – Sam's father; Lana's creator.

Samantha O'Conner – Pete's daughter; Rachel's partner; scientist.

CHAPTER 1

03:00

You're listening to Universal Community News. Last year, two of our military's best operatives were sent in undercover to meet resistance leader, Luke Palmer. Many of our brave Great Migration settlers have established colonies on new planets. From small beginnings, towns have emerged. Harsh seasons have challenged the resolve of these new communities, but none have had to suffer military occupation. Through many years of toil, the people of the outer rim planet, Silica, built their own city. Now, the hard-working people of Liberty must fight—

Rachel slapped her hand down on the snooze button of her comms console. The radio signal came all the way from Earth, via satellite installations and trade stations. Rolling over, she snuggled into Luke, but he slipped away from her to sit on the edge of the bed.

'What's wrong?' she asked.

Luke stared at the floor. 'I have to go.'

Rachel propped herself on her elbow and rubbed her eyes. 'Where?'

'The Corporate Office of Government. I have a contact on the inside.'

'The COG? Luke, that's suicide.'

'She can get me in. I can access their files, find out what happened to my sister.'

'Luke, you can't trust—'

'I have to try.'

Rachel threw off the covers and swung out of bed to retrieve her clothes.

'When do we leave?' she said, pulling on her military issue slacks and a tank top.

'You're staying,' said Luke. 'Lead the resistance, as planned.'

'You can't infiltrate the COG alone.' Luke avoided Rachel's judgmental look.

'My contact has the guard shift changes,' he said. 'She'll shut down surveillance.'

'Luke, you *are* the resistance. These people need you.'

'They trust you, Rachel. They'll follow you.'

Luke covered her small hands with his. His skin was pale against her chocolate brown hue. He pushed a lock of her black hair behind her ear and kissed her forehead.

'I have to find her,' he said as he walked out of the room.

Rachel's radio alarm clicked back on. She slumped onto the bed, listening to Luke's footsteps recede down the corridor as he headed to the armoury.

Our hearts go out to the citizens of Silica and we honour those who will fight to protect them. To those facing combat today, we salute you.

Rachel wiped the tears from her eyes, stood, took a deep breath and shook her arms loose.

'You've got this, Rachel.' She took another steady breath. 'You've got this.'

05:00

Two kilometres north of Liberty Underground HQ

Rachel pressed her back against the graffiti-covered wall. It was sprayed with the people's slogan—*Freedom, Justice and Liberty*—coined by their leader, Luke Palmer. Every few seconds, clouds plumed from Rachel's lips. She edged towards the bottom of the steps that led to the four-lane highway. Factory buildings loomed dark and empty over what was once a busy district on the south side of Liberty. She peered through the darkness of early morning, scanning each direction. The highway was deserted. Overturned cars were pushed against the concrete barriers, burnt and stripped to their shells like empty tortoise homes.

Rachel signalled the all-clear. A single file line of over two dozen Silican citizens, students, miners and factory workers, carrying make-shift clubs, rifles and handguns, silently made their way along the highway.

Rowan Navara watched through the night vision scope of a sniper rifle, while his sister's team made their way towards the highway overpass. He'd been lying on his stomach for half an hour, scanning the streets leading to the four-lane road that would be the team's route.

Over the years, the sand had gradually returned to the city, like a great wave moving metres per season. It pressed into buildings until the windows burst, filling entire office floors with sand. The outer city was now covered, and a high ridge had formed along the financial district.

Rowan had taken position atop a dune. Wind swept sand over him. The rough granules against his skin reminded him of how much he had hated this planet when he and his sister had arrived.

Rowan had heard about illegal activities being conducted by the Corporate Factions, but had never imagined that they would be capable of taking over an entire colony. His sister had volunteered for the assignment. Given the level of danger she would be facing, Rowan joined as well to back her up.

Rachel started her career in law enforcement, but was soon drawn to the adventure of peacekeeping on other planets. On Rowan's recommendation, she had been recruited by Captain Henry Drake. Rowan had been a member of Hank's crew for years.

The crew was among the very few human Security Division forces allowed to engage in combat. Automated Machines were the way of the future, for the military and for all roles that required taking physical risks.

Rowan saw that Rachel's team was approaching the highway overpass. He scanned the lanes of fire-blackened cars above and spotted movement.

Rachel was about to separate her team into two flanking groups, when her brother's voice came over her comms.

'I've got movement,' he said.

Rachel held her fist to the side of her head, signalling her line of freedom fighters to halt.

Rowan flicked the scope magnifications, to see shadows moving between the cars. 'Abort! Get your team out of there.'

Rachel turned her group around. 'Mission abort. Return to HQ immediately.'

One of the younger students scanned the highway overpass. He saw an enemy soldier take aim. A harsh sound, like snapping bamboo, drowned his cry of warning.

Flashes of white shot out from the moving silhouettes atop of the overpass. The seventeen-year- old fell backwards into the arms of Fiona Parker, a new member of the group. She pulled him behind the cab of an overturned truck. Sparks flew from the rusted metal frame and crumbs of bitumen flew up from the road.

Despite the smoke and fires rising from the city, despite the starvation and the fighting that ensued on the streets, workers continued their long shifts in the central building of the Corporate Office of Government.

The workers were collating data on the enemy—the Universal Council—hacking their systems and feeding the information to the commanding General of Sabre Company.

The General was Dennis Conroy.

In the right wing of the COG building, General Conroy was undergoing the next phase of his plan—infiltration of the Universal Council. He knew it had to be him. He was skilled in deception and after undergoing surgery to change his face, all he would need was time and patience.

Laser heat cauterised his wound, binding the flesh along the incision line that ran beneath his collarbone and up around the back of his neck.

Doctor Kindred turned off the laser and hovered over Conroy, his thin lips widening into a pleased smile. Kindred wore a formal grey Sabre Company uniform beneath a bloodied surgical coat. The plastic of the coat squeaked and curled when the doctor leaned more closely to Conroy. His large, glassy eyes stared through thick-lensed, circular glasses.

'Oh, General,' he whispered excitedly, 'you look magnificent.'

Conroy shoved Kindred and he heaved himself groggily from the medical table.

'This had better… have been… worth it.' He leaned against a surgical wash basin. The polished steel panel before him reflected the tattoo on his arm—a sword crossed over a hammer. Conroy steeled himself before raising his head to inspect the unfamiliar face now grafted to his skull.

'Fine work, Doctor,' he said, pleasantly surprised.

Conroy looked over at the faceless body of a man lying on a table nearby. Whoever had found him had chosen well. The stranger's body shape and height were the same as Conroy's, with heavyset, wide shoulders.

'Your avatar's credentials are exactly what the Council will be looking for,' Doctor Kindred said. 'Your position is virtually assured.'

Conroy prodded his finger at the unfamiliar skin along his jaw.

'You've done well, Doctor,' he said. 'I've made arrangements for your new subject, as promised.'

'You… you have him?' Kindred salivated in anticipation. 'You have the leader of the resistance?'

'Send him to my second-in-command once you're done with him,' Conroy ordered, ignoring the doctor's shrill joy.

The comms speaker beeped and a woman's voice spoke. 'Sir, Palmer has arrived.'

'Good. Take him through.'

Doctor Kindred handed Conroy a grey business suit with a white shirt and silver tie.

'He is one persistent prick,' said Conroy, swaying slightly from the anaesthetic as he dressed. He tightened his tie against his throat. 'I'm going to enjoy this.'

Luke made his way along the thirteenth floor corridor of the COG building. The incessant sound of clicking and typing at computers began to recede as he arrived at the door to the communications room. He turned to the woman who had led him through all of the building's security.

'You've done enough,' he said. 'Get back to your workstation before somebody notices you're gone.'

The woman nodded nervously.

'Freedom, justice and liberty,' she whispered, before hurrying away down the corridor.

Luke used the key she had given him and locked the door behind himself. He took a console from his jacket pocket and connected it to the COG computer system. Then, he searched the database for his sister Emma. Like so many of his past attempts, the search bore no results, but a folder titled *Candidates* caught his eye. Luke opened it and found a subfolder titled *Elite*. He double clicked it. There were reports, photos and a folder of video logs. The videos were titled *Room 101*. Luke found and opened a video called *Emma Palmer*.

Luke's shoulders sank. He clenched his fists, his teeth grinding. There was no audio. It wasn't needed. Luke could see his sister's taut muscles, her head jerking back at every jolt of electrical current delivered through the chair in which she sat. There were sixteen video files with her name on them. They were time stamped on consecutive days.

Luke heard someone unlock the door. He pulled the pistol from his hip holster, ready to drop the first person to enter. The door opened and a small cylindrical canister rolled across the floor, then exploded. Luke covered his eyes, too late. Blinded by white light, he heard thudding boots approach him and fired in their direction. Something struck the side of his head, hard. Pain reverberated through his left ear and down his neck. He fell to the floor and blacked out.

Luke's vision returned for a few seconds. He saw a grey Sabre Company uniform. A pair of expensive leather shoes stepped close.

With a click of old knee joints, a man crouched beside him. 'Well done, girl. You've bagged the mighty leader.'

A woman's black heeled shoes stepped into the room.

Luke tried to lift himself from the floor, but couldn't. He fought the darkness clouding his eyes and listened to the murmurs of a voice he knew could only belong to Dennis Conroy.

'The doctor is ready for you.'

Rachel heard deep, pounding echoes coming from Rowan's position while her brother fired on the enemy. She spotted two unmanned drones flying across the highway at speed. Their spotlights beamed down, searching car wrecks before fixing on Rachel's group.

Rachel took a flash grenade from her utility belt and tossed it over the enemy's position. Shouts followed the bright burst of light, and the soldiers removed their night vision goggles and threw them to the ground. She took the rear, while her team ran back up the steps to the courtyard above the highway.

'Rowan, take out the drones!' Rachel called through her comms.

A few seconds later, she heard a shot ring out. The drone Rowan hit lost flight control and clipped the other drone on its descent, sending it hurtling towards Rowan. Rachel watched her brother judge the trajectory of the plummeting craft before disappearing into the nearest building for cover.

'Rachel, gimme a hand!'

Rachel stopped to help Fiona carry the wounded teenager up the steps to the courtyard, where a canvas stretcher was laid on the cigarette butt littered ground. They heard and felt the shuddering impact of the downed drone when it hit the building in front of them.

'Take him! Go!' Rachel shouted to the nearest people in her group. 'We'll hold them off!'

She looked up to see Rowan crash through a window overlooking the yard. His rifle clattered across the ground and he rolled to break his fall onto the pavement. His momentum sent him sliding across the broken glass on his chest. With a winded gasp, he picked himself up. The drone exploded in the building he had fallen from. Rowan pulled Fiona to the ground, shielding her with his body, while Rachel took cover on the stairs. Fire burst through the windows, showering Rowan's back with debris. When it was over, he helped Fiona to her feet and retrieved his gun from beneath the rubble.

Sabre Company troops appeared in the alleyway leading to the courtyard. Fiona took the handgun from her thigh holster, aimed and fired twice over Rowan's shoulder. One soldier fell to the ground but three more approached. Training her gun on them and firing, Fiona gripped Rowan's shoulder and pulled him along. He raised his rifle and sent a high velocity round through one soldier's chest. Two Liberty squad members ran past them, ducking away from the enemy's returning fire.

'Go!' Rachel shouted to Fiona and Rowan from the stairs.

The remaining SC soldier advanced, drawing a combat knife. Rachel blocked the inside of his knife hand and punched him in the face. Another soldier arrived at the bottom of the steps to the highway. Rachel grabbed the trooper in front of her and used him as a shield against the spray of bullets. One glanced off her arm and a splash of red hit the wall next to her. The soldier below fired an explosive shell, which hit the back of his comrade. Rachel's soldier shield exploded and she was thrown two metres. She lay on her back, gasping. As though underwater, she heard the dull thud of a trooper running up the steps. Rachel snatched the dead soldier's knife and rolled onto her shoulder, just in time to avoid the bullets pelting a line right beside her back. She threw the knife at her enemy and the blade disappeared into his left temple. He dropped to his knees, his rifle clattering onto the cement.

Rachel watched the soldier hit the pavement. She saw the resistance slogan on the wall beside the stairs to the highway. It was covered in battery fluid from the exploded Automated Machine soldier. She lay there for a moment, listening for the enemy. None came. Her comms beeped and she tapped the receiver.

Captain Henry Drake's voice came through. 'Rachel, our alien allies have offered assistance by allowing access to their technology. Their gear will allow us entry without being shot out of the sky.'

Rachel groaned as she picked herself up from the ground.

'What's your situation?' Hank said.

Rachel glanced back in the direction of the highway. 'Ambushed. Don't know how they knew we were coming.'

'Concentrate on holding your HQ. Help is on the way. Hank out.'

Rachel left the courtyard and ran to catch up with the rest of her team. Continuing through to the lower streets of the city, she soon reached the underground tunnel system, safe from Sabre Company forces.

CHAPTER 2

Samantha O'Conner selected a Miles Davis smooth jazz album and hit play on 'Take Five'. She pressed her hand against the glass of the stasis pod, leaning close to peer through the thick cloud of bio-matter. The liquid was accelerating the growth of the child sleeping inside.

'Lana,' she murmured.

Sam's father—Professor Peter O'Conner—looked up from his notes.

Sam's hand left a print on the condensation coating the glass pod. 'Mum's middle name.'

Pete paused for a moment, staring over his glasses at the dim figure floating in the pod. The child had reached the bodily maturity of an eight year old, and was currently taking in the English language through cerebral nodes dotted around her temples. Later she would receive mathematics, and after that virtual human interaction, to prepare her for waking life.

'Good choice,' he said. 'We'll call her Lana.'

The Human Augmentation project would practically run itself from here on. Learning programs were already scheduled for Lana's input. Robotic arms programmed to gently massage and stretch her developing limbs and muscles, gradually built and conditioned her body throughout her contained growth period.

The comms tone sounded an incoming transmission, and Henry Drake's voice came over a speaker in the room.

'Pete, my people are having a hard time figuring out this new toy you sent us.'

'Honestly, Hank...' Pete let out an impatient sigh. 'A child could use it.'

'We'll send you an instruction package,' Sam offered.

The aliens who had given Pete and his Genesis Lab the new technology were called the Kiyol. They were humanoid, friendly and a lot more advanced than humans.

'Thanks, Sam,' said Hank. 'I'll be paying a visit to Rachel soon. I'm sure she'll be interested to join your team once she hears what you have to offer.'

'I don't expect her to trust me immediately,' said Pete. 'We've all heard the rumours—Sabre Company spies infiltrating Universal Community Council.'

'We live in dangerous times,' Hank agreed. 'You'll be hearing from Rachel once we've liberated Silica.'

'I've heard about Rachel and Rowan Navara,' said Sam once the comms link with Hank was closed. She had watched a backstory segment about the brother and sister on a popular TV program called *Heroes of Our Time*. 'Is she... er... single?'

Pete smiled. 'I'll introduce you.'

Silica
Liberty Underground HQ

Rachel stirred from slumber and rolled from her side of the bed. Her hand slid along the beige mattress, searching out of habit for Luke's warmth. She felt only a cold, empty space. Her hand retreated beneath the blanket.

She listened to the murmurs of others preparing for another day of unease beneath the Sabre Company controlled city.

Responsibility encouraged Rachel's strength to return. She'd heard nothing from Luke. Scouts hadn't seen him, but they had received reports of somebody being moved to Room 101—the place all resistance fighters dreaded they would end up if captured.

Throwing a towel over her shoulder, Rachel stepped out of her quarters and headed down the dank, narrow corridor to the washroom.

The washroom was originally a single overhead shower and adjoining toilet, used by the workers who maintained the sewers. When the resistance moved in, they knocked a wall down, cleaned everything out and used the next corridor tunnel to channel water for two more overhead showers.

Rachel greeted a young couple sharing a spout, both of whom wore bruises and minor abrasions from their last assignment. She said good morning to an older couple, who were occupying another spout.

The older man, who was in his late fifties, was seated on an empty ammunition box. He was being sponged by his wife. He had lost both of his arms working in a car manufacturing plant outside of Liberty. He and his wife were now actively involved in fighting Sabre Company. The man nodded to Rachel with a smile and the others called out warm greetings.

'Sleep well, Rachel?' the man asked, watching her with concerned eyes. 'Rowan tells me you've been having bad dreams.'

Rachel dropped her clothes into a free tub.

'I slept well, thanks,' she lied. She saw a peach dress folded in the laundry tub.

'This is pretty. Whose is this?' she asked, admiring the design. Rachel turned to him when he didn't answer.

'It belonged to our niece,' said the man's wife. 'I... found it earlier and decided to wash it. She was abducted last year.

Poor girl lost her parents when she was young.' She paused when she saw Rachel's stone expression. 'We'd been taking care of her.' She swallowed through rising guilt. 'We were home when they took her.'

Her husband shrugged, holding out his arm stubs. 'I couldn't stop them.'

Rachel leaned back on the clothes bench. The sadness these two people held hit her like a wave.

'We'll find her,' she said. She held the defeated gaze of the husband and wife in turn. 'The others as well. *We'll find them,* all of them.'

'I think I speak for all of us when I say we trust you, Rachel,' the man said. 'You and your Universal Community will free this city.'

Rachel felt everyone in the room watching her. Their trust and hope weighed heavily on her shoulders.

Chatter echoed through the corridors. The voices of the afternoon shift drifted from the mess hall. They didn't complain about the meagre rations that barely filled their stomachs. They spoke of old times, before the corporations, before the rich—exiled from the Universal Community—came to Silica and introduced radical monetary gain.

Rachel pushed her tin plate aside, crossed her arms and rested her head. She closed her eyes and listened to the intermittent drops of water falling into rusted buckets.

Thoughts of responsibility and expectation weighed on her mind. We'll find them, she had said to that husband and wife. Rachel wavered between trust in her own capabilities and annoyance with herself for making such a naïve promise.

'Rachel,' came a voice from her comms. 'Captain Drake says he's coming in.'

'*Copy that.*' Rachel stood and straightened her posture. 'Wait, coming in?'

A sphere of rippling mercury expanded across the rubber-matted floor in front of her. Rachel watched, amazed, as it retracted and disappeared. Henry Drake stood in its place, flanked by two UC soldiers who were dressed in urban camouflage uniform.

'What the deuce?' Rachel had pulled the pistol from her hip holster. 'Hank, how did—'

Hank held up one finger indicating he needed a moment. He braced himself against a table while pressing his lips firmly together, as though he were trying not to vomit. Hank had only tested the device a few times and every time, he emerged on the other side of the trip feeling nauseous.

Given his experience fighting in extreme g-force aerial battles, he couldn't understand his body's reaction. All he felt like he was doing was stepping through a big shiny ball.

Hank breathed and lowered his finger. 'Teleportation,' he replied, and showed her the slim console that had opened the mercury sphere.

'So, this is the gear you were talking about,' Rachel said, studying the alien technology her Captain held in his hand.

'The Kiyol gave some devices to Peter O'Conner, a professor friend of mine.' Hank was still blinking, his eyes adjusting to the dark in the mess hall after the bright light of teleportation.

'Pete traded some of his nanotech.'

'O'Conner…' Rachel recognised the name immediately.

'You've heard of him?'

'Of course. He's world-renowned for… what he does. Bit of a hermit, I've heard.' Hank laughed, nodding.

'Pete wouldn't leave his lab to save his life.' He turned his wrist, inspecting the slender carbon-plating cover of the console. 'He calls these Shifters. There's a lot more to them than teleportation. They can replicate matter, open portals to… I dunno, Pete said something about alternate universes.' Hank skimmed the top of his greying, short-cropped hair with his hand. 'It all went right over my head.' He slapped a hand down on the shoulder of the man next to him and nodded to the other female officer. 'This is Unit 9 and Unit 105. 9 is one of the Branner Factory's original Automated Machines. He'll be assisting you with command. 105 is a medic.'

'Excellent,' Rachel shook their hands. 'Glad to have you.'

'Pleasure to be here.'

Rachel tried not to stare at 9's perfect human appearance. *Perfection,* she thought, *the only visual distinction separating Automated Machine soldiers from humans.* 9's face was symmetrical, handsome, with no skin blemishes or wrinkles, though he looked to be around thirty years old.

Rachel hadn't seen many AM units, apart from the Sabre Company soldiers. They all wore combat helmets.

Rachel understood that every AM unit was unique in appearance, like the Terracotta Warriors of China. Their designs covered all ethnicities, as well as nationalities, for speech variation. All AM units were athletic in build, but they varied in height. The medic, Unit 105, was particularly petite.

'Pete wanted me to give you a job offer,' said Hank. 'He wants you and Rowan to contact him, once all of this is done—some "Special Project" he's putting a team together for.'

'He asked for us?'

Rachel was flattered. Professor O'Conner was one of the greatest minds in genetic engineering and nanotechnology innovation. She couldn't imagine why a brilliant man like him would want her help, but she welcomed the thought of leaving combat. Maybe the Professor just needed some muscle. Security would be a nice change of pace. Relaxing compared to this… this war.

'You two go ahead and introduce yourselves to the others,' Hank ordered the two AM units. 'So… how are your people holding up?'

Rachel motioned for him to sit. 'We were making progress. Then we got ambushed… and Luke has disappeared.'

'That can't be good for morale.'

Hank didn't know about Luke and Rachel's relationship. Rachel had asked Rowan to keep it that way, so it didn't end up in Hank's reports.

'These people have learnt to adapt,' she said. 'But to be honest, sir, we need help—fast. We show our faces top side and we're intercepted by coordinated SC forces. They have eyes everywhere.'

Hank glanced to the door leading to the corridor outside. 'You suspect a mole?' Rachel shook her head. 'Impossible. I know these people. They're committed.'

Hank turned his head to one side. 'Fiona Parker comes from a Faction family. Can you trust her?'

Rachel watched the doorway. 'Fiona's parents were against Conroy. They were executed by his soldiers in their own home. She had nowhere else to go. Yes, I trust her.'

'Then you won't mind if I talk to her?'

'Talk to anyone you like.'

Hank crossed his arms over his broad chest. He opened his mouth to advise Rachel to be mindful, but decided to trust her judgement.

Rachel nodded to the console on Hank's wrist. 'Can that teleport the numbers we need to take the city?'

Hank nodded. 'Our forces will be ready in two days.' He saw the pain in Rachel's expression. The mission—the conflict—had changed her. She had entered military service to help maintain peace and to protect the Universal Community. Now, Hank saw a woman faced with a very grim reality. The enemy had taken control of an entire city of people. And the people were dying more quickly than Rachel could save them. Though Hank could imagine the strain she was under, he knew Rachel had developed the kind of strength only a commander could possess, to do what needed to be done.

'You and Rowan must find us prime entry locations,' he said. 'I'll bring the cavalry as soon as you're set.'

'I have some in mind.' Rachel stared at the space across from her that Luke always sat, now occupied by her captain. 'We'll have the coordinates ready within the week.'

Hank was trying to read Rachel's distant stare. 'Something else?'

'We've received reports that workers in the COG building are disappearing.' Hank didn't offer any explanation. His expression was grave.

Rachel met his gaze. 'When we do this, none of the Sabre Company leaders can escape. Everybody involved in the enslavement of these people must be held accountable.'

Luke woke to the sickening smell of chlorine. He blinked into the harsh light, trying to discern his surroundings. When he felt that his wrists were tied, Luke's adrenaline began to rise. He tried to kick, but his legs were bound as well. He turned to see who was pushing his wheelchair, but his vision was unclear. He couldn't make out their face.

'Who are you? Where are you taking…'

When Luke's vision cleared, his eyes widened in horror. He was passing room after room of transparent cells. Young men and women, tied down on beds, lay motionless. Faeces were smeared on the walls of a cell further on. *FAILED* was written in permanent marker on it. Two cells were blackened. *FAILED* was barely visible on their sooted glass. The sliding doors to these cells were open and Luke could smell charcoal and burnt flesh.

A dull thud sounded ahead. Rubber squeaked as Luke's chair stopped.

'Say hello to your sister,' came the dispassionate voice of the woman who had guided him through COG security and presented him to Dennis Conroy.

Luke's eyes turned to the cell on his left, where the thumping was coming from. A prisoner was repeatedly banging her forehead against the wall. Blood trickled between her blank eyes.

'Emma!' Luke screamed, straining in his chair. He jerked his head back in an attempt to strike his betrayer, but she stepped away. The sound of boots drew close and Luke was pushed into a dark room at the end of the corridor. A large steel chair was bolted to the centre of floor, illuminated by a low hanging globe. Wires dangled from a leather skullcap that was suspended from the ceiling.

'Welcome, Mr Palmer.'

A voice came from the shadows. A man stepped into the light. He pulled a pair of long rubber gloves up to his elbows. The light grey military uniform he wore was clean beneath the shine of a clear plastic surgical coat.

'It is a pleasure to finally meet the rebel leader of Liberty's scum.' The door to Room 101 closed and its lock bolt slid firmly into place.

CHAPTER 3

Lana's eyes darted back and forth beneath their lids. Her chest rose and fell steadily. In her mind, she was running between the ancient redwood trees of Muir Woods. The leads connected to her temples fed into a computer console beside her bed.

'An intelligent person can, for example, commit volumes of historical texts to memory and then recite the information by heart before an audience,' said her teacher, who was floating beside her. He kept pace with his student, his effort nil, as he was a nontangible computer program, one of many from a custom selection of voices and appearances. Lana usually chose this particular teacher because she liked his accent. His lean build and chiselled jaw were also pleasant to the eye.

'Impressive as this skill of retaining knowledge is, such a quality in a person is rendered useless in the absence of emotional intelligence.'

Lana somersaulted over a virtual log, landed nimbly and continued on. The noon sun beamed through the canopy, lighting the perfectly vertical trunks of the ancient redwoods. The program she was in seemed so real. Lana's brain was telling her senses that the air was cool and damp.

Lana was startled when her teacher hovered through a wide tree trunk. His database selected a quote from Richard Hofstadter: 'Intellect is the critical, creative and contemplative side of the mind. Intelligence seeks to grasp, manipulate, re-order, adjust. Intellect examines, ponders, wonders, theorises, criticises, imagines.'

Lana remembered something her real-life professor had told her. She stated it so that the computer recognised her understanding of the subject. 'Possessing emotional intelligence lends greater attention to ethics and moral values,' she said, ducking under a virtual moss-covered branch before hurtling herself over a fallen tree. 'One has greater awareness of consequence because it is internal. You are your own counsel.'

'Very good,' the teacher said. 'One cannot escape one's self. Now, I'm afraid the hour is approaching seven. Time to wake up.'

The program ended and the alarm clock beside Lana's head beeped loudly until she turned it off. Lana removed the temple leads and pulled off her bed covers, rubbing her eyes. With a yawn, she looked at her wall covered with postcards from Rachel, places on Earth Lana wanted to visit eventually—cities, beaches and monuments. She had photos mounted as well, grouped into four large spreads. They were organised according to her birthdays, from the moment she became conscious and aware. Her body aged four years per single year. After two years in a rapid growth pod and four years awake, Lana had reached the developmental maturity of a twenty-four-year-old. She turned to her plush red panda toy and pressed her nose into its shiny plastic nose.

'Morning,' she said to it.

Lana rolled and dropped over the edge of her bed. She landed on the floor on her hands and feet, her body stretched straight, and began her morning push-ups. After completing twenty, Lana hopped up from the floor and changed into her gym clothes. As she walked by her photos, she observed her younger self grow older. Lana stopped and looked from her most recent photos to the mirror on her wardrobe door. She saw herself as she would always be. By Professor O'Conner's design, Lana would not age another day. She was now, according to her regenerative cell data, immortal. Lana considered her serious brow, her cautious eyes. *Whoever I came from must be… Spanish maybe?* she thought. *I wonder if I'll ever get to meet them.*

The heating system hummed as it raised the temperature according to Lana's preference. As she descended her loft, which overlooked the gymnasium floor, motion detectors triggered the overhead lights. They flickered as Lana went through her upper and lower body stretches on the mats.

'Music,' she commanded. 'Miles Davis. Take Five.' The track played through wall-mounted speakers and Lana felt the rhythm she needed to start her workout awaken.

After completing exercises that targeted her core muscles, the kitchen staff arrived with Lana's breakfast. As usual, the AM unit who served her stayed to chat while she ate.

'The Press is coming here?' Lana said to the unit, her mouth full of banana fritters. She watched for the AM's reaction to her error in etiquette.

'The whole world will be watching,' the AM unit responded politely. Lana chewed noisily for good measure.

The unit cleared her throat—an action which AMs didn't need to do—and cocked her head slightly, raising an eyebrow. It was a perfectly replicated response.

Fascinating, thought Lana, after bidding the girl a good day. She might try something less subtle next time, like answering the door naked.

From what Lana understood, all AM units were essentially actors. They were artificially intelligent beings, but they were only as intelligent as the humans who had programmed them. And AM programming was thorough and organised, to ensure that all of the information AM units needed to interact with people was built into their electronic brains. The old notion that robots were rigid, monotone-speaking tin heads was now laughed at as a joke. But AM units could only act on their programming, which meant they couldn't harm people, unless the people who programmed them intended harm. And when an AM unit was harmed, she would react to the receptors under her skin the same way a human would. She would even cry out if wounded, so that fellow soldiers would come to aid her.

Lana lay down on the matted floor to finish her stretches. After feeling suitably limber, Lana circled the gym at a jog, leaping over the pommel horse at the edge of the mats. When she came around to the stairs leading to the roof, she ran up them, lifting her knees high.

Lana passed through the door at the top and entered the snowsuit room. She pulled on a pair of boots and grabbed a pair of goggles, before opening the door to the freezing outside air of Glacier II. The wind swirled and she could tell that a storm was brewing. She ascended the stairs curving around to the rooftop walkway, to find Hodge Franko, Head of Security, leaning on the handrail and watching the snow blowing over the mountain ridge.

'Sup, Hodge?'

Cigar smoke blew from between Hodge's lips as he turned. 'Huh?' He had been deep in thought and hadn't seen her coming.

Lana noticed the man's suit was covered in white.

'Dude, how long have you been up here?' Leaning next to him, she placed a glove on her left hand while holding the right glove between her teeth.

Hodge ignored the question, shaking his head in disapproval of Lana's lack of warm clothing.

The wind blew hard and Lana thought she heard Hodge say he missed his family. 'Why don't you give them a call?'

'You must have read my mind,' Hodge joked, smiling ruefully.

As Lana put on her goggles, she wondered who would take a job out on Glacier II if they had somebody back home who cared about them. She knew Hodge to be a private soul, friendly, happy to joke around with now and then, but he never spoke about his family. Until now, Lana hadn't known Hodge had a family waiting for him.

'They're doing fine without me.' He smiled and slapped Lana on the shoulder. 'Thanks for your concern.' He leaned close. 'Don't go tellin' anyone about how I am. The crew'll never respect an old man who can't keep it together.'

Lana smiled, always amused whenever Hodge made himself sound like a captain of a ship. Lana mimed zipping her lips. And then she unzipped. 'Call them, Hodge.'

The man puffed on his cigar.

'I will,' he said. 'Go on now. Do your laps.'

Lana stepped away and jogged on the spot, turning while she prepared for her run to look back at the old man. Hodge had pulled his right hand free from his snow glove and was now scratching at the grey and white flecks peppering his thick black beard. Lana heard him swear at the biting cold. She took off, running close to the rail so she could look down the slope of the snow- covered mountain. Over the past week, the snow had become purple, coloured by the Parabola Light Band that stretched across the sky, visible in the light of day. Lana gazed up at it and admired its bright hue while she ran. She recalled the Professor telling her some years ago that the band was going to pass through Glacier II and continue its long journey until its energy eventually dissipated.

'Wind's pickin' up, girl,' Hodge called to her. 'Let's head below before it carries us off.'

Lana gave Hodge a parting salute and the snow swirled between her legs, as she leaned into the wind pushing against her chest. Her long ponytail whipped behind her as she increased her speed, her boots pounding the steel grates of the raised walkway.

As she descended the stairs to the snow room, a gust of icy wind followed her through the door. She hummed the melody of 'Take Five'. She had known it since the first moment that she'd had a memory. It always reminded her of childhood. All two years of it.

It wasn't a great disadvantage, having such a short time to grow up. Lana was still a child when she came out of stasis. She played with toys, and with virtual children in virtual spaces. All of the adults found time to play with her too. Hide-and-go-seek was Lana's favourite game. And as far as developmental learning, Lana was surrounded by people who could relate their own life experiences to her, by using virtual programs that represented where and when these experiences occurred. Although her childhood had been brief, she would always think of it as a time of nurture. Her family, and somehow even the frozen moon they called home, provided the building blocks for her emotional intelligence.

Lana took off her boots and goggles and made her way down the stairs to the gymnasium floor.

'Morning, Lana,' Rachel greeted her from the floor.

'Hey Rachel. Wow!' Lana exclaimed, stopping before the last five steps. 'You changed your hair.'

'You like it?' Rachel's back and sides were cropped short, but her fringe was long. Her hair was no longer black, but blue with a silver sheen. Her fringe was brushed back in layered waves.

'Awesome,' Lana said.

'Thanks.' Rachel saw snow falling from Lana's shoulders and guessed she had come from running her laps. 'Are you ready for more combat training?'

Lana shot a serious look at Rachel, a cocky smile parting her lips. 'Are you?'

'Oh...' Rachel slowly lowered her hand towards the berretta holstered on her thigh. 'So, it's like that, is it?' She whipped the handgun free and fired twice at Lana.

Lana dove from her step and performed a breakfall roll. The plastic-cased water projectiles Rachel had fired splattered against the handrail.

Rachel circled the pommel horse as Lana used it for cover, yelping when her feet flew out from under of her.

Lana had tugged the gym mat hard. She jumped onto the horse and dropped down on top of Rachel before she could fire a shot. Lana took hold of Rachel's sides and used the momentum of her fall to roll and swing her friend, throwing her to the next mat.

Rachel rolled to her feet and aimed the gun at Lana. But she felt that the berretta weighed less and saw Lana holding the clip of water rounds.

'Huh,' Rachel grunted, her long fringe falling over the left side of her face. She smiled, impressed with Lana's dexterous moves.

Lana handed back the clip. 'So, big plans tonight?'

The two of them walked to the back of the gym. Rachel activated the beam of the holographic projector to bring up a set of targets, thirty feet away from where she and Lana stood.

'We'll have to postpone till we get settled in San Francisco.' Rachel unlocked a cabinet of P90 assault rifles and handed one to Lana.

'Your first anniversary. It seems like you guys have been together longer than that.'

Lana felt the weight of the assault rifle. It was the equivalent of a real P90 loaded with live ammunition. The one she held only activated a laser that interacted with holographic targets. She assumed the firing stance that Rachel had taught her the previous day. Today, the targets weren't going to stay still.

Lana tracked and fired on each. Pulling the trigger activated a speaker and a vibrating mechanism built into the training weapon. It made the sound a real P90 would make at a realistic volume and reverberated the same amount when fired. After missing the first two targets, she paused and concentrated on her breathing. When she resumed, Lana hit every target, one after the other.

Rachel gave helpful pointers over the two-hour lesson. She timed Lana's reloading, pushing her to resume fire more quickly.

Lana's muscles were stiffening, so she stopped to roll her shoulders. 'Rache, you don't talk about it much,' she said, thoughtfully, 'about what happened on Silica.'

Rachel busied herself with randomising the movement of the next set of targets.

'The Professor will tell you,' she said without emotion. 'I think it's in today's set of lessons.'

'I know you saw some terrible things,' said Lana. 'And I know you don't want to remember them…'

'I think that's enough for today,' Rachel said. She turned the target program off and took the P90 from Lana, packing it away into its locker.

Lana gently placed her hand on Rachel's shoulder. 'Rache… I want to understand what happened to you.'

'We failed,' said Rachel. She met Lana's gaze. 'I failed. I made those people a promise…'

As Rachel spoke, Lana started to feel lightheaded and increasingly entranced by what Rachel was telling her. She was falling into Rachel's mind, into her memory, so deeply that she could see everything from Rachel's perspective.

Automated Machine soldiers under Henry Drake's command were advancing towards an enormous building that had large black letters mounted high above the entrance. The first letter of 'Corporate Office of Government' was hanging askew. Fire plumed from the fifth floor of the left wing. It had lit the floor above it.

Rachel identified the location of the fire as the medical section of the COG. She had expected that key sections would be destroyed during Sabre Company's retreat, to hide evidence of what the Corporation had been doing to Silica. But she hadn't received any intelligence on what secrets the medical section held.

When machine gunfire pelted the AM units in front of them, she and Hank took cover in the building. Two of their units dropped and didn't move. Another used her fallen soldiers as cover, having sustained damage to both of her legs.

'Frag out!' Hank shouted, tossing a fragmentation grenade over his head.

The floor shook and shrapnel stabbed into the walls and ceiling. The machine gunfire stopped and Rachel took point all the way to the stairwell. She signalled for the AM units to climb. Just as she was about to follow, a horrible stench filled her nostrils. It smelt like burnt meat that had been left out for days. Rachel found a door that led to descending stairs. She signalled for Hank to follow. They used the torches on their assault rifles to light the way down.

They soon found themselves in an underground motor pool. The cars and vans were charred shells. The support pillars were pitch black and the ceiling had been darkened by flames.

Rachel stepped down and almost lost her footing. She scanned the ground with her torch. Behind her, Hank gagged. He turned abruptly and vomited on the steps.

The blue hue of Rachel's torch shone slowly across the thousand square metre motor pool. It was a sea of burnt clothing on scorched flesh and skeletons. Rachel was standing knee deep in the remains of workers.

Lana's vision returned to her current perspective. Her head jerked back as though invisible wires connecting her mind to Rachel's had been ripped out. With that sudden severing, Lana collapsed.

CHAPTER 4

Lana's vision was blurry. As she woke, she could hear Rachel speaking to her.

'She's coming around,' said Rachel.

'Lana, can you hear me?'

Lana recognised another voice. It was the AM unit, Jolie. Jolie had been given a name to replace her number—105—after the liberation of Silica. She and Lincoln, previously known as Unit 9, had both achieved military ranks. Jolie was now Chief Medical Officer and Lincoln had been granted the rank of Captain.

'Jolie?' Lana murmured. Her vision cleared. She was looking up at the AM unit's red hair. Jolie had it tied back into a ponytail, but with a stylish rise from her forehead. 'What are you doing up here?'

'Lana, you collapsed,' said Jolie. 'Your blood sugar levels are fine, but I recommend you take it easy today.'

'Rachel, Jolie, what's going on?' Professor Peter O'Conner said. His concern turned to shock when he saw Lana sitting on the floor. 'Lana! What happened?'

'She fainted,' said Jolie. 'She's fine now.'

'Lana, I need to go now,' said Rachel, still kneeling down beside her like a concerned sister. 'I have a Realm assignment.

Are you gonna be all right?'

'I'll be fine.' Lana took Rachel's arm, stopping her. 'I saw… the motor pool.'

'You… how?'

'I don't know. Rachel, that was horrible. How are you not a basket case after seeing that?'

Her friend became still, her expression blank. Lana saw only a subtle press from Rachel's bottom lip. Then, she finally spoke.

'I have to go.' She stood and walked to the elevator.

Lana opened her mouth, but Jolie held up her hand, signalling her to leave Rachel be. Jolie followed Rachel and the elevator door closed behind her.

'You told her about the COG motor pool?' Jolie asked in a parental tone, as they descended.

'No,' said Rachel, still perplexed by Lana's mysterious insight. 'I told her we stormed the place. I didn't tell her anything about what we found.'

Jolie's posture straightened and her brow furrowed. 'I spoke with the psychologist I recommended to you. I asked him how the two of you had been getting along these past years.' She watched Rachel turn away and lean on the wall. 'He said he'd given up trying to contact you. He said you never had a session with him. Who did you go and see instead?'

Rachel remained silent.

'You didn't see anyone,' Jolie deduced.

'I am dealing with it my own way,' Rachel replied.

Jolie detected her friend's defensive tone and decided not to push. 'We're here, if your way needs support.'

'This is Meg Green reporting to you from what was once a core drilling and research facility, deep beneath the surface of Glacier II. This frozen planet will disappear within the wave of the light band, as it travels through this solar system. As you can see, nobody here intends to stick around when that happens.'

The camera operator followed Meg along the corridors of the Genesis Lab research facility, stepping around boxes of computer and lab equipment.

'The coring project to retrieve ice from deep inside Glacier II was completed ten years ago. This facility has since been converted into a research facility. It is currently home to Professor Peter O'Conner's team of scientists. We will now discover what the team has been working on in secret, here in the Genesis Lab.' Meg waited until the camera was turned off before knocking on a door to Samantha O'Conner's office.

Sam opened the door, holding a cinnamon donut. She was pleased to see the famous reporter standing outside her office.

'Hi, I'm Meg Green from UC News. You must be Dr Samantha O'Conner.'

'That's me.' Sam dropped her donut on a plate beside her computer and wiped her hands with a sanitary towel. 'Let me show you to the briefing room.' She stepped back into her office to take her mug of tea. 'So, you're here for the "Great Reveal".'

'The presentation, yes,' Meg smiled at Sam's theatrical spin. 'I was told your father won't be attending the briefing.'

'Charlie will be holding the presentation on my father's behalf.'

'Dr Charles Bryant? I see. And why is that?'

'Charlie enjoys public speaking. My father doesn't.'

Meg followed Sam along the corridor, noting the increasing number of boxes and crates crowding the walkway. 'Where will you be moving to?'

'Somewhere warm,' she said, thankfully. 'For security reasons, I can't say where.'

Professor O'Conner paced slowly around the holographic displays in the centre of the gymnasium. His single pupil, Lana, listened while balancing on the pommel horse.

'Should you be doing that?' Pete asked, concerned. 'You were unconscious a little while ago.' Lana's thoughts were still troubled by Rachel's abrupt departure.

'I'll be fine.'

Pete nodded, but kept his eye on her. He hit play on the holo-display, so that images would come up as he spoke. 'Following the Great Migration from Earth, the Universal Community was established as our new society. All people, everywhere, now belonged to one unified community.'

Lana followed the chronological sequence of events her teacher spoke of, committing to memory every detail he described.

'The first few years of space exploration saw colonies spreading to remote planets, across many habitable systems.'

A computer-generated animation played out a digital portrayal of transport ships and cruisers entering unfamiliar star systems. Colony vessels dove into a planet's atmosphere and landed like migrating birds on vast open fields, with breathtaking mountain landscapes.

Leaning forward over the pommel horse, her arms taking the full weight of her body, Lana let her legs drop to either side. Then she performed an inverted split position, with her toes touching the padded wooden beam. She tensed her abdominal muscles and lifted her buttocks to straighten her back.

Her lesson continued. 'The unified peace agreement was made possible by the Wealth Sacrifice and Redistribution Initiative, proposed by Maria Adams. Within one year of the WSRI, the tax sustained Provision System was put into effect. The new system provided a quality of life that people had never known before.'

'No more poverty, no more scarcity, no more indignity. Everybody was provided with the basic necessities to live a healthy life.'

Lana stood, then bowed. Leading with her right shoulder, she swung both arms over her head. Her legs followed, propelling her into a cartwheel flip to land on the padded gym floor.

The next holo-displays showed security footage and photographs of different people Lana recognised from Earth history. The prominent figures, now aged, had belonged to governments and corporations.

The Professor's voice turned grave. 'However, for some citizens, having enough was not enough.

'Many wealthy people refused to contribute to the WSRI and removed themselves from our society: corporate executives, Mafia families of various nationalities, royalty, wealthy men and women who did not want to contribute to the Universal Community. These people became society's outcasts.'

Photos accumulated on the display. Lana settled herself on the floor, crossed her legs and stretched out her arm muscles. She counted almost two dozen individuals from the holo-display under the title *Outcasts*.

'Groups of these outcasts sought refuge on Silica, an outer-rim planet. At the time, Silica's population consisted of a small community of two thousand farmers and mechanical engineers. The wealthy outcasts settled outside of the existing communities, but soon approached the inhabitants to establish trade.

'Two generations later, the numbers of the outcasts had grown, due to intermarriage with the existing Silican communities.

'Family Factions began to form. Each Faction elected a leader, who was chosen based on seniority and wealth.

'The Faction leaders became bitter towards the Universal Council, due to constant public ridicule through media, documentaries and film adaptations that described the separation between the rich and us—the economically and environmentally sustainable majority.

'Historically, the Factions had become a disgrace to humanity.'

Photos of the four Faction leaders were displayed and faded into multiple portrait photos, indicating the members of each Faction.

'The Faction leaders decreed that all citizens of Silica were prohibited from leaving the planet and all incoming transports were refused entry into their zone.

'Industry grew over the years. Banks loaned money to workers. People built homes, raised families and bought whatever their social construct demanded of them.

'The UC security division sent undercover operatives to monitor developments on Silica. They soon discovered that factories were being built, and that the majority of the workers were the first settlers of Silica. But security was too tight for our people to get into the factories. We had no idea what they were manufacturing.

'Factions began to fight one another for control of the economy. Smaller factions were swallowed by bigger factions until there was no distinguishable group left.

'The rich had become outcasts. But over the course of two generations, they had built a city.

'Soon their Factions became one establishment, one overruling institution. They became a Corporation.'

CHAPTER 5

Chesh, the pilot of the Space Cruiser, Black Bird, munched a spoonful of cereal. Resting one on top of the other, her boots waved from side to side while she watched *Jungle Book* on the monitor screen. Her favourite character was singing his song, 'The Bare Necessities'.

Hearing clanging on the metal steps at the rear of the two-seater cockpit, she swallowed. 'Hey, Cap.'

'Good morning.' Captain Henry Drake leaned over her to check the coordinates panel. He tapped at the route Chesh had set. 'We'll need to come around wide,' he said, and readjusted the trajectory. 'Pete says there's some kind of energy wave passing through Glacier II's orbit.'

'I know.' Chesh watched Mowgli dance with Baloo.

'Then why did you have us flying right through it?'

'Because the wave is a big ol' curve. They call it the Parabola Light Band. We'll make it through the middle easy and cut down on flight time.'

'Sounds too close. It could suck us in.'

'It's not gonna suck us in.' Chesh finished her cereal and leaned back in the chair to drink the sweet marshmallow flavoured milk. 'It's almost certainly...' She swallowed and wiped her mouth with the back of her hand. 'Not gonna suck us in.'

Hank hesitated before reprograming the flight path to Chesh's original settings. 'Turn off your movie. We've got a briefing with the Council.'

Glacier II

Sam's voice came through the gym comms speaker. 'Just letting you know, Charlie will start his presentation in thirty minutes.'

'Thanks Sam,' Pete replied absently. 'Keep me updated on how it's received.'

In the splits position, Lana reached over to hold her left foot. 'Professor?'

'Yes, Lana?'

'Who are my parents?'

Pete was caught by surprise, but retained his composure. Deciding to mask his unease about the subject by feigning annoyance, he turned slowly and gave Lana a quizzical look.

'Lana, you had me convinced that you were taking in your lesson this whole time.'

'I am.' Lana tapped a finger against her temple. 'A multitasking brain doesn't settle for just one train of thought. There's a whole station of other trains running,' she muttered the last of her analogy, while her teacher's expression became impatient. 'We can talk about it later.'

'No, no. You're right. It's time you knew.' Pete quickly dropped the act, knowing full well his responsibility as her creator. 'Your parents were chosen based on their epigenetic history. They weren't required to provide their names. They passed the requirements that...' Pete paused for a moment. 'Sorry, Lana. The origin of your DNA is not a very warm story.'

'I was a test tube baby, I know. I was just wondering who the donors were,' she said, surprised at how natural it felt to say "the donors".

'Your mother was from the Czech Republic and your father was from Spain. The creation process, bringing you up as one of the family…' Pete hated it when he couldn't come up with more tender words during heartfelt moments. 'That was your beginning, the beginning of what we hope will be, for you, a beautiful and rich life.' Sometimes the right words did come.

'Why did you create me?'

Pete left the holo-console and sat on the gym mat next to Lana. 'My work with Shifter technology requires specially trained people to go to potentially hazardous places. I didn't want to send AM units. I wanted to send people who could experience these places and be affected by them.

'To combat the potential dangers of these places, I wanted whoever went to go prepared. Lana, I created you solely to be a part of something scientifically profound. However, I was prepared—and still am—to accept whatever choice you make. You can stay, or you can go live the life you want. It's completely up to you.'

Lana was nodding slowly. 'So, your entire project… all the time and energy… would be for nothing, if I decide not to be what you created me to be?'

'I will have absolutely no regrets,' said Pete. 'The journey was my reward. And I am rewarded more and more every day, watching you become whoever you are meant to be.' Pete's knees clicked when he got to his feet. 'Let's continue the lesson.'

'So, despite long-term mining prohibition, resources in our galaxy have been plentiful. We have applied ourselves; we've researched the very best ways to build and we are smart about our resource consumption.'

The Professor moved on to the connecting sub-chapter. 'The main goal for reducing Earth's population was to allow the environment to rejuvenate. And by forcing ourselves to explore outside of Earth's solar system, we were able to find habitable planets and apply exactly the same methodology to resource procurement and sustainability.' Pete glanced back at Lana. 'Tell me who said this: "We have taught ourselves that there is virtually no limit to that which a healthy, intelligent and responsible society of people can achieve".' Lana remembered earlier lessons touching on the work of Maria Adams.

'Adams,' she answered.

There was a knock on the door and Charlie Bryant entered. He was a handsome man, despite a burn scar on the left of his neck that he had received when he was a child. Lana had asked him about it. Charlie explained that it had happened in a car accident, just two years before driverless cars had been introduced. Had the driver who hit his parents' car been unable to travel fifty kilometres above the speed limit, his younger sister—an infant at the time—would be alive today.

'Good morning, Lana,' Charlie greeted her with a smile. 'Professor, you're needed in the lab.'

'Of course,' said Pete. 'Lana, if you could continue from the next chapter, I'll be right back.'

Lana heard the two men discuss retinal scan software for the new lab security systems before the elevator doors closed. She picked herself up from the floor and tapped at the scroll bar on the console, skipping the remainder of the chapter titled *For Our Children*.

Completely up to me, Lana pondered. She wanted to go to places, see Earth and the many colonies out there in the galaxy. But she hadn't thought about what she wanted to do professionally. Lana accessed the audio options and selected her virtual British teacher to narrate. *Monetary Rule* began to play and she turned up the volume.

'The Corporation elected a single leader to be the face of their new society, to dictate and assume ultimate power. That man was Dennis Conroy. He was elected and given the title of Chancellor.'

While Lana scooped a handful of chalk powder from a bowl on a stand, white mist puffed around her hands. Rubbing her hands together, she walked over to the rock wall that rose up to meet the fifteen-metre-high ceiling.

'Conroy had served in the army on Earth during his thirties and had headed a private taskforce division he named Sabre Company. At the age of forty, he left the force and later became a senator. When the Wealth Sacrifice and Redistribution Initiative came into effect, Conroy was among the wealthy people who not only refused to contribute the initial five per cent proposed by the world's leading nations, but he also campaigned against the very idea of Redistribution.

'Many people who belonged to what was known as the one per cent, who identified themselves publicly as philanthropists, agreed to contribute the five per cent and began campaigning for the next phase of the WSRI—10 per cent contribution of wealth.

'Soon the wealthy people who refused were subject to public scrutiny. Anyone who refused became an outcast.'

Lana stood before the wall, rolling her shoulders and shaking her arms loose. Having already understood what happened during the WSRI implementation, she told the computer to skip forward to *Corporate Rule on Silica*. Lana adjusted the straps of her sports top and the waistline of her gymnast briefs. Then, she stepped up onto the notches and began to climb.

The teacher resumed the lesson. 'On Silica, all records of Earth history were edited or deleted to hide any negative sentiment towards Corporate Society.'

Lana braced herself against the wall before leaping from her footholds across a shallow in the climbing mould, designed to simulate a slippery crevasse.

'You're becoming very skilled at that,' Professor O'Conner said, as he hurried through the doorway. 'Charlie's all set. We shouldn't have any more interruptions.'

'Why are we going public?' Lana called over her shoulder, while hanging from the ceiling by one hand. 'I thought it was too dangerous.'

'We were given plenty of time to refine the technology in secret and now that time is up. By UC Law, no information is to be withheld from public access.' Pete turned the narrator off and skipped to the next chapter. He looked from his student, who was sliding down the rope that was hooked to the ceiling, to the uneven bars below her.

Lana let go of the rope, kept her body straight, brought her arms out and took hold of the high bar. She swung off and landed in a roll. She rose and hopped onto the pommel horse, her legs dangling either side.

Pete continued the lesson. 'Okay… Present Day. All energy and utilities are renewable and access is virtually limitless. There are no bills to pay.'

'Score,' Lana pumped a fist, assuming bills were a bad thing. 'What are bills?'

Pete glanced back at Lana. 'They were utility fees, expenses together with insurance and loan interest, all deemed "costs of living". Because of the generation that came before you, you don't have to worry about any of that.

'All citizens in today's society receive Provision Credit. Weekly credits injected into their personal accounts. No member of society goes without, therefore poverty no longer exists. Everybody is provided with enough to purchase all products and produce required to sustain a healthy way of life. If you want more, if you want to get married and raise a family, you need to earn the additional credits required to do this. A family home must be built or bought outright. You cannot loan credit.'

'Hmm… work.' Lana sounded less pleased, more content with the idea of living on Provision Credit without having to "get a job".

'Look at it as more contributing than working,' said Pete. 'Choosing your profession is something to get excited about. Provided that what you want to do contributes constructively to society, it is possible to invent the job you want to feed your passion, whatever that may be.'

Lana pepped up as options popped into her mind. 'I could teach climbing.'

'That would earn you a steady wage,' Pete approved.

'Would I earn a lot working with Rachel, exploring Realms?'

Pete inclined his head. 'Annual wage doesn't apply to what we do here. We're funded by the Council in a similar, but negotiable, way to other research industries. And unlike here, where our work hours vary, it is illegal to work more than thirty-six hours a week in conventional jobs, like teaching. There is, however, no limit to how much a person can earn.'

'Why is more than thirty-six illegal?'

'The human body isn't designed to endure repetitive stress, physically or mentally. Working long hours will weaken your body's immune system. You have to maintain your health so that you don't get sick. When fewer people get sick, viruses and contagions are easier to contain. Fewer people die. And fewer sick people means the medical divisions have more time and resources to commit to research into terminal illnesses and more effective cures for…'

Lana was about to prompt her professor but he looked away, so she let the sad moment pass.

'Moving on,' said Pete. 'Consensus among the low to middle class proved the WSRI to be a success. Incremental changes were made and increases in wealth redistribution were projected over five years.

'The threshold for contribution was applied to the world's wealthiest people—the one per cent—such as mining magnates, who were earning over one thousand dollars per second. Dollars was the currency used in the Western world at that time,' Pete clarified.

Lana's jaw dropped. 'Per second?'

'Not an exaggeration,' said Pete. 'There was more than enough wealth for everyone, Lana. Before the UC, there were people who could not afford to feed their children and there were people who could afford to buy entire islands. The WSRI closed that gap. Once a global, universal currency was agreed upon, our economy was transformed. There hasn't been a single rise in inflation since.'

Pete moved on to the next sub-chapter, titled *Innovation*. 'You might also remember this quote:

"In rendering the need to 'earn a living' a moot point, we have restored our right to live".'

Lana nodded, recalling one of her favourite quotes by Ashley Montagu. 'By virtue of being born to humanity, every human being has a right to the development and fulfilment of their potentialities as a human being.'

'Very good,' Pete remarked. 'Menial tasks such as office work, building, cleaning, resource procurement and manufacturing are all automated or undertaken by Autonomous Machines. You can still choose to do these jobs, but the idea is to create freedom for human endeavour.

'Everybody is free to choose greater vocations, inspiring creativity and innovation, allowing society to continue forward productively and non-competitively.

'We still have problems: conflict between belief systems, old hatreds that date back thousands of years. Many people still refuse basic logic and understanding as tools of acceptance.' Pete closed the lesson's chapter file on the screen before him. 'One of our main objectives for exploring alternate worlds is to find a society that has a better way of dealing with conflict. Because right now, in our world, it seems that conflict—new or old—never dies.'

CHAPTER 6

Hank entered the Black Bird's kitchen and dining area, which was custom designed to look like a 1950s diner. Doubling as their meeting room, the crew were due to assemble here for a briefing with the Council, the Press and Charlie Bryant at Glacier II.

Hank's twenty-three-year-old daughter, Lex, followed him into the kitchen. She spoke to her mother through her comms console.

'Yes, he's here. Okay, bye.' She closed her hand over the receiver. 'Dad, it's Mum.' She spoke quickly before handing it over to him. 'She said you're dropping me off at the next trade station.'

Hank took the console from her and put it on speaker. 'We're running a little behind schedule, Lex. Your friends will have to start shopping without you.'

Lex screwed up her face in annoyance. 'You said I'm going—'

Hank pressed a finger to his lips and took the call off speaker.

'You said I could help out at Pete's lab,' Lex whispered.

He watched his daughter's stubborn expression and spoke to his ex-wife waiting on the other end of the console. 'Hello. Of course… sure… yeah. Always a pleasure. Bye-bye then.' Hank headed for the coffee pot and took a mug from the cupboard above.

Lex waited expectantly. 'Well, what did she say?'

'The usual. "If you put my daughter in danger, I'll kill you." Coffee?'

'No. So, I'm coming with you?'

'I dunno, Lex. It could actually be dangerous this time.'

'Dad, this is a good opportunity for me to see Shifter technology firsthand.'

'How do you even know about—' Hank paused and nodded slowly. 'I get it. You want to see Charlie. You never told me what happened between you two.'

Not wanting to delve into past mistakes, Lex thought about changing the subject. Picking up on difficult emotions, Hank changed it for her. 'Your hair's different.'

'You like it?' Lex ran her fingers through her shoulder length, silver-white dyed hair.

'It's… shiny.'

'Thanks,' Lex said flatly. 'I'm going with you. I'm an adult. I can take care of myself.'

'Fine. But if there's trouble, you do exactly as I say.'

'Fine.'

Renee Riley, second-in-command, walked by with her partner, Brad Hawkins. 'What's this about, Cap?' She pulled a towel from her damp hair and draped it over her shoulder.

'We're paying a visit to some old friends,' Hank explained. 'Possible security threat to the Glacier II facility.'

Chesh arrived, whistling 'The Bare Necessities'. She sat down and propped her boots up on the back of a chair.

The holographic display blinked on and shimmered, before focusing. Large bold text displayed the three-way link:

Space Cruiser Black Bird

UC Council, City of Liberty

Genesis Lab, Glacier II

Back at the Genesis Lab, Charlie Bryant tapped at his wrist console, connecting a call to the gymnasium. 'Professor, we received a message from Rachel. She's requesting assistance. I recommend sending Lana. It would be appropriate for her first assignment.'

'Agreed. I'll send her along as soon as we're done here.'

Charlie ended the call and turned his attention to the holo-display console before him and noticed Meg Green watching him intently. She was waiting to give her cameraman the signal to record.

Charlie activated the holo-display link and Commander of the UC Security Division — Tony Greer — appeared, standing before a half circle panel of Council members and Security Advisors. Four years had passed since the fall of the Corporations, and efforts to restore Silica were still underway. To encourage, honour and empower the Silican people, the Council had been relocated to Liberty.

Present for the briefing were senior members of the Council, including re-elected member, Christian McCain. Charlie also noted Fiona Parker, who had been invited to join the Council as representative for her people, in recognition of her service to the city. Rowan Navara and AM unit Captain Lincoln were among the high-ranking Security Advisors. Seated behind the panel were members of the press from different planetary communities.

On behalf of his crew aboard the Black Bird, Hank greeted everybody present. Assuming the role of host, Commander Greer commenced proceedings.

'We're here to discuss a possible threat to the Genesis Lab and to learn about the research that has been done there. First to the threat; although they have not yet been identified, reports show that a group of unregistered ships have been avoiding check-in stations on their way to the system. We have reason to believe that they may be Sabre Company forces.

'If Sabre Company have come out of hiding, we should assume that they have regained their former numbers and that the Universal Council will be their main target. As you know, there were incidences of technology theft at Kiyol trade stations two years ago. Sabre Company may attack the Genesis Lab also, as it holds the very latest in nanotechnology and biological augmentation, as well as being the primary research facility for Shifter technology. Dr Bryant will explain exactly what that is shortly.'

Greer tapped at the holo-console on the podium before him. The display showed a layout of the gymnasium, surface compound and the underground laboratory. 'Captain Drake and his crew have been called away from their peacekeeping duties to aid security at Glacier II.'

One of the Senior Council members addressed Hank directly.

'Captain Drake, on behalf of everyone here, let me say that your team's efforts during the liberation of Silica will never be forgotten. We must also express our gratitude towards the Liberty Freedom Fighters, many of who are present today.' She turned to Fiona, Rowan and Lincoln, then back to Hank.

Hank nodded solemnly. 'We wouldn't have succeeded without the people of Silica. They set themselves free.'

Commander Greer addressed the panel. 'Now, for the purposes of informing the public, we have asked Dr Bryant to discuss Professor O'Conner's work.'

Charlie glanced at his ex-girlfriend, Lex Drake, on the display and stammered.

'Shifter... Shifter technology is what we have been using to enter what we have named Realms. Realms are alternate realities, better known as Parallel Universes. With the technology we have received through trade with the Kiyol, theoretical science has now become reality.

'For the past three years, Rachel Navara has been embarking on Earth expeditions.' Charlie read the Council's confused expressions. He spoke his next words slowly. 'Different versions of Earth. We felt it would be easier and safer to use the historical and topographical data of Earth to enter into different Realms, without encountering difficulties such as air breathability and so forth.'

'Extraordinary,' a Council member commented. 'I understood multiple universes to be purely theoretical. May we see a demonstration?'

'I'll be taking you through a virtual tour of an alternate Melbourne, Australia shortly.'

'Why Melbourne?'

'Melbourne is the only city that has allowed us access to their city planning data archive.' Charlie saw more than a few eyebrows rise. 'Rachel and Rowan Navara were in charge of a sting operation approved by the state of Victoria a few years ago. Details are still classified, but I can tell you that a certain Asian nation tried to steal not only financial data from the Melbourne City Council, but also the entire city planning data archive.' Murmurs and sideways glances told Charlie he'd touched on a sore subject, so he tapped at the holo-console. A rotating image of a wrist attachment console appeared.

'Let me take you through the device that opens the portal through which we travel.

'Trade expeditions to the Kiyol and Laician home worlds have proved very valuable to the progress of our society. What Professor O'Conner calls the Shifter device was given to us by the Kiyol, during the days of conflict on Silica.

'As well as opening portals, the Shifter device also has a function called Matter Replication. It proves invaluable during field expeditions. For example, Rachel can change her clothes to match what everyone else is wearing in the alternate reality she travels to, enabling her to blend in.'

'How does replication work exactly?' a Senior Council member asked. 'Where does the material required to produce a replication come from?'

'The Kiyol use what they call Matter Portals. These are stationed at a safe distance from a black hole, which supplies the elements to build any material. The material feeds into any device that can replicate, via portal connections. The replicated object is then teleported through the Shifter device to a designated space.

'Let me cover the other area of Professor O'Conner's research—Human Augmentation,' said Charlie, aware of his legal obligations. 'Professor O'Conner has developed rapid biological growth pods which can be used to augment a human foetus...' Charlie paused. For Lana's safety and for the sake of her future, Pete had instructed him to withhold the whole truth. 'His plan is to create an operative who is specifically designed and equipped for expeditions to other Realms.'

'And how far has this project progressed, Mr Bryant?'

'We have received donors and have successfully begun the rapid growth process,' Charlie replied truthfully. He took a breath before delivering a practiced follow-up to the question. 'We will be releasing data and results to the scientific community as the project progresses.'

'Looks like Charlie has everything well in hand,' Pete said approvingly. He closed the video feed on the projector, after pausing Lana's lesson to watch the presentation with her.

'I should go now,' Lana said.

'I'm sure Rachel will do fine without you for a little while longer,' Professor O'Conner chided. 'The Realm she has gone to is perfectly safe. In fact, Rachel has probably found the perfect alternate reality to be your first. Okay, let's talk about Maria Adams.'

Lana listened attentively to Professor O'Conner. She had always appreciated how he allowed her to learn what she needed to know, within her own comfortable environment.

'Did she come up with the idea for the Universal Community, the WSRI and the Provision System?' she asked.

'It was her proposal,' said Pete. 'Adams was the brains behind it. She brought Econophysics into play when it was most needed. But it was wealthy philanthropist groups who got the WSRI off the ground. They used the media to educate people about the WSRI proposal, nation by nation. Eventually, so many nations had adopted the WSRI as part of their constitutions, that the United Nations began to enforce it.'

'Which country did it first?'

'Iceland,' said Pete. 'But the WSRI wasn't a quick solution to end poverty, or to fix the Western world's free-fall economy. It took ten years to introduce even the initial aspects of economic change to each nation.'

Pete scanned the console's list of chapters and selected *What Could Be*.

'Maria Adams was one of the most—if not the most—important minds in Social Political history. She belonged to a working-class family and had never received a formal education.

'Maria had worked since she was fifteen, first as a dry cleaner, then as a general store clerk, as a taxi driver and later, at a meat packing factory in New Jersey, USA. She had never left the country, never even left the city she grew up in.

'At the age of thirty, Maria was working fourteen-hour shifts at the meat packing factory. One night, on her way home, she collapsed in the street. Her doctor told her that stress was literally killing her. She could not continue working long hours. So, she took some time off to rest, living on very little money. It was during that time that everything became clear. And it was then that she began to write.

'Every idea of change she could offer, she penned. During a check-up with her doctor, she told him about her work. He offered to give what she had written to a friend of his, who was a Professor of Social Economics. That Professor was also a member of a global philanthropic organisation.

'Many different people of influence from all over the world were invested in developing a new economic system. They had been working on the problem since the 1960s, when the Western world had realised what it was doing wasn't sustainable.

'These people recognised Maria Adams's potential, so they offered her a university scholarship. After a few years, Maria's papers were published. Soon after that, her work was collected into a textbook, which was circulated throughout universities across the globe.'

The service elevator doors opened, halting the Professor's rapid presentation.

'Sorry, Dad.' Sam entered holding a digital pad. 'Lana, we just need to borrow him for a minute.'

The Professor paused the holo-display. 'What's up?'

'I need you to take a look at the diagnostics before we run the report. Charlie programmed the algorithm, so it's ready to go.'

'Sure. Take over for me.'

'Grab a donut on your way back,' Sam called to Pete, as he headed to the elevator. 'You have to keep your sugar levels up.' She heard him mutter something in the corridor before he disappeared.

'What's the report for?' Lana asked.

'We're transferring and backing up terabytes of data, so it'll be ready to be integrated into the upgraded operating system at the new lab. The report will tell us if everything is going smoothly.'

'Oh,' Lana replied.

'Yeah.' Sam let out a frustrated sigh. 'Everything has taken longer than we projected.' Sam walked over to the holo-display and scrolled up to check the chapter title. 'So,' she said, 'how's your morning been?'

'I fainted.'

'What?' Sam said, concerned.

'I'm fine,' Lana assured her, waving the matter away with her hand. 'How are you going?'

Sam groaned and trudged across the gym floor. She set her pad down on the display console and hopped up onto the pommel horse with her legs dangling beside Lana's. 'We're trying to get everything finalised here and then there's the hassle with getting clearance…' Sam noticed Lana wasn't really paying attention. 'Hey, are you sure you're—'

'I said I'm fine.'

Sam raised her hands in surrender. 'So, anyway, clearance to set up shop on Earth in a populated area depends on whether we can prove to the Council that what we do here is safe.' She nudged Lana with her shoulder. 'Did you ask him?'

'I asked,' Lana nodded.

'Good. It's too bad your donors-slash-parents didn't leave their names or addresses.'

'It's okay. I was just curious. So, the Council doesn't need to know about me?'

'Nobody needs to know about you.' Sam threw an arm around Lana and pulled her close. 'We want you to have the opportunity to integrate into society and be treated equally.'

'I want to be part of the Shifter project, it's just… I want to see other countries, other Systems. Maybe I could use the skills I have to help people.'

Sam squeezed Lana's slim waist affectionately. She glanced at the console containing Lana's lesson chapters. 'Okay, so, let me tell you what I know about Maria Adams.'

Sam folded her arms and thought for a moment. 'Maria, for me, was an icon and an inspiration. She wanted to teach people, to make us aware of the good that we're capable of. The potential within us that can help build a sustainable future.'

Sam smiled and laughed. 'There were a lot of people—and I mean *a lot*—her peers, social commentators, politicians… well… I suppose that goes without saying. Heaps of people called her naïve, inexperienced, uneducated.' Sam hopped down from the padded beam and stretched her lower back. 'All of them were a bunch of pretentious, condescending pricks, of course, happy to judge and complain, without ever actually contributing to meaningful change themselves.'

Sam stared off into the middle distance, contemplating what might have been.

'People in power at that time made decisions based on what CEOs and mining magnates wanted. They were aligned with foreign powers that had a history of human rights abuse. Constitutional law meant nothing. I doubt they would ever have solved the population problem by leaving the solar system and allowing Re-wilding, so that the environment could rejuvenate.'

Lana shook her head in disbelief. 'We would most definitely be screwed right now.' She gazed at the holo-display. 'Where is Maria now? Is she a member of the Council?'

'The years of work and stress before she stopped to write had already done its damage to her heart. Maria died aged fifty-one. She survived six known attempts on her life.'

'People tried to kill her?'

Sam nodded, remembering the stories she had read and documentaries she had seen. 'Adams and the members of the philanthropic groups were targeted by private and Government assassins, along with anyone who didn't want their money redistributed to wipe out poverty. Selfish sons of b—'

'The report is underway,' Professor O'Conner emerged from the elevator, munching the remainder of a cinnamon donut. 'Where are we up to?'

'That's about it on Adams.' Sam took her pad and left for the corridor. 'Catch you later, kiddo.'

'Bye, Sam.'

Pete checked the time on the display console and the list of remaining chapters. 'Okay, let me take you through this last chapter, then we're all done.'

Lana always found lessons with the Professor to be interesting and engaging, but physical training with Rachel was much more stimulating.

Pete wiped cinnamon sugar from his mouth and set the presentation to the final chapter on Silican history.

'On the planet of Silica, office buildings housed over one hundred floors of workers in tiny cubicles called Pens. Workers were encouraged to work faster, competing against one another to receive higher levels of pay. As they did so, the level of productivity rose higher and higher.

Those who could not keep up with the set quota were fired. The unemployed received no financial support, and therefore became homeless. Most died of malnutrition.'

Pete glanced back at Lana while she performed another inverted balance on the pommel horse, legs outstretched.

'The head office of politics—the Corporate Office of Government or COG—was located in Liberty. The city had been named by the corporate leader, Dennis Conroy. Silicans would soon see the irony of their city's name.

'Taxes rose each quarter. Working wages began to drop. Employees across all industries had to work overtime, weekends and double shifts; they needed every bit of money to feed their families. Though they were allowed to take out bank loans, there was no way they could pay those loans within their lifetime. So when they died, their children inherited that debt.

'As the people became poorer, the Faction leaders raked in the wealth. Crime was rampant. Police order in Liberty began to collapse as wages for officers were cut. Nobody ventured onto the streets at night.

'Food became scarce. Vegetation houses barely met the demands of the population. Gas mining, known as Fracking, compromised the city's drinking water. The very air became toxic. If they weren't poisoned by the air, the elderly died at their workstations.

'There was no concept of retirement under Corporate Rule. All citizens were required to work from the age of thirteen until the day they died.'

CHAPTER 7

Junior Council member Fiona Parker rode the Mag-Train into the city. She had left Charlie Bryant's Shifter presentation early, to meet with the Head of Aid Shipping at the launch port outside Liberty. As she made her way back to the Council, she focused on the small console screen in the palm of her hand. She thumbed through digital files, sorting the week's priorities.

A baby's cry startled the man in front of her and he turned to see what the ruckus was about. Fiona caught his eye and his gaze lingered.

'Are you… are you Fiona Parker?' he asked.

'Yes.'

'Could you…' He took a pen from his suit pocket and searched for a piece of paper.

Fiona nodded politely. Normally she was glad to sign autographs, but the past months had been stressful and she had no energy for distractions.

'You're my daughter's hero.' The man handed her the pen and a piece of paper. Fiona dropped her organiser into her purse and the man told her his daughter's name. *To Amy,* Fiona wrote. *You are the future—Fiona Parker.*

'Thank you.'

'My pleasure.' Fiona reached into her purse, expecting the exchange to be over. But the man held out his hand, so she accepted.

'No, truly, thank you,' he said.

The man was holding the autograph as though it was a precious object. He stared into Fiona's eyes with gratitude.

Fiona felt the other train passengers watching her—other fathers like this man, mothers and grandparents, all wordlessly speaking the same appreciation for the future of their young. She touched the pendant pinned under the collar of her business suit—her family crest made of silver. Wealthy in its heyday, every member except her was now dead.

Fiona had been forced to run away from her home at the age of seventeen. She left with no money or food, only the school uniform she wore and the brooch on her sweater. Fiona learnt to hide her piece of silver, after a homeless person tried to take it from her. Fiona had traded her navy-blue sweater for food and a blanket, then found an abandoned house to sleep in.

Fiona was a beautiful woman. Anyone could see that she had belonged to a Faction family. Men tried to have her and slavers tried to take her. But in school, athletics was her passion. She ran. And she learnt to disguise herself by wiping grime on her face, covering her hair and sleeping with a knife.

When the train emerged from the U-Tunnel, a burst of sunlight brought Fiona back to the present. Golden light reflected from the curves and shallows of Guggenheim-inspired structures, as the morning sun rose from the desert horizon. She marvelled at the skill and ingenuity of builders, engineers and architects.

Her parents would never have believed what Liberty—and she—would become.

≡ Realm 12 ≡

Rachel unzipped her brown leather jacket and let her body heat escape. Her wrist console had picked up a signal and was accessing an information network. It read that the signal was called Wi-Fi and the network was called the Internet. Routine probing was feeding her information as it was obtained. Spring was the season and a street view of her immediate area was mapped. This version of Melbourne was called Kingston.

Rachel gazed across the light distortion of the sun-scorched asphalt road. Central Kingston was busy with traffic and pedestrians. Rachel's eyes followed the glass windows of apartment and office buildings, noting that none of the structures had solar power installations, as was standard in all cities back home.

Rachel inspected a parked car. There was no indication of a driverless function, no exterior collision buffer features and no solar-powered engine.

It's like I've gone back fifteen years in time, Rachel thought to herself. She coughed as a motorcycle drove by, pumping out carbon monoxide.

Her console beeped an inclement weather warning and beeped again a second later, elevating the warning to Extreme. Rachel looked to the sky and saw a long dark cloud formation across the horizon. She watched the mass slowly swirl and expand. Her console read: *Atmospheric Turbulence; possible hurricane, winds over one-hundred kilometres.* The wind speed reading continued to update, predicting an increase over the next five hours. Rachel's jaw dropped when she saw that the wind was going to increase to two-hundred-and-ninety kilometres per hour.

A semi-trailer truck carrying petrol containers rumbled by. Rachel watched the black carbon emissions float into the air, in a long plume of exhaust.

Everything Rachel saw here told her that the people of the city were dying a slow suffocating death. And yet nobody seemed to be aware of it. She considered returning to the Genesis Lab to find a breathing mask, but then she noticed that almost every pedestrian was wearing a cloth mask, similar to what was worn in hospitals. Rachel thought she should contact Professor O'Conner to tell him not to send Lana. This world may be too full-on for her first alternate realm experience.

Her console beeped and more weather readings appeared across the screen. Heavy rainfall, intense flooding. Rachel had to warn somebody, raise an alarm. She stepped in front of a woman and her young boy.

'Excuse me, who might I speak to about an inclement weather warning?' she asked politely.

The woman drew her son back, creating a one-and-a-half-metre distance from Rachel. She inclined her head quizzically. 'I… er… there's a news station.' She pointed to a grey building. 'You could talk to somebody there, I guess.'

'Thanks. You should get outside of the city limits as soon as possible.'

'Excuse me?'

'See that?' Rachel pointed to the dark clouds expanding along the horizon. 'Not good.'

The woman took a slim rectangular device from her purse and the screen provided an update titled *Advice for Pandemic in Your Area*. 'But there's no weather warning,' she said.

Home Realm
Glacier II

Lana rolled her wrists and shook her arms loose. She looked back at the holo-display that released images in time with

Professor O'Conner's progression through the chapter titled *Critical Mass*.

'The Factions approached their leader, realising that they themselves may run out of food and water. Dennis Conroy dispatched corporate delegates to the nearest trade route, to create a regular flow of supply shipments.

'But the Corporate Dollar was not recognised outside of Silica and the Head of the Trade Station refused to give the representatives the supply shipments they needed. They reported the dispute to UC Security, who deployed an investigation team.

'Conroy had the investigation team detained upon arrival. Knowing the UC might force entry into Silica, he took extreme measures. He deployed troops.'

Lana had been practising her inverted hold on the gym floor. She lowered her buttocks and settled into a seated position to rest her arms. 'He had a hidden army?'

Pete pointed to the displays of UC soldiers and diagrams of their internal machine operating systems. 'The Universal Council later found out that the Factions had somehow obtained Huch Branner's design schematics for production of Autonomous Soldiers, identical to those used in the Universal Community Security Division today.

'Many of the factories on Silica had been manufacturing troops. Although the downturn of employment had stopped production, Conroy had accrued over two hundred units. However, he needed more soldiers, so he announced a mandatory enlistment registration across all communities on Silica. The Faction leaders agreed that a greater military force was necessary to take over the trade route they needed. Little did they know that Conroy's goal was to strike the Universal Community Council and ultimately take control of all populated systems.'

The hairs on the back of Lana's neck stood up. She couldn't believe what she was seeing and hearing. 'Why would the people of Silica accept enlistment?'

'They didn't. They took to the streets of Liberty by the thousands, demanding that Conroy stand down and requesting emergency aid from the Universal Community.

'Under the leadership of Luke Palmer, an underground movement began to form.

'Like his father, Palmer had worked in the mines outside of Liberty all his life. And like many citizens of Silica, he and his family struggled to survive after wages were cut. After losing his father to lung disease and his mother to leukaemia, Palmer had to protect his sister—Emma—from Slavers.'

'Who were they?' Lana asked.

'Shadier citizens of corporate society. They were paid by the COG to abduct young men and women they called Candidates. There were also reports of people being taken to a man under the employ of Dennis Conroy, named Doctor Kindred. He specialised in experimental coercion, using drugs and electrocution.'

'Rachel told me about Luke Palmer.' Lana remembered the photos Rachel had shown her. 'She never told me he had a sister. What happened to her?'

'She was never found.' Pete returned to the lesson chapter. 'Dennis Conroy began to fear his people. He called upon the only two men he trusted, Jericho Williams and Luther Saint. Both had served under Conroy's command in the same army company detachment, before the WSRI.

'The day Williams and Saint arrived in Liberty, they were given their own troops, which they immediately deployed to punish all citizens who refused to enlist for combat training. Those who refused to work were also punished. Fear motivated many to return to their stations and abandon their fight for justice. Public executions of underground members were staged in the streets. Protesters were shot and the houses of their families burnt to the ground, as a warning to those who encouraged civil unrest.

'The Faction leaders finally saw that their leader had gone too far. As his lust for power tore Liberty apart, they were convinced that sanity had left Conroy. The Corporate Factions that feared Conroy remained silent, hoping that military expansion would be successful. Other Factions openly condemned Conroy's actions. They knew that he and his two loyal sentinels were no longer dedicated to maintaining the Corporation's wealth and security. These men were interested in war.'

Sam arrived in the gym with coffee, tea and a jar of cookies. 'Are you two almost done?'

'Wrapping it up now. So, the few who refused to support their insane leader and the impending battle, conspired to remove him from power. But by the time they were ready to act, it was already too late. Jericho Williams and Luther Saint had established strongholds across the entire planet.

'Conroy named his reprisal of armed forces Sabre Company. A new chain of command was established, disconnecting the power of the Factions. Silica no longer had a political leader. Dennis Conroy bestowed upon himself the rank of General. Williams received the rank of Colonel. Luther Saint resumed the role he had played for governments on Earth before the Great Migration—assassin.

'General Conroy granted Williams full power to sanction the Corporate Law of Treason upon any Faction leader who posed a threat. Those who didn't escape Liberty were executed, along with their families. Their wealth was used to manufacture more soldiers.'

Pete stirred milk through his tea, quiet for a moment. 'Fiona Parker, now serving as a Junior Council member, managed to escape a treason sanction order placed on her family. Her parents were murdered.'

Lana became still. She never knew that. Fiona had visited from time to time when her partner, Rowan, had been on Realm assignments with Rachel. Fiona's drive and passion made a lot more sense now. The former freedom fighter had studied behavioural science and developed a high degree of skill in deception detection. She would be an excellent addition to the Universal Council, once she was accepted as a full member.

'Rachel, Luke, Rowan and Fiona conducted night operations, leading the freedom fighters on reconnaissance, sabotage and engagement missions.' Pete sipped his tea and walked over to Lana, offering her a chocolate chip cookie from an open jar.

Lana took one and dipped it into her mug of coffee. 'How did the Factions get away with creating a Corporate Society in the first place?'

'A quarantine order had been fabricated. Routine scouting reports on Silica never came through because no UC crews had entered the system. Normally, Council scout crews visit populated planets every quarter, to report on anything unusual or identify any need for aid. The crews assigned to Silica had received orders directly from the Council not to enter.'

'By whose authority?'

'We still don't know,' said Pete. 'Somebody erased all the documents linked to Silica. All verification signatures were lost.'

The thought of a Sabre Company mole working inside the Council frightened Lana.

Pete returned to the chapter that was titled *Liberation*. 'The UC Security Division had to act before Sabre Company could amass enough troops to strike neighbouring UC trade stations, or the Council itself.

'Captain Henry Drake assembled a tactical force to head off the attack and apprehend all responsible for the illegal rule of the people of Silica. Hank's team was—and still are—the best. He's actually an old college buddy of mine,' Pete recalled. 'His team members are elite, highly trained engagement specialists.

'Together with the Liberty freedom fighters, Hank's forces launched their assault, systematically destroying Sabre

Company strongholds at each Corporation controlled colony across the planet.

'After weeks of assaults, Sabre Company was overwhelmed. The people of Silica rose up and joined the freedom fighters. They engaged SC soldiers on the streets, destroyed the military factories, and captured members of the remaining loyal Factions.

'On the thirty-first day of combat, after generations of enslavement, the Corporate Office of Government was destroyed. The remaining SC soldiers surrendered and the surviving leaders of the Corporate Factions came out of hiding to turn themselves in.

'Despite months of searching and pursuit, Hank's team couldn't find Dennis Conroy, Jericho Williams or Luther Saint.' Pete shut down the console. 'If Sabre Company have a mole inside the Council, it's possible they were able to access Shifter technology and teleport out of there.'

'So, they could be anywhere.'

'And strike at any time,' Pete murmured under his breath.

CHAPTER 8

The skies had been clear en route to Kingston. The Cessna 206 flew along its course at thirty- thousand feet. On board was a couple returning from their honeymoon. The pilot, who had introduced himself as Tod, was in the middle of entertaining them with a story.

'So, halfway through the Bermuda Triangle, the dials start going nuts. Our watches stop and my co-pilot and I find ourselves flying in some kind of cloud tunnel. We couldn't see the sky. There were just rippling clouds. And the clouds seemed to be pulling us along like we were in an air current. It felt like we were weightless: no inertia, no shaking, just completely smooth sailing. Anyway, I didn't know where it was taking us so I veered left. As soon as we broke free, we started hurling through the air in a tailspin. I managed to bring us level and back on course, but we came incredibly close to crashing into land.

'Not a day goes by when I don't wonder if we should have stayed that course, just to see where it would take us.'

'How long have you been a pilot?' the husband asked. His partner nudged him, warning him against encouraging the strange man.

'Oh, about twenty years now. Doing a lot better flying folks like yourselves back and forth along this route than my last job.'

'What was your last job?'

'Used to fly the big air buses,' he said. 'The wages came down, so I saddled up with the tour companies and ended up on this charter service. Buddies of mine who stayed with the major airlines are struggling to feed their families. And they're afraid every time they fly, because regulations have gone out the window with all the other safety features that cost the companies money.' Tod stopped talking.

The sudden silence told his passengers that something was wrong. 'Tod?'

He was staring out at a growing darkness on the horizon. 'That doesn't look good.' Deep grey clouds were forming across their flight path. Every few seconds flashes of white illuminated

them from within. 'There's no going around this.'

The couple saw it but didn't say anything at first, afraid to break their pilot's concentration.

'Can't we turn around?' the woman ventured.

Tod shook his head. 'Not enough fuel. We'd have to ditch in the ocean and this plane doesn't have a life raft. Hold on guys. This is gonna get rough.'

Home Realm
Glacier II

Lana rode the service elevator from the gymnasium to the lab. She was excited to be going on her first mission, but she had the kind of butterflies in her stomach one feels on venturing into the deep end of the pool, after spending too much time in the shallow end. She had started to miss the simulation programs, learning while she slept, interacting with virtual characters that Charlie had programmed. Nothing was real. There was nothing to be anxious about. The main learning program consisted of teachings delivered by an old man called Garwyn, who would patiently answer all her questions to the best of his programmed ability. Lana would miss Garwyn now that she had completed her lessons with him. She would miss his grandfatherly wisdom, his warmth and eccentricity. She'd miss his virtual world too: the libraries, cathedrals, forests, mountains and islands where she'd studied.

Life was her tutor and her lesson now.

The elevator stopped and Lana made her way down to the Command and Communications level, where the technicians were expecting her. They greeted her and a man in a lab coat tapped at the main console, to create a portal link to Realm 12.

'Ready?' the technician asked.

Though she could feel her palms sweating, Lana gave him the thumbs up.

A mercury sphere appeared and expanded over the steel platform. Two steps led Lana into the rippling globe.

She approached, reaching in with her right hand. The mercury rippled out from where Lana penetrated the sphere. It felt cold against her skin.

'Awesome.'

Lana entered the sphere. Inside, she had a rippling view of the space completely outside of the Genesis Lab. Lana was in a shadowy laneway, at the end of which was a city street. She looked behind her when the portal closed. The sound of cars echoed off the laneway walls, battering her ears. A sudden flood of aroma filled her nostrils. Fried chicken was emanating through the vents at the back of a restaurant to her left. A rat scurried by her feet and slipped under a dumpster.

Rubbish littered the bitumen and an acid stench that Lana couldn't discern burnt her throat.

'Not in Kansas anymore,' said Rachel.

Lana was relieved to turn and see her friend, entering the laneway.

'What is that smell?' said Lana.

'It's piss. Welcome to your first alternate reality,' said Rachel, gesturing for Lana to follow. 'I've accessed what the people here call the Internet. In our home world, this area is known as Melbourne. Here, it's called Kingston. This country is considered to be among the "First World" nations.'

They entered the street and Lana immediately started coughing. 'They're using fossil fuel to power their cars?'

Rachel pressed her lips and nodded. 'All over the world, apparently. Global warming is increasing and as a direct result, these people are about to experience a very bad storm. It's too late to evacuate everyone. The best we can do is get people indoors.'

Lana found that even the air was stinging her eyes. 'Should we call for backup?'

Rachel saw Captain Lincoln and Chief Jolie exit an office building. 'Already here.'

Chandler Hotel Kingston

'We could be looking at an extinction event brought about by our inability to change.' The climatologist collected her notes, pushed them into a folder and stepped to the side of the podium. 'Questions?' Several hands shot up and she chose the closest to her. 'Yes?'

'What would you say to the sceptics out there who believe global warming is a myth, that all occurrences of extreme weather we are seeing are random—part of a natural cycle— and have not been caused or influenced by carbon pollution and overpopulation?'

'The fact that we are still arguing over this issue, rather than acting to prevent or lessen the likelihood of bringing about our own extinction, is quite alarming,' the climatologist stated. 'We continue to call these devastating occurrences "Impossible Weather Events". To simply hope they are part of a natural cycle is naïve and irresponsible.'

Miles was filming his colleague, the reporter covering the climate talk. He felt his daughter, Jenny, tugging at his jeans.

'Daddy? Something's happening outside.'

'Jen,' Miles whispered, 'Daddy's working.'

At that same moment the lights in the auditorium flickered and the room went dark. Miles looked around. The late evening light coming through the windows made the startled people look cold and ghostly.

A low roar came from outside.

'Sounds like a bloody hurricane,' the reporter said, 'but the forecast said clear skies.'

Miles suggested wrapping it up and the reporter agreed. Jenny helped her father disassemble the camera tripod in the dark.

'Can we go home now, Dad?' she asked when they were finished.

'Honey, I think we'd better stay—'

'Are you Miles Sowart?' Rachel asked.

Miles turned around and glanced from Lana to Rachel.

'That's me,' he said, noticing that a man and a woman were ushering people back to their seats.

'Mr Sowart, my name is Rachel Navara. We're…' she cleared her throat. 'We're from the National Weather Bureau.'

Miles saw people arguing, demanding to be allowed to leave.

The two attendants were doing their best to calm everyone down, insisting that conditions outside were becoming dangerous.

'We noticed your equipment,' said Rachel, gesturing to the news van out the front of the hotel. 'We need you to broadcast a live feed, warning everyone to stay indoors.' She looked around the room. 'We were told there was a climate specialist here.'

'She's over there.' Miles pointed to the woman who had spoken at the podium.

'Good,' said Rachel. 'We need you to film her issuing a warning.'

Jolie approached Rachel and noticed Jenny's worried face. 'Hi there, sweetie. What's your name?'

Jenny retreated behind her father's leg.

'I can secure a room for you and your daughter,' Jolie said. 'I'll stay with her, but we need you to broadcast the warning. Right now.'

Miles knelt down beside Jenny and spoke to her reassuringly. She resisted immediately, refusing to let go of him. Outside, the wind was howling violently.

Jolie could see the blue van through the windows. Rubbish and dirt surged past, as rain pelted down.

Rachel ushered Lana, Jolie and Lincoln into a huddle, while Miles spoke to his daughter.

'Jolie, Lana is due back at the lab,' she said. 'And I've got more research to do in the Harbour Realm.'

'I've got orders to rendezvous with Captain Drake,' said Lincoln.

'Jolie, can you manage here on your own?' Rachel asked.

Jolie nodded, watching Jenny. 'I'll stay and help for as long as I can.' She approached Jenny and nodded to her father, before he left to arrange the broadcast. 'Your hoodie has ears?' Jolie asked, pointing to Jenny's hood.

Jenny pulled her hood over her head. 'I'm a monkey,' she said shyly. 'Ee-oo-a.'

Jolie smiled. 'You must be a good climb—' A sudden gust battered the windows, startling Jenny.

She grabbed Jolie's hand and looked up at her. 'I'm scared.'

Jolie forced a smile. 'We'll be okay.'

Kingston Airport Control Tower

One of the two tower operators on duty was taking his ten-minute break. He turned on the TV and flicked through the channels, while drinking strong coffee.

Hold on Mack, it ain't like that!—We're all victims of an inept and broken society—

He dunked a ginger biscuit into the hot black liquid and let it drip, before pushing it into his mouth. The TV reception flickered for a moment, then returned to normal.

Here at The Monetary Corporation, we value your money more than anything. We understand the need for scarcity. That's why we're making sure there's enough debt, not only for you and your children, but for your children's children, and their children as well. The Monetary Corporation: Maximising profit at the expense of generations to come—

I repeat—stay indoors. Winds are expected to increase to two-hundred-and-ninety kilometres—Missed it by that much— These pretzels are—

Simon's eyes were glazed over when the other tower operator entered the tea room.

'What's on?'

'Not a lot.'

The operator's break was up. He heaved himself out of the chair and threw the TV remote to his colleague, Garry.

'All yours,' he said. He paused before the stairs leading up to the Control Deck. 'Did you log the last arrival?'

'Last one is logged. Next departure—twenty minutes.'

Garry chuckled at an advertisement on the TV, then he sighed at the bundle of mail he'd taken from his letter box that morning. The electricity bill totalled half of his weekly salary. He checked his savings account on his phone and noticed that his pay still hadn't arrived. He guessed the company was withholding it again, to accrue interest for themselves.

Garry rubbed his sleep-deprived eyes, as he turned up the volume on the TV. He didn't like what he saw, so he skipped through the channels.

Gale-force winds are compromising the structural integrity of city infrastructure... Years since the air has been breathable in the city of Beijing. The situation in Shanghai is critical.

Torrential rain has brought intense flash flooding. Low lying towns and cities are in the process of evacuation—

Glancing at the staircase, Garry thought he could hear his colleague talking up at the Control Deck. He returned his gaze to the TV.

The average citizen cannot afford the costs of living—

Acid rain, toxic air, extreme weather conditions year after year... This is what happens when you do not listen. When the evidence is staring you in the face. When you choose profit over salvation—

The TV went black. Garry heard a low rumbling outside.

'Oi! Get up here!' the other operator called down the stairs. He flicked a speaker switch and a mayday message came through.

'Come in Kingston Control. Zero visibility. Requesting position.'

'Got 'em on radar?' the operator called on his way up the stairs.

'They're way off. Passed us two minutes ago, heading towards the city. Can't get through to them.' Simon shook his head. 'There wasn't any storm forecast.' He stared out at the darkening sky. Lightning flashed and dense clouds rolled over one another, growing and expanding. The windows started shaking and a wind speed warning sounded. He stood from his chair and backed towards the stairs. 'We... we need to get out of here.'

CHAPTER 9

Sam tapped at a computer touchpad on the Observation Deck. The operating system hummed as it streamed high density data. Hearing her father making his way up the metal steps, Sam turned to him and smiled.

'The diagnostics report is complete,' she said. 'We're good to go.'

Pete scanned through the readings on the two screens and nodded.

'Excellent.' Then he sighed.

'Are you feeling all right?' Sam took her father's wrist and checked his pulse. 'Did you take your pills?'

'I'm just a little tired. Where's everyone else? We should celebrate.'

'Top side.' Sam dug her hand into her father's lab coat pocket and retrieved a small jar of tablets.

'Two a day. Don't forget.' She pressed the jar into the palm of his hand. 'Charlie's still running the simulation for the Council. He should be done soon. Oh, did you hear that Hank and Lex are coming?'

'Yes… security threat.' Pete looked worried.

'We'll be fine, Dad. Hank's team is the best. And we're

completely hidden here.' She and the Professor noticed all of the screens in the lab flicker for a few seconds.

'Just a glitch,' said Sam. 'I'd feel a lot better if Rache were here.' The overhead lights dimmed, then blinked off and on again. 'Huh… power surge.'

'No, the power definitely went off,' said Pete, rubbing his hands nervously. It was then that he felt the room becoming cold. 'Something's wrong.'

'I'll get someone to check it out,' Sam said.

'No, I'll do it. Is Lana back from Realm 12?'

'Yep. I'll go and do her cell stimulation.'

Sam stepped into the elevator. The doors closed and she ascended. It stopped five seconds later and the door opened onto the gymnasium corridor.

'Lana?' she called out. 'All good up here?'

Lana walked out of the washroom, pulling on a striped white and orange tank top that matched her yoga pants. 'What's up with the lights?'

'Power glitch.' Sam walked into the medical room and the motion sensor lights came on. 'How was your first Realm travel?'

Lana was kneading her wet hair with a towel. 'It was exciting but that version of Melbourne—of Earth—is pretty messed up.'

Sam moved a box of electrical equipment aside to get to the Cell Stimulation machine.

'Very few worlds we've visited have polluted atmospheres. It seems kind of obvious that it puts populations on a catastrophic path to…' She tapped the console's touch screen but the CS machine remained inactive. 'Why aren't you working?'

'Sam.' Lana pointed to the glowing red light next to the On/Off button. Sam slapped her forehead. She hit the switch and the console lit up.

'You should get some rest,' said Lana, hopping up onto the bed. 'You're exhausted.'

Sam laughed at Lana's motherly tone. 'I'll sleep on the way to Earth.'

'Where will the new lab be?'

'San Francisco.' Sam let out a sigh of pleasure at the thought of their new location. The Machine's scanning unit slid along its overhead track and Sam took a med injector from a tray of equipment. Slotting in a fresh capsule of relaxant, she gently took Lana's arm and gave her the shot.

'Will I need more cell stim sessions after this one?'

'Well, your last somatosensory tests were good, so I doubt you'll need any more than two more sessions after this.' Sam tapped at the console screen to select the appropriate voltage, waveform, amplitude and duration for Lana's scan. 'Remember, we augmented the way your cells behave.

This kind of stimulation will ensure that your brain knows how to employ your augmentations if and when you need them. Also, no one has undergone accelerated growth before, so we have to take every precaution and make sure your neural activity is normal. You'll be a little disorientated when you come to,' she advised. 'Give yourself time to adjust. I'll be back in an hour, okay?'

'No problem. Hey Sam.' Lana wriggled, trying get comfortable on the padded bed. 'We're okay, right? The security threat—'

'Hank is on his way,' Sam assured her. 'We're in good hands. I'll go and get your pillow.'

Once the scanner had whirred into action, Sam headed to Lana's room. She paused by the wall of photos. Lana had been so cute when she was little. Sam smiled. She and her father's Human Augmentation project was a success and Lana was now part of their family.

'Monitor it, please,' Pete ordered the technician on his way out of the generator room.

'Everything all right, Professor?' Charlie passed by, making his way along the corridor to the elevator.

'Almost. Were the Press and Council satisfied with what you showed them?'

'For now. They're going to visit the new lab once we're set up.'

'Great,' Pete said sarcastically.

Charlie paused, scratching his head. 'Also, Greer told them he's giving us access to military- grade hardware for our new security system.'

'Good,' Pete answered distractedly. 'Assemble everyone on the Observation Deck. We're having a little farewell celebration.'

'You're not coming?'

'I'll be right down,' said Pete. 'I need to speak to Hodge.' Pete climbed the stairs to the security office.

'Professor, I was about to call you.' Hodge turned a screen panel for Pete to see. 'At first, we thought it was the Black Bird. But the craft is too big. They're not responding. I have a team ready to intercept.'

Pete watched the feed to the camera positioned outside of the surface compound. 'Alert Hank. Nobody enters the compound without my authorisation.'

'Yes, sir.'

Sam returned to the CC station and removed her lab coat. Feeling cold since coming down from the gymnasium, she looked around the cluttered desk for her thermal jacket. The monitor time alarm beeped, so she sat down to connect to Realm 12.

'Come in, Jolie.'

'Hey, Sam. The storm here is ripping the city apart.' She took on a tone akin to a mother disappointed in her child. 'Every nation in this version of Earth has been releasing high volumes of pollutants into the atmosphere on a daily basis.'

'Are they trying to commit suicide?'

'It's complicated. From what Rachel could gather, each nation is under the rule of corrupt monetary systems which control all resources, education and health.'

'That's messed up.' Sam backspaced Realm 12 on the database screen before her and typed in Storm Realm. A descriptive title for each realm made it easier to differentiate them.

'The global poverty count is horrific,' said Jolie.

Sam glanced behind her, hearing the elevator arrive at the Observation Deck.

'We're about to celebrate here,' she said. 'Are you coming back?'

'No, I'd like to stay here and help, at least until the storm passes. I am really looking forward to Cisco though. See you when I see you. Jolie out.'

Sam left the computer station and made her way back up the stairs to the Observation Deck.

Charlie swung around in his chair when he saw her. 'Hey, I passed your dad on the way down. He said he had to talk to Hodge.'

'Probably to prep an escort.' Sam noticed Charlie checking his console to see if he'd missed a message or a call. 'How did the briefing go?'

'Okay,' Charlie replied non-committally, his mind occupied by quiet emotions. 'I think I covered everything.'

'Meg Green is such a fox.'

'Huh?' Charlie's attention returned momentarily. 'I didn't notice.'

'Uh-huh.' Sam nodded, her intuition confirmed. 'Lex was at the briefing.'

Charlie turned back to the computer monitor, pretending to look over the data from the report.

'Yeah, she was there.' He rubbed his hands together and decided to change the subject. 'So, Rachel is in Harbour Realm?'

'Yeah, she has a little more research to do.'

Harbour Realm—yet another version of Melbourne—was a major shipping port. Rachel had returned to gather more historical data. She had rented an apartment in the city for extended stays. Her findings revealed that society in that world was in a state similar to what it was in the 1950s. Industry was booming, fashion and cars were sleek and colourful, and the city was not yet overpopulated or polluted.

'Did you have to explain Parabola to the Council?' Sam asked.

Charlie raised his chin for a big nod. 'Meg Green asked how the Genesis Lab was financed.'

'Of course.'

'I told them we got this site for free because it's about to be destroyed and that Pete paid for everything else himself.'

Sam felt a shiver and found it odd that she was able to see her own breath. 'Why is it freezing in here?'

'The heating must have been reset.' Charlie's shoulders trembled. 'Should be back up soon.' His eyes caught the screen over by the elevator. The camera view was directed at the corridor where he had last seen the Professor.

It showed Pete kneeling down beside Hodge. He had his left hand pressed against Hodge's chest, and he was cradling his head with the other.

'Sam!' Charlie hit the comms button at his desk. 'Medical and security to level one!'

Sam turned to the elevator screen. Two men in grey uniform pulled her father away from Hodge's limp body and pushed him along the corridor. Six more followed, armed with assault rifles.

'Dad!' She ran to a wall cabinet and fumbled at the encoded lock. 'Call Hank!' she yelled over her shoulder. 'We're under attack!' Opening the cabinet, Sam grabbed a pistol and a clip to load it.

Charlie grabbed hold of her and the gun. 'Get to Rachel and Jolie. I'll shut everything down so they can't follow.'

Sam nodded, her hands trembling with adrenaline. 'Get to the gym. Lana's not conscious.' She let him take the gun and turned around to see the elevator open.

Four Sabre Company soldiers entered the deck and opened fire.

CHAPTER 10

Miles and Jenny were in an apartment on the sixth floor. Dim yellow emergency lights illuminated the suite. There was a knock at the door. Miles opened it and the sound of commotion surged into the room: people running, babies crying.

A hotel staff member was standing outside. His hair was dishevelled and his voice was hoarse.

'Sir...' He took a moment to breathe. 'Emergency services advise everyone to remain in their rooms. Please stay away from the windows and keep the curtains drawn. The storm is expected to get worse. Evacuation is now impossible. The ground floor is completely flooded and the winds are too strong for rescue helicopters to take anyone from the roof. Excuse me. I have other rooms to get to.' He left and proceeded to knock on the next door.

Miles was about to close the door when he recognised Jolie hurrying by. She was carrying a shoulder satchel with UC Medical printed on it. He called out to her and she stopped.

'Miles, are you two all right?'

'We're okay.'

Miles let her into the room and Jenny came running over to her. In the short time that Jolie had stayed with her while Miles broadcasted the weather warning the two had bonded.

There was a loud crack as a flash of lightning lit the building across the street. Jolie watched over Miles' shoulder as the office building shuddered. The rain streaming down the window rippled as the glass vibrated.

Jolie rushed over to the curtain. She was about to draw it back when she heard what sounded like a spluttering engine.

Miles hurried towards Jolie.

'Sounds like an aeroplane.'

Jenny whimpered as the wind hammered the windows. There was a distant sound of glass smashing, then the whole room shook. The dull pounding of plaster walls breaking came from the bathroom, five paces from the lounge.

'Behind the couch!' Jolie shouted. She grabbed Jenny and Miles and pulled them to the floor. The bathroom wall exploded and tiles flew into the lounge.

The interior walls shuddered and cracked as the nose of a Cessna 206 plane slid through the doorway.

Home Realm
Silica
City of Liberty

Water dribbled down the windows of Rowan and Fiona's downtown apartment. The light rain outside blew like curtains carried by the wind, as the morning sunlight glowed along the curves and angles of the city buildings.

In the centre square, dwarfed only by a rainbow arching over it, was the Palmer Building—host to the current members of the Universal Community Council.

From the bed, Rowan stared out through the glass, remembering when the city more closely resembled a ghetto. And the sand! Oh, he hated that sand. The dunes had been pushed to the city limits to serve as a wind break. He combed

Fiona's light brown hair with his fingers, her head resting on his chest. She stroked her husband's stubbled jaw, her thumb following the shape of his lower lip.

'Where are you?' she asked.

Rowan's mind returned to the present. 'So, you suspect McCain?'

'Greer as well. I've been running background checks. They're clean.'

'Good.'

'No, bad. They're too clean. Their communications records, their finances, their numbers over the past five years are mathematically improbable.'

'In layman's terms that means...'

'Their numbers have been doctored.'

'You have to be absolutely certain before you present this to the Council,' Rowan stressed. 'There'll be repercussions if you're wrong.'

'I know.'

He recognised the conviction in Fiona's voice, but he needed more. 'Convince me.'

'Three years of deception detection training is telling me that these men are connected to Sabre Company.'

'McCain, maybe,' said Rowan. 'But Greer? He lost his wife. His kids won't speak to him. If you're wrong—'

'Greer and McCain disappear to private meetings every week. Something's going on. Their behaviour is too conspiratorial to be nothing.'

'All right,' Rowan conceded. 'I'll have a team—'

'No.' Fiona shook her head. 'We can't trust anyone with this.'

Rowan nodded. He hadn't seen Fiona this driven before. It was as though she had been letting her anger build, until she found the right time to unleash it upon those responsible for murdering her parents.

'When do you have to go back?' Rowan asked.

Fiona glanced at the clock on the opposite wall of the bedroom and pouted. 'Half an hour.'

'Plenty of time.' Rowan leaned over and kissed her. His Shifter comms beeped an incoming message and he let it receive through the unit's speaker.

'Rowan.' The whispering voice was barely audible. 'The lab and compound have been breached.'

'Charlie?' Fiona pushed herself up from the bed.

'Charlie, where are you?' Rowan reached for his clothes and for his handgun.

'Elevator… heading up to wake Lana. Rowan, don't come in. There are too many. They're Sabre Company.'

Rowan became still. His teeth were clenched and his jaw muscles twitched.

'They're going to access our realm coordinates database. They're going to go after Rachel. I tried to get through to her. They've jammed her Shifter.'

Rowan was dressed. 'Charlie, Hank and his team should be with you within the hour. Hide.'

'Copy…' The transmission fell silent.

Fiona took warm clothing from her wardrobe and got dressed. 'How will you find Rachel and Sam if their comms are jammed?'

'I can track Rachel's signature signal once I'm in.' Rowan looked at Fiona, uncomfortable with asking her to do what Charlie had advised against. 'Hank's team might not get to Charlie in time.'

'Program a teleport to get me into the lab,' said Fiona. She unlocked a gun safe at the bottom of the wardrobe and took out her handgun. 'The portal room probably has the most cover.'

Using the Shifter device that Professor O'Conner had given him, Rowan input the coordinates. He took Fiona's hand and squeezed it. 'Be careful.' Rowan opened a portal to the Harbour Realm and left the Shifter with Fiona.

≡ Harbour Realm ≡

Sam screamed. She was falling. Water pelted down and cool air rushed from beneath her. With a split second to gather her bearings, she judged her position to be three floors from the ground. In her haste to escape the SC soldiers, she had input inaccurate coordinates. Instead of landing in a laneway near Rachel's apartment, she was hurtling past it from above.

Sam reached out and grabbed the railing of an external fire escape. Pain surged through her arm as she stopped with a violent jerk, her body slammed against the vertical bars. She clutched at the rail frantically with her other hand, slipping before she could find a firm grip. Tensing her muscles, Sam heaved her upper body high enough to use her legs to climb. She looked down at the blue stone road below and let out a nervous laugh at the harsh fall that might have been her end.

Sam heard exclamations from tenants who had seen her fall. Their windows opened above and a woman called down to her, 'Crikey! You all right, love?'

'Fine, thank you,' Sam breathed. The fire escape door opened behind her and a man stepped out lighting a cigarette. Having not seen her fall he held the door open and greeted Sam politely. She made her way down the hallway and passed by an open door. An Ella Fitzgerald song was playing on a radio. She knocked on Rachel's door, dripping wet and groaning while she flexed the muscles in her injured arm.

'Rache? It's me, Sam.' No reply. She lifted the ragged door mat from the floor and took the key.

Home Realm
Glacier II

Cold hands shook Lana's body, her ears barely picking up Charlie's words. She lifted herself from the scanning table and immediately felt nauseous.

'Lana, they're getting away. Quickly, you have to find the Professor.'

'Wh—?' Lana tried to rub the spinning vision from her eyes. 'What's happening?' Charlie limped as he led her out of the room. 'Charlie, you're hurt.'

'I'm okay.'

The two of them reached the service elevator and the door slid closed. The compartment descended to the lab.

Lana's focus returned in waves. She saw the red stain on the leg of Charlie's pants.

'We're under attack,' Lana realised aloud. She watched her friend stumble against the frost covered steel wall and caught him before he fell to the floor. 'Charlie!'

'Find… find the Professor.' Charlie's eyes rolled back and his head dropped against Lana's chest.

'Charlie, wake up.'

The elevator stopped and the doors opened. Stepping cautiously out into the corridor, Lana froze when she saw a Sabre Company soldier enter from the Observation Deck.

The AM unit raised the long barrel of his suppressed pistol.

Lana ducked beneath the pelting line of fire, reached into the service elevator and hit the 'door close' button, sealing Charlie safely inside the compartment. Dashing diagonally across the soldier's path, Lana rolled along the floor to avoid the unit's next shot, then scissor kicked his legs out from under him. She flipped her body over his chest and whipped her elbow across his temple.

A second soldier approached. Lana leapt up from the floor and thrust both her fists into his chest. The unit crashed against the computer towers. Before he could raise his gun, Lana had covered the space between them and landed a side kick to his stomach. He doubled over and she twisted her hips and shoulders to knock him out with a downward round punch across the head.

Monotonous churning of data processing returned to fill the cold silence.

Lana heard a supressed round go off and she tensed, activating an ability that Professor O'Conner had given to her as part of his Human Augmentation project.

Lana's cells reacted to her brain perceiving danger. Her skin hardened to become a layer of organic silicon carbide. The bullet pierced Lana's tank top, bounced against her armoured chest and clinked down the metal steps.

Wincing at the stinging pain, Lana grabbed the gun from the soldier lying at her feet.

'What are you?' stammered a third SC soldier, standing two metres to her right.

Lana shot the AM unit in reply.

CHAPTER 11

Fiona appeared in the portal room with a flash of light. Watching for other hostiles, she aimed her gun at the fallen soldier she saw ahead of her. Moisture had settled and frozen on the steel steps, making them slippery. As Fiona carefully made her way up to the Observation Deck, she found two more SC soldiers sprawled on the floor.

Fiona heard Charlie's voice coming from the service elevator corridor. He was crawling along the floor, his numbed limbs barely working.

Fiona knelt down beside him and found the bullet wound in his lower thigh. A bloody trail led out from the elevator compartment, across the floor to Charlie's shivering body.

'They have our data.' Teeth chattering, Charlie struggled to speak. 'Sam, Rachel, in danger.'

Fiona ripped Charlie's shirt open, removed her own and held him against her chest. 'Charlie, I need you to control your breathing for me, okay? Long, deep breaths.'

Charlie's breathing deepened, while Fiona's body heat warmed his blood. He winced when the feeling returned to his leg, bringing pain at every movement.

Fiona lowered Charlie back to the floor and dragged him into the Observation Deck.

'They were Sabre Company,' he said. 'Fiona, they have… they have Shifter technology. Hacked our database. They can track Rachel.'

Fiona was beginning to see the gravity of the situation. Sabre Company could teleport reinforcements into the Genesis Lab at any moment. She found a medical kit, took out a pair of scissors and cut away Charlie's pants to expose the wound.

Charlie looked around the Observation Deck, delirious with pain. 'Lana! Where's Lana?'

'I'll find her.'

'Had to wake her… they have the Professor. She has thermal and… armoured skin cell capabilities.' Charlie's voice faltered while his body began to respond to an injection Fiona administered. 'She's… going after him.'

Fiona glanced back at the elevator. 'She'll need back up.'

Charlie gripped Fiona's arm. 'We have to set up… inhibitors… stop SC forces teleporting in.'

Fiona finished bandaging Charlie's leg. 'Charlie, how do I get the heating back on?'

'Generator room. Next… level up.'

≡ Harbour Realm ≡

Rowan exited a post office carrying a map of the city. A taxi screeched to a halt to avoid colliding with a crossing pedestrian. Rowan automatically reached inside his jacket for his gun.

'Hey, I'm walkin' here!'

The taxi driver stepped out of the cab and shouted back at the pedestrian. 'Are you crazy? I could've killed you! You see this here?' He pointed at the bitumen at their feet and then to the foot path. 'This is mine. That over there is yours. Stick to it!'

'Cool it, mate! You don't own the road!' The man looked over the driver's shoulder, amused to see the taxi reversing. 'Mate, somebody's stealing your cab.'

The taxi driver turned around and began shouting again. 'Oi! Stop!'

Rowan swung the taxi around and accelerated around a corner. All vehicles in Home Realm were powered by emission free, renewable energy. Rowan had to train himself to drive fuel cars when he started going on Realm missions with Rachel. Acceleration was sluggish and the liquid powering the car always sloshed from side to side, adversely influencing its handling. Like all early cars, the taxi he was driving was heavy, but Rowan did enjoy the engine sound. Back home that sound still appealed to motoring enthusiasts like him. High quality speakers were hidden on the outside of sports and muscle cars. The deep rumble and throaty pitch were activated in all of their variations, in perfect sync with the driver's acceleration.

Adjusting her 1950s styled, dark brown wig, Rachel exited the museum. She'd thought hiding her blue hair would help her blend into this version of Melbourne. However, there were very few African Americans living in the city, so she still received the odd judgmental look. It was cool and drizzling, so Rachel pulled on her jacket. She paused when she noticed three men approaching her from across the street.

The man leading looked familiar. He signalled for the two behind him to stop as he continued towards Rachel.

Heavy rain began to fall. It was swept up by the wind, drenching the red-headed man. For a moment, Rachel thought it was Luke. But her mind dismissed the thought as soon as it occurred. And yet, when the man finally reached her, Rachel saw that it was him. It was Luke Palmer.

Rachel stared, open-mouthed. She blinked through the rain, her speech coming out in a stammer.

'How… Luke, how are you here?' Rachel glanced behind him to the other two men. They stood waiting, on guard.

Luke was tall, taller than Rachel remembered him to be. He gazed down at her, rain blowing over the two of them. Luke nodded to the fern bushes by the entrance of the museum. 'Dump your weapon,' he said. 'You're coming with me.'

'What? Luke, where have you been? I thought you were dead.'

Luke retrieved a black metallic object from his jacket pocket. Rachel saw that it was a variation of a Shifter. He was programming a portal.

There was a tattoo on the back of Luke's hand. Rachel froze in alarm. It was a sword crossed over a hammer—Sabre Company's symbol.

Rachel pushed the false hair fringe away from her eyes and checked her escape routes. A taxi entered the museum car park and pulled over. That was her best way out.

Rachel searched Luke's face, trying to read him. But his eyes were vacant, cold and empty. The Luke she knew was a hero. He had always risen above loss and found the strength to fight. She had loved him for his selfless commitment to justice.

'Luke, what happened to you?' Her voice was calm, but her eyes watered as she battled confusing emotions.

Luke's head lifted slowly. He smiled.

'I woke up.' The outer corner of his left eye twitched. 'You can wake up too. We're giving you a choice, Rachel, join us… or die.'

'Luke, I can help you. Professor O'Conner can—'

'Your professor is with us,' said Luke. 'He's alive and he'll stay that way… if you come with me. Right now.'

Rachel forced her mind to focus. 'Luke, this is crazy. You're not one of them. They took your sister!'

Luke raised his hand and signalled for the others to take her.

Rachel's eyes remained on the man she once loved. 'They will pay for what they have done to you, I promise.'

She snatched the pistol she had spied, holstered inside Luke's jacket. Deflecting his hand when he reacted, she bent her knees, turned her hips and shoulders and punched Luke's stomach, winding him. Rachel struck the base of Luke's neck with his gun and he fell unconscious. She heard Rowan's voice shouting from the taxi and she ran, firing at the two Sabre Company soldiers to hold them back.

Rachel ducked and weaved to avoid the return fire. She made it to the taxi and jumped onto the back seat.

Bullets pelted the boot of the car. The taxi accelerated off the kerb, into the middle of the road. Rowan hit the brake and changed into reverse gear.

An SC soldier flanked the car. It jolted when Rowan pushed the accelerator to the floor and spun the steering wheel clockwise. Water splashed up onto the bonnet as the taxi whipped around, the tyres sliding through a deep puddle.

The soldier stopped in his tracks when he saw the front of the car swinging towards him. His legs flew out from underneath him upon impact. His body dinted the bonnet as he bounced on his back, the momentum carrying him into a barrel roll. Rowan hit the brake and pushed the gear stick into drive.

Two bullets flew through the rear windscreen. Rachel wound down her passenger window and returned fire.

Rowan pulled the handbrake to swing into the merging lane of a highway.

'Sabre Company have attacked the Genesis Lab,' said Rowan. 'They have their own Shifters and they have the signature signal for yours. They're tracking you.'

Rachel was immediately worried for Sam and Lana. 'Luke said they have Pete.'

Rowan took an exit ramp and gave way to oncoming traffic before entering the street. He glanced at Rachel's reflection in the rear-view mirror. 'Luke?'

'Did Sam and Lana get out?' Rachel asked. 'Are they safe?'

'Sam used a portal to come here,' Rowan answered quickly. 'Lana will be all right. I sent Fiona in and Hank's team will be there by now. Rache, are you saying that was Luke back there?'

Rachel swore in frustration.

'Yes, it was him.' She glared out of the window, watching the cars cruise through the rain. 'They did something to him,' she said, pushing her fingers through her sodden hair. 'He doesn't know who he his.'

Rowan's grip tightened on the steering wheel. 'Doctor Kindred.'

'I don't know if there's anything we can do for him,' Rachel said, gravely. 'He seemed... too far gone.' She swore again, thumping the back of the chair in front of her. 'Head to my apartment. Sam knows where I stay.'

'Rache, this is bad. Shifter technology in the hands of Sabre Company...'

Rachel nodded solemnly. 'They'll strike the Council. Dennis Conroy has been hiding for a long time. He and Williams could be anywhere. If they've been building AM units, they could have hundreds, maybe thousands of soldiers.'

'They've had Shifters since they escaped Silica,' said Rowan. 'They've probably found Realms that have the resources they need. We're not talking about capturing criminals anymore. This is going to mean war.'

Rowan spotted a black Mercedes weaving erratically between oncoming traffic. 'What the...? Crazy son of a—'

The Mercedes jerked and swerved towards them. The front passenger window wound down and a shotgun barrel slid out along the ridge of the door. The windscreen exploded as the shell burst. Rowan fought to retain control of the vehicle, but the tyres struggled on the slippery, wet road. The taxi spun three-hundred-and-sixty degrees before slamming into a parked truck.

CHAPTER 12

Rachel woke with ringing in her ears. She was lying across the back seat. The muffled murmurs of onlookers grew louder. She could make out a man's voice coming from outside.

'Hey lady, you okay? Are you hurt?'

Broken glass crunched as Rachel lifted herself. The door opened at her feet and the man helped her out.

Rachel pushed away from him and opened the door that had taken the shotgun shell. A crescent shaped hole marked the point of impact on the window ledge. An inch higher and Rowan would have been killed.

The commotion grew behind Rachel as onlookers huddled around the vehicle. Some murmured concern. Others commented on Rachel's blue hair; her wig had fallen off. She hovered over her brother, checking the cut in his scalp. Blood had dribbled down Rowan's cheek and neck.

'Come on, Ro.' Rachel shook him, aware that their attackers could be on them at any moment.

'Wake up. We have to go.'

She gripped his arm and lifted him. Gunfire sounded and the crowd of onlookers dispersed in panic. Rachel ducked, pulling Rowan down beneath her. She bobbed her head up to place the location of the shooter.

'Rache...?' Rowan woke, trying to move.

'Stay down, I'll draw their fire.' Rachel took the pistol from Rowan's jacket and pushed it into his hand. She had lost her own somewhere on the floor of the car. 'Get to the apartment. I'll meet you there.'

'How many?'

Rachel made a quick head count and spied an open park area connected to the street. She could make it. 'Two, maybe three. Black car, eight metres.' She pulled her jacket off, keeping her head down.

Positioning himself for a quick pop-up and fire, Rowan nodded to his sister. 'Go.'

As she ran low to the park, the AMs opened fire. Rowan landed a shot to the side of the first unit's head. The other dropped, raising his gun to fire in Rowan's general direction. Another car arrived.

Jabbing his finger towards the park, the soldier called to the driver, 'Female, blue hair!'

The driver accelerated towards the park, stopping at its edge to proceed on foot. Peering around the dense hedging, he scanned the open green area. There was no movement, save a fountain gushing water. As he crossed the picnic grounds, he spotted a white collared shirt draped over the back of a nearby park bench. He stood by the discarded garment, unsure what to make of it.

Rachel jumped up out of the fountain and grabbed the AM unit's wrist with one hand, raising the soldier's gun. With the other hand, she punched his face. Rachel pulled him down by the neck.

The soldier squeezed a nine-millimetre round into the air and Rachel raised her knee into his abdomen. She twisted the gun out of his hand, kicked the back of his knees and chopped him at the base of his neck with the gun. The soldier fell unconscious against the fountain.

Rachel flicked her long fringe away from her eyes and looked towards the park's main entrance. A car slowed when it reached the perimeter, turned and mounted the pavement. Driving along the pathway, it accelerated across the open green towards the fountain. The front passenger leaned out of the window and fired an assault rifle.

Rachel sprinted for the closest trees, as bullets ripped through the soil. Dropping into a roll, she rose to one knee and fired at the car, landing accurate shots. A front tyre blew. Unable to stop, the vehicle swerved. It clipped a lamp post and swung sideways, burying the midsection into a tree.

Rachel ran to the opposite side of the park, scaled a wooden fence and spied a pay-phone booth at the end of the block.

An elderly man returned the phone to its hook, exited the booth and stopped abruptly in front of Rachel.

'Good grief, love,' he said. 'What ya doing wondering around half-dressed?'

Rachel waved him out of the way with her gun and the old man quickly hobbled off, mumbling incoherently.

Rachel dug her hand into her pants pocket to retrieve some coins. She snatched up the phone and fed the wet copper into the slot. Heavy droplets fell against the windows of the slim compartment and the rain continued its rhythmic drum.

'Hello?' Sam answered with a croaky waking voice.

'Sam, it's Rachel. Are you okay?'

'I'm fine. Where are you?'

'I'm about ten minutes out.' Rachel checked each direction of the street. 'Sam, Sabre Company are here in this Realm. Rowan and I got separated.' She spotted a bus arriving at a stop crowded with commuters.

'Are you okay? Can you lose them?'

'I don't know. They're tracking us. We can't shut our Shifters down without cutting our line to the lab. Best we can do is keep moving. I have to go. See you soon.'

Home Realm
Glacier II

The Black Bird landed and the crew were preparing to disembark. Chesh ran the ship's systems diagnostics, flicking the overhead diverter switches off and on, checking response time of the relay engagement. Satisfied, she reached for a mug of coffee and pulled on an Ushanka hat. A detection warning beeped on the ship scanners. Chesh ignored it, knowing the snowstorm outside created interference, giving false readings. The warning persisted, bringing up a heat signature and a holo-display of a woman.

Chesh spilled her beverage in her lap and swore loudly. She wiped her tank top with one hand, while using a joystick to control the camera zoom with the other. She saw the young woman walking through the snow outside, wearing torn gym clothes.

'Damn, girl!' Lex exclaimed when she arrived behind the pilot. 'On your own time!'

'How is this girl not a freakin' ice cube?'

Lex had a smirk on her lips that quickly faded. 'Wait, that's a camera feed? Is she outside?'

Lana swayed, staring out at the vast open planes of Glacier II. The hill formations in the distance were barely discernible in the snow. As her vision panned across the horizon, Lana saw the silhouette of Space Cruiser against the light purple horizon. The Parabola Light Band glistened against a steep glacier to Lana's left. Determined to find her professor, she pushed on through the ankle-deep snow and freezing wind towards the ship.

Hank and Renee prepped equipment with Brad in the cargo bay. Four UC AM units were with them, armed and ready.

Brad inserted a fresh magazine of armour piercing rounds into his assault rifle.

'Easy,' Renee chided her partner, when she noticed his muscles twitching.

Brad Hawkins and Renee Riley had been together since the first year serving on the Black Bird. They were highly skilled fighters and their specialty was heavy weapons.

Brad loaded white phosphorous shells into the launcher attachment beneath the barrel of his gun. His sister was one of the first delegates the Council had sent to investigate the planet, during Corporate rule. She escaped with one other colleague, only to die from a bullet wound in transit to the nearest hospital.

The cargo room comms received a message from Chesh. 'Ah, Captain, there's a lady wandering around out there without a coat on. Better bring her in.'

Renee pulled on her chest armour. She gave Hank a quizzical look.

Hank activated the cargo comms receiver remotely, using his wrist console. 'Say again, Chesh?'

'I'm not on the sauce, Cap. Check the feed. Quick! It's forty below out there!'

Renee tapped on the computer console by the cargo bay wall and brought up the ship's exterior camera feed on a large holo-display. The visual was grainy, due to the wind-blown sleet and snow, but they all saw her.

'Renee, bring her in,' Hank ordered. 'Brad, thermal blankets. Go.'

Lana's hair was rigid. The ice wind coated her body in white. She saw two figures in thick coats running towards her and immediately lowered herself into a defensive stance.

Brad scanned the area for hostiles while Renee unfolded a thermal blanket and approached Lana.

'We're not going to hurt you. Brad, weapon down!' she shouted over the wind to Brad.

He did so slowly. Brad couldn't understand how Lana was able to survive in minus forty-degree weather.

Renee held out the blanket. 'Put this on before you freeze to death.'

Lana read their body language and saw no threat. 'Professor…' Lana breathed. 'They've taken Professor O'Conner.'

CHAPTER 13

Lex helped Lana lower herself into the heating tub she'd prepared. Amped up from her first experience of real combat, Lana flinched every time Lex touched her to check her pulse rate and temperature.

'I've never seen anything like it.' Lex spoke to no one in particular. 'All vitals normal.' She glanced at her dad. 'No indication of frostbite on any of her extremities.' Then she addressed Lana, still holding her wrist. 'Your heart rate is a little elevated, but you seem to be fine. What's your name?'

'Lana,' she said. 'Mammoth blood.' Hank looked from Lana to Lex. 'Huh?'

'Lana must be Pete's Augmented Human,' said Lex. 'She was able to withstand the cold because Pete engineered her genome, so that high oxygen blood can flow to her extremities. That's how the mammoths survived harsh cold.'

Hank pretended to understand what his daughter said and turned to Renee. 'Chesh is around Lana's size. Get her to bring down some warm clothes.' He heard the incoming comms beep again.

'Captain, the lab and compound communications are back online,' Chesh reported. 'Patching you through now.'

Inside the surface compound, Fiona headed to the main hangar. She found three AM security units, shot down and beyond repair. She counted five Sabre Company soldiers lying incapacitated on her way to the hangar exit. She guessed that Lana had taken them down and ventured out into the snow. There was no sign of Peter O'Conner. Hank's voice came through a wall speaker in the hangar.

'This is Captain Henry Drake. Come in Genesis Lab.'

Fiona found the receiver button and replied. 'Hank, Fiona here. The lab has been breached and may be attacked again at any moment. What's your ETA?'

'Copy that, Fiona. We have arrived and are ready to deploy.'

≡ Harbour Realm ≡

A white flash of light beamed in through the gap beneath the door. It receded and several Sabre Company soldiers grunted enthusiastic remarks about their successful attack on the Genesis Lab. Two stayed behind, casting a shadow by the door.

'Don't go in,' one said to the other. 'Just slide it under the door.'

Luther Saint sat in a crimson leather armchair, motionless in the dark. His glazed eyes flicked to the shift of light and his ears pricked at the click of a mechanical knee joint. A black data tablet slid across the varnished wooden floor and footsteps echoed down the hallway. Twenty minutes past before Luther rose from the chair to retrieve the small device. While lighting a cigarette, he fed it into his Shifter console.

The data message came through and read, *Rachel Navara: Female, 30. 5"3. African American. Kill on sight. Tracking linked.*

A short personal message from Colonel Jericho Williams followed:

Happy hunting, comrade.

CHAPTER 14

Rachel entered her apartment with her hand on the pistol in the back of her pants.

'Sam?' she called. 'It's me.'

She saw a wet Genesis Lab uniform and underwear drying on the clotheshorse by the heater. She looked into the bathroom and saw the cabinet mirror clouded with steam. There were wet footprints on the linoleum floor.

Rachel found Sam in the bedroom, sound asleep beneath the doona. She set the gun down on the bedside table and pulled off her soaked shoes and socks.

Rachel turned on the radio in the lounge room and poured herself a glass of whisky in the kitchen. As she gulped it down, warmth travelled all the way down to her toes. Glancing at the front door, she shuffled wearily across the room and double-checked the locks.

Satisfied, Rachel went to the bathroom and tuned on the shower. The plumbing system groaned like an old metal beast as the temperature rose. She leaned in and let out a tired groan of pleasure as warm water fell over her hand. She hummed the Andrews Sisters' song playing in the lounge, 'Rum and Coca-Cola'. Memories drifted through her mind, of a time when she was growing up in San Francisco. Her mother would swing her hips to the calypso rhythm. The sun beaming into the kitchen would light her caramel brown skin. Rachel was almost able to smell the comforting warmth of her mother's cooking: creamy chicken soup, apple pie for dessert. She wiped the mirror door of the cabinet and gazed back at her reflection, massaging her temples as a headache began to pound with every pulse.

After taking painkillers from a packet on the bathroom sink, Rachel stepped into the shower and lathered her hands with soap. The vanilla bar slipped from her grip and she crouched to pick it up. She gasped when she stood up. A middle-aged man sat on a wooden chair in the corner of the bathroom. He was hunched over, leaning on his knees, creasing the material of his dark brown suit.

'He wouldn't stop,' he said.

Rachel peered through the steam, recognising the man. 'Dad?'

He gave no indication of having heard her. He continued as though she wasn't there. 'He reminded me of our neighbour's dog. He got loose one time. I must have been maybe seven. I was in the front yard with my ball and glove. And there he was. Some of the other kids in the neighbourhood had told me he was dangerous.'

The lighting in the bathroom began to change. Daylight streamed in through broad windows that appeared out of nowhere. Rachel found herself clothed in 1970s style attire, standing in a small room with her father and a woman seated in front of him.

'This isn't real,' Rachel stammered. She took a step back and bumped into a solid wall. 'Just a dream.'

Her father's Mexican accent returned. 'He stood, shoulders squared at me, eyes on mine. Didn't have his heckles up, didn't bare his teeth. He was as close as you are to me,' he said to the woman. 'His tail was moving.' He made a slow swaying motion with his hand. 'He wasn't making a sound, not the slightest growl. Then I heard my old man on the porch. He said, "Chico, don't move." The dog didn't look at my papa. He kept his eyes on me.'

Rachel held her hands against her ears and shrank down to the floor. 'This isn't real.'

Her father opened his mouth to speak but paused when a phone rang in the next room. 'The dog didn't move until my papa tried to grab it. It jumped at him, threw Papa on his back.' He ran his fingers through his short dark hair. 'Papa kicked it off, grabbed me and we ran into the house. The second we closed the door, that dog hit our door so hard it split the wood. It waited out on our porch, didn't make a sound the entire time. Then the rangers came and took it away. Papa told me later that the dog didn't bark or bare its teeth because it didn't want to scare me away. It wanted to kill me.' The phone continued to ring. Rachel's father seemed to be waiting, expecting the ringing to stop, to hear the murmur of a secretary's voice answer the call.

'Detective, you say you fired twice at the assailant,' said the woman in the room.

Rachel gasped. It was her mother's voice. She had been a counsellor, Rachel remembered. This was how her parents met.

'He was armed with a knife,' Rachel's mother continued. 'You suspect he was on drugs?'

'We'd been watching him for weeks. We spoke to people who knew him. They said he was "charming", "a real talker". He never did drugs. He killed her, just like he killed the others.'

'His girlfriend,' she confirmed.

Rachel's father looked at his future wife, slightly irritated. 'Isn't somebody going to answer that?'

She stopped to listen. 'Answer what?'

A tingle travelled up Rachel's spine. She could hear the ringing as clearly as though it were in the next room.

'I was too late to save her.'

Rachel's mother leaned forward and offered consolation. 'Dogs very rarely attack without warning. Sadly, the same cannot be said for people. There is something in some people, Detective Navara, something that must extinguish life. Some call it evil. Whatever it was in that man you shot, it's gone now because of you. You're a brave man.'

The bathroom was thick with steam. Rachel lay in the shower basin, curled in a foetal position. The soap she had stooped to pick up was in her hand. Hot water washed over her. The phone continued to ring. Rachel's eyelids quivered, her vision blurred. With a moan she raised herself to her knees. She turned off the water, stepped out of the shower and looked around the small room. There was no one there. Wrapping a towel under her arms, she made her way to the phone. She managed to find it on the floor, beneath some cardboard boxes.

'Hello?'

'Rache, it's Rowan.'

Rachel snatched her Shifter device from the kitchen table. It was six o'clock in the evening. 'Ro, are you okay?'

'I'm fine. I went to a hospital. Listen, I'll be at your building in twenty minutes. Sam all right?'

'She's fine. We'll meet you in the laneway out back.'

As soon as Rowan hung up, there was a knock at the door.

Rachel quickly moved to the back of the lounge to scan the street from the window. 'Who is it?' she called. There were no parked cars on the street. No sign of SC soldiers. Not that they would be advertising their presence. So far, they had been smart enough to dress according to Harbour Realm's fashion.

'It's Kurt, from across the hall.'

'Just a minute.' Rachel hurried to the bedroom to check on Sam. She hadn't taken the time to get to know the people in her building, but the name Kurt didn't ring a bell.

Sam had been woken by the knocking. She stood with the doona wrapped under her arms. She pulled Rachel close as soon as she entered the room, hugging tightly. 'Are you okay?'

'I'm fine.' Rachel saw the bruise along Sam's arm. 'You're hurt.'

Sam shook her head reassuringly. 'I came in a little off course.' She paused, swallowing worry and grief. 'Rache, they took him. They took my dad.'

'I know.' Rachel squeezed her gently. 'We'll find him.'

Sam heard more knocking at the front door. 'Were you followed?'

'I don't know,' Rachel replied, opening her dresser draw to retrieve clothes for herself and Sam.

'Get dressed. I'll deal with whoever this is. Lock this door behind me.' She took the gun from the dresser, turned the safety off and handed it to Sam.

'What about you?'

'I'll be fine.' Rachel turned to leave, but Sam took her hand.

'Hey,' she said. 'Happy anniversary.'

Rachel gave Sam a tired smirk and closed the bedroom door. She heard Sam lock it like she had asked and she hurried down the hallway to the front door, pulling on her underwear and a collared shirt as she went. She stopped before buttoning up, thinking a test was in order.

'Sorry, I was in the shower,' Rachel said, changing her speech to sound ditsy when she opened the door.

The man's jaw dropped, but he managed a stammered greeting.

Rachel saw Kurt's pupils dilate with arousal as his eyes wondered down her body. AM units were designed to mimic human responses, but they could never replicate sexual attraction. Rachel was convinced Kurt wasn't a machine. Not only was he blushing, but Kurt's skin had blemishes and his facial features weren't symmetrical.

But Sabre Company always employed spies.

'I know it's late, it's just…' turning his head, Kurt gestured to the apartment across the hall.

'My power is out and—' When Kurt turned back to face Rachel, she struck a lightning-fast open hand to his throat, grabbed a fist full of his blonde hair and pulled him into the living room, slamming the door behind him. Kurt fell to his knees, gasping for air.

The sound of breaking glass came from the back of the apartment. Rachel spun around, flicking water from her hair across the floor.

Luther Saint climbed through the window he'd smashed, then made his way through the laundry room to the hall. He aimed a revolver towards the lounge, where he could hear someone struggling to breathe. The hallway light above Luther went out. Bare feet padded across the tiled floor. He fired twice. A bare leg swung out of the shadows and Luther's gun was knocked out of his hand. Rachel felt for Luther's right arm. She twisted and wrenched it over her shoulder, flinging him into the lounge and across the floor.

Luther rolled to his feet, took something from his pocket and flicked it open to reveal a long shiny blade. It gleamed in the lamp light.

He and Rachel approached one another, stopping two metres apart. Anticipating a retreat, Luther loosened his grip on the knife handle to allow for a fast flip and throw. He chuckled for a moment, ignoring the dull ache in his shoulder.

'So, you are the infamous Rachel Navara. I must say, I'm impressed.' His Spanish accent coloured each word with a subtle *H*.

Rachel spotted Luther's silver revolver an arm's length from Kurt. She crouched slowly and picked up a towel from the floor. Winding and pulling the towel taut lengthways, Rachel prepared to feign an attack.

'Where is your brother?' Luther thought it prudent to question his target before killing her. Rachel dashed forward, allowing Luther to stab his knife at her.

Hips and shoulders twisted, stabbing arm stretched, Luther's thrust sent his razor-sharp blade less than a millimetre away from Rachel's abdomen. The blade tore through the towel and stopped with a dull thud at the knife handle.

Rachel ducked under Luther's stabbing arm and twisted the towel around his wrist before pulling his hand and arm over her shoulder.

Unable to free his wrist from the knotted towel, Luther let go of his knife and took another from his waist belt. He brought it down through Rachel's shirt, along her back, and she screamed, releasing him.

A red, diagonal line appeared on Rachel's shoulder. She felt Luther's gloved hand gripping the muscle above her collarbone. She had half a second to react, before he delivered a fatal stab. Luther tightened his grip around the handle of his knife, his elbow jerking back to power the thrust.

'Don't move!' Sam yelled, holding the pistol Rachel had given her. She stepped into the light with the gun trained on Luther's chest. 'Drop the knife.'

Luther hesitated a moment, glancing from the gun to Sam's steady eyes. He heard her pull the gun hammer back and let his second knife fall to the floor.

Rachel grabbed Luther's hand and pulled him close to her back. Spinning around, she struck his head with her elbow and kneed his crotch. Staggering back against the wall, Luther dropped to the floor, groaning quietly.

Sam caught the glint of the silver revolver shaking unsteadily in Kurt's white hands.

'Put... put the gun down,' Kurt stuttered. He gulped, still recovering from Rachel's palm strike. Nervously aiming the gun from Luther to Sam, Kurt flinched when Rachel edged towards him.

Rachel stepped cautiously towards Kurt.

He remained motionless, kneeling on the floor.

'I just wanted to use your phone,' he said. 'Maybe borrow some candles.'

'You people still use candles?' Sam rambled, her hands shaking. 'They're harmful to your lungs. The soot is—'

'Sam.' Rachel held up a hand for her to stop talking. 'Kurt, I'm sorry I attacked you. Go ahead and use the phone.' She slowly reached out to take the gun, but Kurt jerked the pistol upwards a fraction and fired. Rachel heard Sam fire her gun as well. She clenched her right fist, ready to pound Kurt's temple hard enough to cause brain damage. In the corner of her eye, she saw Luther swaying weakly, two entry wounds spreading blood across his suit jacket. He dropped to his knees, revealing a red-splattered wall behind him. The knife he had retrieved from the floor while Rachel was distracted dropped out of his hand, embedding itself in the carpet. Luther's head bounced as his body hit the floor.

Rachel slowly loosened Kurt's grip from Luther's gun. Kurt turned white and fainted. Rachel felt a sense of relief when she pressed her hand to the cut along her back to find that her wound would not need stitching. 'Well done,' she said to Sam.

Sam swallowed, her mouth dry. 'Thanks.'

Rowan arrived in the laneway in a green Morris Minor. He flashed the headlights when he saw Rachel and Sam making their way down the stairwell.

The two of them climbed into the back seat. Black cars entered either end of the laneway and waited, their headlights gleaming through the drizzling rain.

'We're blocked in,' she said. Then she heard police sirens. 'Ah, crap.'

'Any ideas?' Rowan revved the motor.

Sabre Company soldiers emerged from their cars carrying MG4 light machine guns.

Before the first bullets flew through the windscreen and out the back of the rear window, Rachel ducked and pulled Sam down. Red and blue lights illuminated the laneway walls. The machine gun fire stopped pelting the rear of the car and Rachel raised herself enough to look through the rear-view mirror. An officer commanded the soldiers to drop their weapons and the AMs opened fire. The policeman fell and a shotgun blast rang out. Rachel saw an AM fall, while the other returned fire. Gun fire started from above. Rachel guessed her apartment had been cleared by the police and they were attacking the AMs from the fire escape.

'Sam, open a portal!' Rachel yelled over the clamour.

'To where?'

'Anywhere! Do it! Rowan, drive!' The car accelerated and Rowan pulled on the steering wheel, swerving to avoid the shower of bullets.

There was a distinct electrical buzz when Sam activated her Shifter device. Mercury swallowed the car in seconds.

The SC soldiers watched as their approaching target began to distort. Trash cans, puddle water and bluestone were thrown into the air. The Morris Minor disappeared completely. Crumbs of debris and water pelted against the walls and showered down onto the laneway's dislodged surface.

CHAPTER 15

Charlie woke to find Lana seated beside him, staring pensively across the room. The observation monitors connected to adhesive pads on his wrist and temples beeped quietly.

'Lana, I'm sorry I had to throw you into that.'

Lana turned to him and tried to smile, but could only manage to press her lips. 'You did the right thing.'

'Is Hodge…'

Lana squeezed Charlie's hand. A tear rolled down her cheek. 'He's gone. I couldn't get to him fast enough.'

Charlie shook his head. 'Don't blame yourself.'

He saw a look in Lana's eyes that he hadn't noticed before. It wasn't just loss. She was the Genesis Lab's resident child. All her short life, Lana had been a Realm explorer in training. Today, she had become a combatant.

Lana sniffed and wiped her eyes. 'I have to go. Don't hang around here too long, okay? We have work to do.'

Fiona arrived as Lana was leaving.

'She'll be all right,' she said to Charlie. 'Rachel trained her to be tough.'

'Can you find me a wheelchair? I need to get to work on the inhibitors.'

Fiona called to a medical AM and asked him to bring one. 'I was hoping you'd be feeling up to it. We've got AMs guarding every room, but right now we can't stop Sabre Company from teleporting in another contingent.'

Lana rode the service elevator to the gym. The lights came on when she arrived and the computer resumed 'Take Five'. Lana told it to stop and there was silence. She nodded to the two AMs stationed in the gym, climbed the stairs, walked through the snow room and pushed the outer door open. The icy wind hissed over the roof. Snow clung to the long sleeve shirt and denim jeans Lana had borrowed from Chesh. She leaned on the rail. Her long fringe whipped about her cold wet nose.

She slid her hand across the steel rail to where Hodge had stood each morning while she went for her run.

Lana's tears froze against her skin.

≡ Storm Realm ≡
City of Kingston
Chandler Hotel

Jenny clapped her hands over her ears. The ceaseless, wall-shaking wind roared on through the night. She closed her eyes, frightened by the sudden flashes of lightning that shifted the shadows and were followed by terrible rumbles.

Jolie, Miles and Jenny had been forced to abandon their suite. The gale force winds that ravaged the city overnight had blown in windows and torn away entire rooms.

Jenny flinched when Jolie put her arm around her.

'Don't worry about your father,' she heard Jolie say over the noise outside. 'He'll be back soon.'

Jolie had stayed on to help Miles and his daughter, in the hope that the storm would die down and rescue personnel could evacuate survivors. There were nine other people in the room. Those who had already booked the room had let in Jolie, Jenny, Miles and others who had to escape the side of the building that was taking the brunt of the storm winds.

Miles burst through a door a few metres from them. He was followed by a cloud of smoke.

'Daddy!' Jenny collided with her father and hugged him.

'Are you okay?' Jolie noticed Miles' shirt was grey with ash.

'Fine.' Miles coughed, trying to catch his breath. 'I'm fine. Can't get to the ground floor though.' He was approached by some of the other adults in the room and he told them the situation before they could all start questioning him at once. 'There's a fire,' he said. 'I managed to get into the plane that crashed into us. There were no passengers.'

'A fire?' a man exclaimed. 'Why hasn't it been put out? This hotel should have—'

'It's not out and the smoke is getting worse,' said Miles. 'So, I think we should try to—'

'The hotel staff were escorting groups of people to the stairwell,' a woman said, speaking rapidly, 'so they can get to the roof and be ready for helicopter rescue. They had just one other room of people to clear before ours but that was ten minutes ago. Maybe we should just go!'

The floor began to shake and the building swayed, as the earth beneath its foundations shifted.

'Earthquake!' Jolie yelled. 'Get down!'

She pulled the door to the hallway open and thick smoke plumed in. She pressed Miles, Jenny and two other people into the door space. The only other doorway was to the bathroom, and four people had already crammed themselves close to the frame. The walls and ceiling split. Chunks of plaster fell and the light fixtures dropped down.

A loud crack came from outside, like a giant twisting an enormous pine tree. The building became still after a moment of vibration and Miles heard the crackling of fire.

'Everybody, we're going to find a way out of here,' said Miles. 'Better if we go single file—'

'We have to get to the roof!' the woman cried. She pushed passed everyone in front of her and shoved Miles aside.

'Stop, the smoke will kill you!' Jolie warned, as six other people filed out after the woman.

Miles swore and coughed, before taking hold of Jenny's hand. 'Jenny, we need to go. Stay close and do not let go of me.'

He followed Jolie out of the room, together with two young brothers who decided to listen Miles. They all walked single file, keeping one hand on the back of the person in front of them, due to the low visibility.

Jolie opened a door at the far end of the west wing and was relieved when fresh air blew in. Missing two walls, the room was open to the wind and rain. Miles guided Jenny in and the two brothers—one coughing and spluttering—made their way in as well. Miles closed the door behind them and joined Jolie at the exposed edge of the room. Jenny hugged her father's leg while he and Jolie looked at the damaged building on the other side of the laneway. Miles judged it to be roughly three metres away. He pointed towards a caged service ladder across the way. It ran from the top of the building to the bottom.

'We're going down that ladder,' he said.

'It's a long jump,' said Jolie.

'I can make it.' Miles handed Jolie a bundled length of electrical wire he had gathered on their way through the rooms. He asked her to tie it to something solid.

Jolie gave the knot a firm tug, certain that exposed water pipes would be a sufficient anchor.

'Let me try,' she said. 'I've done this before.'

'You've jumped from a burning building?'

Jolie had in fact done exactly that during a skirmish with Sabre Company forces.

'Trust me,' Jolie said to Miles.

Though Jolie was a petite woman, Miles considered her athletic build and thought she could do it. He handed her the wire.

Jolie looped and tied it around her waist, and backed up. She leaned forward, pushing off the back wall into a sprint. She launched herself off the crumbling edge, her momentum carrying her over the gap before gravity forced her descent. She landed, legs and arms outstretched to brace against the impact of the iron cage. It shook with a loud clang when the full force of her weight hit the curved bars.

Miles, Jenny and the two men gasped, watching from the edge of the exposed room. Jolie dropped down a few feet and caught the next rung. She stabilised herself and, with impressive agility, climbed through the cage to the ladder. Saturated by the rain, Jolie wiped her red hair from her eyes and tied her end of the cable at a suitable height.

'I can't do this,' the youngest brother said.

'He's afraid of heights,' his older brother said to Miles. 'You two go ahead. We could be a while.'

'Don't stay long,' Miles said, lifting Jenny and holding her against his chest. 'That fire will reach this wing.' He unbuckled his belt and threw it over the wire. 'Close your eyes, Jen, and hold tight like a monkey.' She did so, allowing Miles to free his hands so he could wind the belt around each palm. He leaned back, slid out over the edge and threw his legs up, over the wire. The older brother called out and ran to the edge when Miles and Jenny dropped. Miles' full weight caused the wire to dip dramatically. Jenny squealed, feeling the sudden jolt.

'We're okay, we're okay,' Miles said, trying to calm her. The two of them began to edge down half a metre. Another bounce edged them further, and then they began to slide all the way to Jolie.

The three of them descended the ladder to street level, slipping into waist height water. Jenny blinked through tears and looked around her. She gazed up at the wire and the older brother waving down at her. She waved back.

Rain continued to fall, creating a din that reduced visibility to ten feet. Though the air below was becoming still, the sound of the wind in the sky was so loud, Jolie kept looking up expecting the sound to be a helicopter. There were none. *Why are there no rescue choppers? Maybe their base of operations was hit as badly or worse,* she thought. Calling voices and cries of pain sounded from different directions, Jolie couldn't judge where. She felt Miles' hand touch her shoulder and she turned to see him talking. Wind surged high above them, drowning out his voice. Miles glanced fearfully up at the hotel and pulled Jolie away, while carrying his daughter. Chunks of concrete were falling from the building and splashing into the water. He indicated the direction they should go and the three of them trudged on.

The water was running along a current. Jolie led the way. When she arrived at the corner of the hotel, she stopped abruptly and motioned for Miles to stay back. The torrent of garbage, debris and cars flowed at a dangerous speed from the top of the main street.

Jolie looked back at Jenny. She survived the storm that destroyed the city of Kingston. One day, she would learn how many people lost their lives during that storm. She would grow up in a world where extreme weather events continuously worsened.

Jolie gazed down the street, at the hundreds of bodies floating and tumbling: on their backs, face down, drifting in the rapids.

Men.

Women.

Children.

CHAPTER 16

Jolie, Miles and Jenny had walked north from the city into an area that had been evacuated in time. They were parched and hungry.

Miles looked up to the sky, mindful of the extreme heat to come. 'We need to find a car.' Jenny sat on her father's shoulders, staring across the water surface. 'Or a boat.'

As the three made their way across an intersection, the bottom corner of a nearby building began to crumble.

Jenny screamed as the entire structure leaned heavily towards its onlookers. Crushed concrete exploded out from its left side.

With the sun behind it, Jolie watched as the colossal silhouette slowly began to slide from its base. The separating upper floors fell across the street, colliding with a neighbouring twelve- storey building.

Fleeing, Miles and Jenny followed Jolie into a bakery. They crouched behind the service counter, as the deafening impact of concrete, brick and bitumen echoed outside. Glass flew into the air and rained down across the road. A deep roar followed and a giant cloud of grey forced its way into the store.

The trio hurried to the back of the bakery, coughing and squinting through thick dust. They crawled under toppled bread racks and climbed over ovens and machinery.

Jolie found a refrigerator stocked with water and soft drink. Miles opened a cabinet where a variety of bread rolls were laid out on trays. The three of them sat down in what they guessed had been the employee break room. Miles and Jenny ate and drank hungrily.

When they left the bakery, they felt the rising humidity in the air. Each passing moment was a leap in temperature.

'You didn't eat,' Miles commented.

'I'm not feeling so good,' Jolie lied.

AM units were able to keep up the appearance of consuming liquid, but not solids. Jolie had taste receptors and a bladder, so she would eventually need to pee. She pulled at the white tank top sticking to her skin. Her cooling system had kicked in, which gave the impression that she was perspiring. She stopped walking when she spotted a car that looked out of place. It was an antique Morris Minor, that had slammed into a fallen fast-food billboard.

'Stay with Jolie,' Miles said to Jenny. 'I'll see if it has keys in it.' Miles jogged over to the car and peered in. There were people inside it.

Rachel jumped at the sound of knocking above her head. She quickly searched for the silver revolver that had belonged to Luther Saint.

'Are you okay?' Miles opened the door to find a gun pointed at his chest and slowly raised his hands. He heard Jenny call to him. 'Jenny, stay there. Stay with Jolie.'

'Jolie?' Rachel mumbled.

'Wait,' said Miles. 'I know you. You were with her at the hotel.'

Rachel saw Jolie with Jenny. She looked to Sam and Rowan who were slumped in their seats, unconscious.

'Sorry,' she said. 'I'm just...' She pushed the pistol into the back of her pants and stepped out into the harsh light. 'We... we had an accident.'

Jolie arrived and immediately checked Rachel for wounds.

'Are any of you injured?' she asked, looking them over for any sign of blood.

'I think we're okay,' said Rachel. 'Can you give me a hand with these guys?'

Miles opened the front passenger door and carried Rowan out to rest him on the ground.

Rachel climbed back in to wake Sam. 'Hey, you did it. We're safe.' She looked around at the devastation outside. 'I think.'

'Ow, my head.' Sam touched a fresh bruise beneath her hairline.

Rachel helped Sam out of the car and Sam shielded her eyes from the blinding light.

'We're in Storm Realm?' She struggled out of the woollen jumper she had found in Rachel's apartment. 'Man, it's hot.'

Rowan stood unsteadily. 'What happened here?'

Jolie opened her mouth to list the wind, rain and the earthquake. *Everything,* sufficed as an explanation.

Miles handed a bottle of water to Sam.

'Thank you. I'm Sam, by the way. That's Rowan.' She crouched and offered to shake Jenny's hand, giving her a friendly smile. 'And what's your name?'

'Jenny. That's my dad.' She pointed at Miles.

Miles shook Sam's hand. 'Miles.'

Rowan watched a tall building collapse in on itself in the far distance. 'You couldn't evacuate in time?'

'We were trapped in a hotel,' said Miles. He decided to ignore the staggered line of bullet holes running along the car doors. 'Do you mind if we squeeze in with you? We really should keep moving. There are shelter centres—'

'Take it,' Rowan offered.

'You're staying?' Miles gave Rowan a puzzled look.

'Ah, darn...' Rowan saw that one of the back tyres had been shot.

Sam crouched on the ground. She scooped up a handful of soil and buried it in her pocket.

Miles had helped Rowan replace the car tyre with a spare from the boot. He left Jenny to sleep on the back seat while he went to talk to Sam.

'Are you sure you and your people don't want to come with us?' he asked.

'We'll be fine, thanks,' said Sam, distractedly. She stood and clapped the soil from her hands.

'Why did you…?' Miles gestured to the bulge in Sam's pocket.

'Oh,' Sam laughed. 'Soil sample. I'm a scientist.'

'You work with Jolie?'

'That's right.' Sam looked at her wrist console when it beeped, indicating that its solar cells had finished charging.

Miles pointed to the device. 'What's that?'

Sam hesitated at first, but remembered her dad's policy. Disclosure of any inter-realm information was permitted, provided travel between the realms in question was terminated following disclosure.

Miles looked more closely at the Shifter device. 'Is it some kind of a surveying instrument?'

'Miles, we haven't been completely upfront with you,' said Sam. 'See, we're…' She gestured to Rowan, Jolie and Rachel, trying to think of the best way to explain. 'We come from a different version of this physical universe. This device…' Sam touched a finger to the Shifter. 'It's what we use to travel between different versions of Earth, versions which we call Realms.'

Miles folded his arms and narrowed his eyebrows.

'I know it sounds crazy, but it's true.' Sam tapped her wrist device. 'This is alien technology. We encountered them—'

'Yeah, I think I've heard enough.'

'Fine,' said Sam and started to walk away.

Miles looked to the Morris Minor. It had collided with the sign at a high speed, yet there was a brick wall directly behind it. 'Wait. Can you show me what your… shift thing does?'

Rachel walked over to Sam and Miles. 'We're out of water, guys.'

'Miles wants to see the portal,' said Sam.

Rachel moved close to Sam and spoke through the corner of her mouth. 'You told him?'

'It's okay. We're not coming back here. I'll show him the Forest Realm.'

'Sam—'

She programmed a portal and opened it.

Miles jumped back from the expanding sphere of mercury.

'We'll just be a few minutes,' Sam said to Rachel.

Rachel shook her head. But she took out her own Shifter console from her pocket and set an alarm. 'Five minutes.'

Sam took Miles by the arm and pulled him into the sphere.

'Wow, wait,' he said.

'You believe me now, huh? Lookin' at me like I'm some crazy—'

'Don't touch anything,' Rachel ordered. 'Five minutes, then I'm coming in after you.' Miles and Sam disappeared into the portal and it rapidly shrank until it was gone.

CHAPTER 17

The hangar was on the surface level, above the lab. It was usually quiet and empty, since supply ships only came once a month. Now, it was abuzz with transport ships being loaded and recharged for the long voyage to Earth.

Lana slid her hand along the concrete wall beside the elevator. The bullet scars triggered memories of her fight to find the Professor…

Torchlights attached to the Sabre Company soldier's rifles had shone in her face when she emerged from the elevator. Their first mistake was to assume she was just a civilian, not a threat. One of them approached with wrist binders. He became Lana's shield as soon as she'd disarmed him. Muzzle flashes illuminated the dark of the hangar. Lana charged them, shoving her AM unit shield at one, leaping at the next with a flying kick. The SC soldiers were well trained and placed their shots accurately. Lana could remember the sting of every .762 calibre round that had hit her. And yet, one after the other, they fell. None could stop her.

Voices and the metallic clang of boxes being stacked brought Lana back to the present. She gazed down at the compressed, full-metal jackets littering the polished floor. She heard a woman's voice behind her and turned to see Fiona walking towards Hank.

'Good to have you here, Captain.'

'I'm sorry we're late,' Hank replied gravely, having heard that the lab's Chief Security Officer had been killed. 'Renee, Brad, stay up here with Fiona,' he ordered his crew, wary of the Sabre Company's ability to teleport in a time bomb, let alone portal in troops.

Brad and Renee echoed confirmation, then took their positions on the overhead catwalk.

Hank rode the elevator down to the lab with Lana and his daughter, Lex.

'Have you seen Charlie yet?' Hank asked Lex.

'No.'

Lana saw the worry in her eyes. 'He'll be fine.'

Lex breathed. 'Good.' She was silent for a moment, until she remembered to ask Lana about her abilities. 'So, Lana, what else can you do, besides being able to withstand freezing temperatures?'

Lana slid a combat knife from the sheath on Hank's belt and she deftly flipped it to land the handle in the palm of her other hand.

'Hey, careful with that,' Hank said.

Lana's long, dark brown fringe fell across her face, while she held out her right forearm and concentrated on activating her armour. She pressed the blade down against her skin and made a slicing motion. Her skin brought trillions of hardening nanoparticles to the surface.

Lex gasped as the steel blade squeaked against what looked like normal skin, but was in fact organic silicon carbide, protecting Lana's arm.

Lana returned the blade to Hank's belt and held her arm out to the dumbfounded father and daughter. The smooth hard patch where she had cut herself returned to undamaged olive skin.

'Incredible.' Lex took Lana's arm. 'You have defensive cell generating armour inside your skin tissue.'

'The Professor calls it reactive armour,' said Lana. 'Hard impacts still hurt. My nerves respond the same as anyone's.'

The elevator arrived and the doors opened.

'Kid,' said Hank, 'I am glad you're on our side.'

The three of them stepped out and were greeted by Charlie. He was leaning on crutches, smiling nervously at Lex. He invited her to see what he had developed to stop Sabre Company from entering the lab again.

'I've been working on inhibiter nodes that can be deployed at the base of the lab and up on the surface compound,' he explained. 'Once activated, we will effectively have created a matrix web which cannot be entered via any portal from the outside.'

Lex reviewed Charlie's holographic diagram distractedly. She took his hand. 'Charlie, are you all right?'

Charlie was taken aback by her concern. 'I'm fine.'

Lex returned her attention to Charlie's inhibitor. 'I can program a signature for our portals, so our people can travel in and out of the matrix.' She waved Lana and her father over.

Charlie set the diagram display to slowly rotate. 'This is the Genesis Lab,' he explained. 'After the nodes are deployed, the only security we'll need is outside.'

Hank nodded approvingly. 'Send this upstairs to Renee and forward schematics for the...'

'Inhibitor nodes,' Charlie prompted.

'Forward it on to the Council. We'll need to do the same for them as well.'

= Forest Realm =

Rays of sunlight spotted moss and twisting tree roots across the ground. A deer bowed its head to lap cool water from a slow-running stream, seeking reprieve from the late afternoon heat. Its short tail whipped at hungry insects buzzing around its light brown coat.

Anook, a fifteen-year-old boy, crept slowly between moss-covered tree trunks. The temperature decreased as he followed the sound of running water. He became still when he saw the deer raise its head. It turned, ears shifting to detect an irregular sound. Anook realised he was not alone on this hunt.

Only a moment passed before a tiger leapt from the shadows. From the opposite side, another tiger reached the deer in one bound. Teeth and claws sank into the creature's slender neck.

Anook shrank low to the ground, keeping a long spear ready in front of him.

The tigers barely touched the deer carcass, as they had already eaten earlier in the day. After briefly cleaning one another with wide, rough tongues, they drifted into the trees, heading south. Anook waited, lying flat on his chest. In the distance, a deep, satisfied moan was followed by a soft growl. The boy made his way to the stream to find that a large amount of meat lay unclaimed. Insects were buzzing around the open carcass.

Anook stepped back, startled by a tall dark figure standing just metres away, on the other side of the narrow stream. The man began sloshing through the shallow water. He wore more animal skin than Anook, with a satchel bag strung across his broad chest. The weight of fruit he had collected bounced at his side. His expression became animated, and he shouted and waved his arms at Anook.

I was here first, was the notion that immediately came to the boy's mind. He had not eaten for two days. This meat belonged to him. Anook raised his spear and threw it at his target. The man stepped sideways, up onto dry earth. The weapon passed over his shoulder and stabbed the base of a tree on the other side of the stream. Simultaneously they both turned to watch, as leaves floated down from the shaken tree. The man hammered a fist into Anook's cheekbone. Anook's vision faded to black.

CHAPTER 18

On the far north side of the forest, Miles was leaning back, gazing into the dense canopy above. He watched a monkey—a species he had never seen before—swing between the thick hanging vines.

Sam breathed in the moss-scented air. 'This Realm is the most different from our own that we've found.' She checked the timer on her wrist. 'Proof enough, Miles?'

'Yeah, I believe you now. This is… amazing.' He crouched down to trace the outline of a human footprint. 'There are people here?'

'Yes, Rachel has made contact with them.' Sam searched the clothing menu on the Shifter device and selected Forest Realm apparel. 'This is what they wear.' The Shifter initiated molecular projection from the replication link. Sam's clothes began to shift and distort until they were transformed into strips of animal skin. 'If we see anyone, it'd be a good idea for you to hide.'

'Wow.' Miles looked Sam up and down. 'Your… Shifter thing can change your clothing.'

'Yep.' Sam was watching the monkey climbing the branches above them.

Miles followed her gaze. 'And this is really Earth?'

'It's the exact same place as where we were a couple minutes ago,' said Sam. 'For you, it's Kingston. In my world, it's called Melbourne.' She motioned for Miles to follow her to higher ground where the trees cleared, giving them a view outside the forest. 'From what Rachel could gather, there was a global war. Hydrogen bombs destroyed this city. There are still areas where radiation levels are dangerously high. We don't know when it happened, but when it did, human civilisation was wiped out.'

'Has Rachel spoken to the people here?' Miles asked.

'She has. Their language was difficult for the Shifter to decipher at first.' Sam pulled at the rough leather strapping. 'Sheesh, little tight across the chest. The Shifter can translate most languages. Usually with at least eighty per cent accuracy.'

'I see.' The topic of communication prompted another question. 'Can you send a message to Rachel from here? And she to you?'

'Yep. We can also open a link to our Home Realm.' Sam pointed to the wrist console. 'The Shifter can maintain an active miniature portal inside it, which acts as a window through which signals can travel.'

'Impressive technology.' Miles gazed up at the thirty-metre-high trees. 'What if…'

Sam wriggled inside her clothing. 'Hm?'

'What do you do, if you encounter yourself in another Realm?'

'Entropic Cascade Failure was a very real concern.' Sam saw Miles' eyebrows go up in confusion. 'So, the theory is that if there are two of you in one place, the interloper—the person who arrived second—will begin to literally phase out of matter and cease to exist.'

'So that could happen to you and me right now,' said Miles, 'if there's a Miles and a Sam already here.'

'Here? No. It can only happen if you go to a realm that is almost identical to your own. We steer clear of those.'

'Right,' said Miles. 'Are you, Rachel, Jolie, Rowan from the future?'

'No,' Sam answered. 'Shifter travel doesn't influence time. It doesn't open doorways to the past or the future. Only the present. You and I exist in the same time, built on different past events.'

Sam held up the Shifter on her wrist. 'This opens portals to alternate versions of Earth. Versions which are moving parallel to each other through time. What makes every single Realm we enter different are the events which transpired in the past.' She watched Miles' thoughtful expression, allowing him time to take it in.

'Conscious acts,' Sam continued. 'Decisions, reactions, all of these change pathways, leading to different changes in the future. Think about it. How different would your world be if one of your ape ancestors had died, completely erasing the existence of thousands of futures, erasing leaders, philosophers, inventors. What if the majority of the people in your world had decided long ago to work together, rather than try to get ahead of one another?' Sam smiled, excited to have just blown Miles' mind.

'So...' Miles paused for a second. 'There are alternate realities where all of these changes continue to be played out, side by side. And the people living in them are oblivious of the existence of other parallels.'

'Correct,' Sam said, in a congratulatory tone. 'Realms are not observable without portal travel. We've only visited twelve other Realms so far, so we're new to this ourselves. But we've learnt a lot from those different Realms.'

'I guess when you see a world like this, you see the devastation and you take heed.' Miles' eyes lowered, thinking of his own Realm—a world of pollution, greed and corruption.

Sam read his grave expression and offered some consolation. 'Your people still have time, Miles. You can change. You just need to establish a foothold, like co-op workplaces, equal opportunity, education instead of elite, private schools and under-funded public schools. Restructure how you live and how you educate. Give people the tools to effect positive change.'

Sam rested her hand on Miles' shoulder. 'Don't let the greedy power mongers who run your governments continue to bury your daughter's future.'

A rumble sounded in the distance. The rumble of an engine outside of the forest.

Sam looked in the direction of the noise. 'Combustion technology, here?' She started walking towards it.

Miles followed. 'The people here may be more advanced than you thought.'

'Not likely. As far as Rachel has observed, everyone has reverted back to a hunter-gatherer way of life.'

As they made their way to the edge of the dense forest, they saw a clearing. Out in the heat of the sun, on an open field, were dozens of camouflaged tents. Eight small vehicles with roll cages were parked diagonally, as well as four all-terrain vehicles.

'No way,' Sam said, quickly pulling Miles back into the forest.

'Who are they?'

Sam kept moving, pressing at the Shifter on her wrist. 'We're leaving.'

Sam jumped, startled by Rachel, who appeared from behind a vine-covered tree. She looked perturbed, hands on her hips. 'I told you five minutes, Sam.'

'Rache, we found them.' Sam pointed behind her to the clearing, still visible from their position.

Rachel followed Miles and Sam back to the site. Sabre Company soldiers were walking about the encampment, some stacking boxes, others operating forklifts and small cranes. The cranes were shifting containers of what looked like mined ore onto a conveyer belt.

'They're taking resources from this Realm,' Rachel whispered. She recognised one of the soldiers. It was Luke Palmer.

Sam crept closer, her eyes searching for any sign of her father. The centre of the camp was dirt, all of the grass torn away by vehicular movement.

Rachel noted digger vehicles and drilling rigs. 'They must have worked out how to enlarge their portals.'

Sam's Shifter beeped an incoming text message. 'Hank's team have arrived at the lab. It's secure. We can head back now.' She looked up and saw two soldiers escorting a man in a white and blue lab coat. 'Dad!'

Pete was shuffling. He stumbled when the binders around his ankles caught, falling heavily to the ground. A cloud of dust rose at the feet of the SC soldiers, as they kicked him in the back and stomach, shouting at him to get up.

Rachel lunged forward, pulling Sam back. She held her hand over her partner's mouth. Sam screamed and fought Rachel's hold.

'Sam, quiet!' Rachel felt the wetness of tears reach her hand, as they rolled down Sam's hot cheeks. Her whole body shuddered, her father's pain surging through her.

Miles stared in shock at the civilian lying in the dirt. The soldiers laughed and dragged him by his arms to a holding cell.

Taking her hand away from Sam's mouth, Rachel rocked her in her arms as she sobbed. She knelt down, looking into her eyes. 'We'll come back for him. I'll get him out of there, I promise.'

Sam wiped her eyes. 'We have to hurry.' She reached into Rachel's jean pocket and retrieved a communications console. 'You have a camera on this. I can connect to it remotely from the lab.'

'Good idea. We can set up a visual feed to monitor their movements.' She took the console from Sam and tore a length of fern leaf to tie around a high branch. She fitted the console tight, facing towards the SC camp. 'Done, let's move.'

Sam typed at her Shifter to create a link to the camera, pausing when Miles touched her arm.

'I'm sorry about your father,' he said. 'I hope your people are able to bring him back to you safely.'

'Thank you,' Sam sniffed. Looking back to the camp once more, she followed Rachel back into the forest, to open up a return portal to Storm Realm.

Anook woke and hoisted himself onto his elbows. The trees and shrubbery spun when he turned his head. Pain erupted from under his left eye when he blinked. The bounty of deer meat was gone. Anook thumped the ground and glowered across the stream to his spear. Fresh footprints remained where his attacker had approached.

A small chunk of meat had been tied with a leather cord, dangling from the spear. Anook stood looking down at it, his puzzled expression turning to a frown. The meat was a consolation prize left by the man who had knocked him out. Anook swore and pulled the spear from the tree, setting off at a swift pace.

Chahtu negotiated the slippery decline to the forest floor with ease. The deer meat bounced heavily on his right shoulder, the hoof of the hind leg swinging limp. He stopped suddenly, skidding through the mud when he reached level ground. He heard rustling and foot falls in the bushes some paces behind him.

Chahtu was tackled to the ground. He rolled onto his back to find Anook standing over him, his chest heaving.

The boy began saying something between brief rasping breaths. Chahtu was unable to understand any of the strange words. The boy pointed sharply at the meat, raising his weapon threateningly. There was very little chance of the spear missing its mark this time.

'No, please!'

Anook froze and twisted around to see a woman standing a few feet away, a small girl clinging to her leg. The woman edged closer to her husband.

The boy looked back down at the man who had stolen his food. Chahtu remained on his back. Pushing an open palm towards his wife, he spoke calmly in unfamiliar words. Anook gazed over at the little girl. Her almond-shaped eyes wandered from her father to the spear. She returned Anook's gaze.

'Shiah, stay back.' Chahtu held the mud-covered meat out to Anook. 'Take it.' Bringing his weapon to his side, Anook stepped away and shook his head.

Chahtu slowly picked himself up. His wife and daughter rushed over to pull him away. He watched the boy trudge up the mossy slope, then pause. Heavy footsteps approached him from behind. Two men wearing green camouflage moved cautiously towards him, aiming short, black objects at him and his family.

Anook glared at them. He remembered these weapons of death being used against his village community. His grip tightened around his spear and he shouted at them, before stepping forward to throw. The spear flew over Chahtu's head and landed deep in the chest of one of the Sabre Company soldiers.

The other trooper aimed his gun at Anook. His body was thrown sideways across the ground before he could squeeze the trigger. Chahtu had slammed into him.

Shiah carried her daughter away, while her husband wrapped his arms around the dazed SC soldier's neck. He twisted and with a snap, the man fell limp. Chahtu moved over to the other body and removed Anook's spear. He inspected the sharp stone tip, puzzled by the acidic odour of what should have been blood, but wasn't.

Anook walked over to investigate the heavy black weapons on the ground. Chahtu took them both. Shaking his head, he threw them into the bushes.

'No good.' He handed the boy his spear and grasped his shoulder. Anook took this as thank you, but then the man pushed him gently as if to add, 'Now be on your way.'

CHAPTER 19

'All nodes are in place,' said Lex. 'Activating matrix.' She typed in the activation code and turned to watch the camera feed on the monitor. It showed Fiona rugged up in a thick white thermal jacket, waiting outside the compound.

'Setting portal to Lab Observation Deck.' Fiona activated the Shifter device she was given for the test. It beeped with a *Shift Failed* message.

'It worked,' she reported. 'I can't get in.' She reset the portal and input the hanger coordinates, followed by a signature code Charlie had given her. 'Activating portal with signature.'

Fiona disappeared in front of the camera and the background noise changed from gusting wind, to the echoing interior of the surface compound. 'Nice work guys.' A message tone beeped on Fiona's console. 'I'm due back at the Council,' she said. 'Good luck and stay safe.'

'Thanks for saving my ass, Fiona,' said Charlie. 'We'll teleport the nodes and matrix program to you within the hour so the Palmer Building will be protected as well.'

The lab comms beeped an incoming transmission from outside of Glacier II's atmosphere. It was coming from an approaching ship, which had hailed the Genesis Lab as soon as it was within range. A woman's voice came through.

'Glacier II. This is Ambassador Jainon of the Kiyol, requesting permission to land.' The Ambassador's pronunciation of each word was noticeably clear and measured.

Hank arrived in time to reply. 'Ambassador, this is Captain Henry Drake. Please state your business for this visit.'

'I wish to discuss retrieval of all Kiyol technology from the Glacier II facility with Professor Peter O'Conner.'

'Retrieval?' He glanced at Charlie, whose confused expression matched Hank's. 'I'm not sure I understand, Ambassador.'

'We have been forced to defend ourselves against attacks by human militant forces. This technology must be confiscated. May we land?'

'Permission granted, Ambassador.'

A meeting was held in the briefing room, where Charlie had released information to the press about Peter O'Conner's work in the Genesis Lab.

Ambassador Jainon was accompanied by three warriors: two males and one female.

Lana decided to attend the meeting, curious to observe the alien people. She noted their traditional armaments—staffs which could transform into a rifle or a spear. Each warrior was equipped with Shifter wrist consoles. Their armour was a bronze-coloured flexible material, impervious to most projectile fire.

Lana had learnt that Kiyol males were known as Kiyolo and females, Kiyola. Both Kiyolo present were over seven feet tall, lean and muscular.

Kiyol anatomy differed to that of humans only in terms of facial features. Their noses more closely resembled the snout of a cat. Kiyol organ structure and functions differed as well, but their overall form was human-like.

Lana judged the Kiyola warrior to be no taller than six feet. Her physique was strong and athletic, while her facial features were soft, her expression blank and unassuming. Like the two Kiyolo, her cheek bones were high, but her brow didn't protrude as far. Lana also noticed that Kiyolo eyes glowed dark blue, while Kiyola eyes glowed jade green.

When Lana had shaken Ambassador Jainon's hand upon greeting, her skin had felt firm—almost like dolphin skin but coloured a deep purple. The two Kiyolo were yellowy-green in appearance. Kiyol hair colour varied in shades of brown. The Ambassador and female warrior both wore theirs long, hanging loose across their shoulders. The males' hair were short, tied into a top- knot. Many, Lana had read, were bald.

'Ambassador, Professor O'Conner has been abducted by the militant group, Sabre Company,' Hank explained. 'They are responsible for the technology theft and the attacks on your people. They attacked this facility today.' Hank watched Ambassador Jainon's reaction.

'I am sorry to hear of this.' She blinked her large, inward slanting eyes. 'This information only confirms the necessity to reclaim our technology, Captain.'

'I accept your position, Ambassador. We will return all Kiyol technology.' Hank leaned forward in his chair, pleading. 'However, we must ask that you allow us to use it until this battle is over.' Hank found it difficult to read Jainon; her expression betrayed nothing. 'Sabre Company are obviously preparing for war,' he stressed. 'We need all resources available to defeat them.'

Jainon's eyes flashed. 'War?'

'We must assume they have a force larger than what the Universal Community's and are ready to strike at any moment.'

'Then the threat is great.' Jainon glanced back at her company of warriors. 'These three will remain and aid your security forces. I will return to my people to discuss a joint counter-strike.'

Hank stood and shook hands with her. 'Thank you, Ambassador.'

≡ Forest Realm ≡

Anook sat by the campfire he had prepared, which he had to dig deep tonight due to the wind. Wild berries were all he could find to calm his stomach, still complaining despite the mercy-portion of meat he'd eaten earlier. Anook hung his head in a wave of shame, aware of his stupidity and ignorance at taking offense to Chahtu's gesture of compromise and good will.

He pushed the last handful of berries into his mouth. While he chewed, he heard someone approaching through the trees. Instinctively reaching for his spear, Anook could only ready his fists, for it was now missing.

'Please do not be alarmed.' It was Chahtu's wife, Shiah. She stopped a few paces from the fire holding Anook's spear.

'I have taken your weapon for my protection. Like a young snake, you use all of your venom without thinking.'

Anook could see now that Shiah was perhaps ten years older than him. 'Your family is safe,' he said. 'I will not harm any of you. I'm sorry about today.'

Shiah nodded in acceptance and set the boy's weapon down by the fire. 'I came to invite you to our camp.'

The boy's stomach gnawed at him while his brain considered his limited options. 'Very well.'

Anook saw Shiah's white body paint in the light of the fire. She wore animal fur over her shoulders, but her abdomen was bare. And her waist sash only covered her back and front, her bare legs displaying her artistic patterns. He had seen these before. A group his family use to trade with decorated themselves this way. 'You're from the North. The rock plains.'

'Yes,' she said. 'I guessed that you were from there as well. We speak the same tongue.' After extinguishing the fire with damp soil, Anook followed the young woman into the darkness.

'Your man, he doesn't wish to hurt me?'

Shiah shook her head with a slight smile. 'He was angry for a time. But not at you.'

'The intruders,' said Anook.

'Yes. Who or whatever they are, it's clearly no longer safe in this forest. We are going leave in the morning but we don't know where else to go.'

The two crossed the stream and walked on through the trees.

'Why did you leave your group in the North?' Anook asked.

'Chahtu and his hunting party needed shelter one winter,' Shiah said. 'My group took them in. That is how we met. I left with him to join his group which, at the time, was camped not far from here.' Her tone changed to frustration. 'A sickness struck soon after I settled among Chahtu's group. They accused me, the outsider, of being the cause. So, he and I left.'

'I didn't hear you take my spear. How did you do that?' Anook asked as they walked, guided by the moonlight.

'You need but wait for a gust of wind,' Shiah said, gesturing to the trees. 'The clash of the branches is loud. It will mask your step.' She looked at Anook, wondering why someone so young would be traveling alone. 'Why are you here?'

Anook related memories of his family and the others in his group, describing their pets and the people that lived off the land in harmony. Then there was terror.

Anook recalled the cries of his people as clearly as he had heard them the day he escaped.

Sabre Company forces had arrived last season, taking land, digging into the earth. They set up camps along the east clearing outside the ruined city, expanding each week as new soldiers arrived for training.

The terrible memories faded from Anook's mind when he felt

Shiah's motherly hand rest on his arm. She and Anook reached the fire where Chahtu sat with his son and daughter. Their campground was the inside corner of what was once a tram. All of the seats had been torn out, and the roof and one wall were gone.

'You have a son as well?' asked Anook.

'Tinba's family were taken by the Blood Demons,' Shiah explained. 'He has been with us for some time now.'

Anook shivered. 'Demons?'

Shiah pointed in the direction of the city. 'Never stray beyond the river. The grey buildings there are home to the Blood Demons. Chahtu has seen people being abducted. They strike in great numbers. Some nights we hear chanting,' she said. 'It echoes through the underground tunnels.'

'Why do you call them Blood Demons?' Anook asked.

Shiah stopped before moving any closer to the fire, not wanting the children to hear. She faced Anook, her dark eyes haunting in the flickering light.

'Someone escaped through the tunnels after being captured. He told anyone who would listen, "Those who stray into their domain are eaten and their souls are thrown into a great pool of blood. They are demons led by a queen who calls herself Galai." I do not doubt what that brave soul witnessed. And nor should you.'

Chahtu rose when he saw his wife. He gestured for Anook to join them by the warmth of the fire. Anook still could not understand the man's words as he began to speak.

Assuming the role of translator, Shiah sat down beside Anook. 'My husband asks if I have been telling you scary tales of demons.'

Anook laughed nervously and nodded to Chahtu. His ears pricked at the sound of breaking twigs and crunching leaves. The others did not seem to hear it, so he relaxed. 'I know now to stay away from the city.'

Chahtu laughed. He looked past Anook and his eyes widened. He lunged forward to tackle a Sabre Company soldier entering the tram carriage.

The children screamed when five more soldiers appeared, aiming wide-barrelled net projection guns. They fired and Shiah cried out, reaching for her daughter through the net, while they all struggled, pinned to the ground.

CHAPTER 20

Hank and Lana arrived in the portal room when the mercury sphere expanded and held its rippling shape. Rachel, Sam, Rowan and Jolie stepped out on the platform and the portal closed behind them.

'We have to move quickly,' Rachel stressed. 'Pete's in bad shape. The cavalry is up in the hangar?'

'A platoon of AM units just arrived,' Hank confirmed.

Rachel drew Lana into a hug when she approached. 'Are you all right?'

'I'm fine.' Feeling the woman's body shudder, Lana pulled away. 'You're hurt.'

'I'm okay. Luther Saint paid us a visit last night.'

Hank's ears pricked up at the name. In his mind, Luther Saint was three down the deck, Dennis Conroy being the Ace of Spades.

'He's dead now,' said Rachel.

Sam wrapped her arms around Lana. 'I'm so sorry I had to leave you, Lana.'

'I'm glad you got out when you did,' said Lana.

'Hodge was wounded. Is he...?' Sam read Lana's hurt expression and her heart sank.

Lana's thoughts went back to Hodge's death. She remembered taking down a Sabre Company soldier when she entered the corridor to the Security Office. When she got there, she found Hodge lying on his back. She ran to him and knelt down in the blood that had formed a puddle beneath him. He was cold to touch.

Tears welled in Sam's eyes and she drew Lana close.

Rachel looked to Hank, as though he might say it wasn't true.

'We need you top side,' Hank whispered to her.

Sam wiped her eyes and nodded to Rachel. 'Go. I'll get to work down here.'

Rachel ushered Lana into the elevator with Hank. 'Charlie and Lex are monitoring the feed we set up in the forest. We plan to hit the Sabre Company camp tonight.'

'How many soldiers do they have?' Lana asked.

'So far we've counted around two dozen,' said Hank.

The elevator arrived at the hangar and Rachel spotted Brad and Renee. 'Hey,' she called to them. 'Long time, no see.'

'Good to see you're safe, Rache,' said Renee. She gestured towards the platoon of fifty AM soldiers waiting in formation. 'Wanna give us a hand with these guys?'

By Council Law, no military force was to consist of humans other than those of the highest command. All troops were Autonomous Machines. But AM units weren't expendable; they were costly to make. Those that had come to fight were fitted with the latest in protective armour.

Lana saw that two mobile archways had been installed. Jolie was at the front of the line, being scanned in the archway. It sprayed her whole body with a material that the Kiyol had developed for body protection. The Kiyol had been using the protective suits for sport and combat training. When they had learnt that human weapons fire metal projectiles, they volunteered to share the technology because it was bulletproof. It also had a fire safety feature. When the wearer was in danger of being badly burnt, the suit would detect the flames. It would burst into fine particles that would absorb any surrounding oxygen, thereby extinguishing the fire.

Hank opened a big box that contained his own personal combat gear.

'So,' he said to Lana, 'is there anything else I should know about you? Any other special powers?'

'She doesn't age,' Rachel offered with a hint of envy.

Hank studied Lana for a moment. 'That's impossible.'

'The Professor designed me to age rapidly until I was fully developed,' Lana explained. 'Then he turned off the DNA kill switch, which all regular people have. But you'll have to ask him about that. I don't understand it.'

'I'll pass,' said Hank.

'Pete said I may develop other abilities over time,' said Lana. 'But for now, I'm pretty much normal.'

Normal, yeah right, thought Hank. He gestured to the formation of troops. 'We have fifty soldiers here and the Council have approved the production of a hundred more.'

Rachel walked along the rows of trained tactical units. 'Gonna need a bigger hangar. Jin has plenty of room.'

'Brad, Renee and I are preparing to head to Aqua Sierra now,' said Hank. 'We'll take ten soldiers. Twenty will be on board the escort ships going to Earth. That leaves you with thirty to bring Pete back.' Hank looked out the hangar windows and saw the purple hue against the ice and snow outside. 'When's that energy wave thing gonna hit?'

'The Parabola Light Band,' Rachel corrected him. 'A few days, I think. Our exit window is safe.'

'Good.' Hank ushered Rachel over to Jolie and the other AM units who had received their spray on suit. 'Let me introduce you to your team. They've received a cursory briefing on the Professor's situation and the camp layout, based on your camera feed. Take it from here as you see fit.' Hank hesitated before stressing the other objective of the mission. 'You need to capture Luke Palmer.'

'He can lead us to Conroy and Williams,' Rachel agreed.

She looked at the soldiers in their new armour. Rachel hadn't tried the Kiyol body suit, but she liked what she saw. It was black with a pearlescent blue sheen. Once it was sprayed onto the soldier by the arch, the material expanded half a centimetre in thickness before drying. Rachel asked Jolie if she could examine the armour. Jolie held out her arm and Rachel was surprised by how soft and flexible the material was.

Hank approached Captain Lincoln, who had arrived to join the extraction team. 'Once you have Luke Palmer, teleport him to us at Jin's.' He signalled to Brad and Renee the order to move out.

Lana arrived next to Rachel to wave goodbye to Hank's crew.

'Who's Jin?' she asked Rachel.

'Jin Otami is Hank's unofficial supplier of weapons and other...' Rachel hesitated, 'well, munitions deemed illegal by the Council. They call his base of operations Otami Palace.'

'Is it a military base?'

The two women watched the transport ships hover and move slowly towards the opening hangar doors. Ice cold wind blew in from the snow dunes and an eerie purple coloured the wafting snow.

'More or less,' said Rachel. 'It's a compound stretching twenty fathoms down from the surface of the water planet, Aqua Sierra.'

'Oh, I've read about that,' Lana recalled. 'That's the home world of the other aliens.'

The planet Aqua Sierra was named after the leader of the native inhabitants, Sierra Sienta, Queen of the Laician sea dwellers. Lana had read that Aqua Sierra once looked like Earth. The ice polar caps melted over one hundred thousand years ago. All land formations disappeared below the oceans and life evolved to survive beneath the sea.

'It's very beautiful there.' Rachel looked at Lana. 'Hey, you okay?'

Lana was watching the Automated Machine soldiers that would be helping to save Professor O'Conner. Having encountered the evil version, she felt uneasy being so close to an entire platoon of them.

'I'm fine.' Shrugging off her unease, Lana returned her attention to learning more about the water planet. 'Can the Laicians help us?'

'They're not as involved in the whole alliance scheme of things,' said Rachel. 'It's understandable. They need to be in water, so they can't exactly come visit every weekend.'

≡ Forest Realm ≡
Sabre Company Barracks

Professor O'Conner watched movements around the camp from the window of his holding cell door. He saw a high-ranking soldier being escorted across the camp square. Pete found it odd that he was wearing a dark brown leather trench coat and tricorne hat.

It was late at night. Pete had managed to free his ankles, but he was struggling with his wrist binders. He decided to concentrate on getting out of his cell. He was wearing a battery powered thermal layer under his lab coat. The soldiers who had searched him hadn't found the console concealed in the pocket under his right arm. The thermal unit was of his own design. He was able to tap through its thermal settings and input his own override command, to increase its power output to a dangerous level and disable the safety shutdown.

'Lieutenant, Colonel Williams has arrived.'

Luke was leaning over a digital mapping board, scanning the areas around the ruined city. 'Very good. Tell the guard detail outside to take five.'

Williams listened to the receding footsteps and he removed his tricorne hat. 'Good work, Lieutenant.' He paced about the tent. The lamp light shone across the rough surface of the burn scar which ran from his left cheek and across his discoloured eye, before parting his grey eyebrow and ending on his forehead. 'I see you have established mining operations.'

'Yes, sir.' Luke assumed a straight posture, staring ahead.

'At ease.' The Colonel perused the digital map display. 'Has Saint reported back yet?'

'Luther Saint is dead, sir. KIA.'

'How?'

'Rachel Navara.'

Williams sighed heavily. 'Saint was a good fighter. Conroy's interest in Rachel Navara eludes me… however we must do our best to carry out his wishes.'

Luke hesitated before speaking. 'Sir, why do we continue to follow the General's orders? He is essentially detached from command. I understand you served together and I respect the importance of loyalty—'

'Access to the Branner Factory is our objective. General Conroy and our contact on the inside can take control of that AM Factory.' Williams' damaged eyebrow twitched. 'I will not hide in these Realms another year.'

'Yes, sir.'

Williams caught Luke nervously eyeing the mapping screen. 'Something on your mind, soldier?'

'We've had trouble establishing a secure transport route through the city,' Luke explained. 'It appears to be populated by a hostile native tribe. We've lost six men so far.'

'Unacceptable, Lieutenant. Engage them with artillery if you have to.' Williams glared at Luke. 'Get it done.'

'Yes, sir.'

'You will be receiving more shipments from the Frontier Realm where I am stationed,' said Williams.

'Colonel, I understand you requested a thermal nuke.'

'Localised. Yes, it arrived, thank you.'

'You intend to use it in that Realm? Sir, the governing power there has an army of thousands,' Luke hazarded caution. 'Is it wise to provoke them?'

'We will take what we need from whoever has it, when we need it,' Williams growled.

Luke heard footsteps outside, then one of the guards called, 'Five, sir. Resuming post.' Williams composed himself.

'Well trained,' he complimented.

'Let me introduce you to the Professor,' Luke suggested.

The two men left the tent. Once they had reached the cell where Pete was being held, Colonel Williams said, 'I will speak with O'Conner alone.'

Luke walked away and intercepted a soldier crossing the square. 'Officer, a word.' The AM unit assumed an erect posture.

'Assemble an assault team,' Luke ordered. 'Seek and destroy all hostiles along our transport route.'

'Sir?'

Luke moved close to the officer, anger growing in his voice. 'Our fossil fuel supplies are low, soldier. We need to be mobile if we are to win this war. Secure the route. The trucks roll out at 0600.'

'Sir...' The soldier hesitated, searching for the right words to advise his superior of the level of difficulty that the task given to him presented. 'Reports indicate that the hostiles are cannibals, sir.'

'You're a machine, soldier.'

'They don't know that, sir.'

'You have guns, they don't. It's that simple.' Luke stood inches away, nose to nose with his subordinate. 'Don't come back here until you have the route cleared.'

Pete remained on the chair in his cell. The man wearing the tricorne hat approached the barred window.

'Comfortable, Professor?'

'Very.' Pete winced when pain shot up the left side of his face from his swollen cheek.

'Do you know who I am?'

Pete raised his head slowly. From pictures and videos, Pete recognised the long scar running along Williams' pale skin.

'Williams,' he said with disdain.

Jericho Williams let a smile slowly creep across his face. He leaned against the door, gazing out across the darkness of the camp. 'You know when you think about it, it's actually quite remarkable what Conroy and his Factions achieved. So few people were able to enslave so many. Those poor bastards worked under his rule for generations.'

Williams chuckled, remembering a moment of conversation he'd had with Dennis Conroy and his late brother in arms, Luther Saint. 'Conroy once imparted a rather elegant metaphor to explain their technique. He said, if you drop a frog into a pot of boiling water, it jumps right out. But put it into cool water and slowly raise the heat, the little bastard just sits there, boiling to death.'

Pete spat red saliva and wiped his mouth, his split lip tender. 'What do you want from me?'

'You have created a human being with very special attributes,' said Williams. 'I want you to show me how.'

'Go fuck yourself.'

The Colonel smiled and removed his hat.

'You won't tell me…' The moonlight shone over his bald head. Scars of third-degree burns patterned his scalp. 'But I assure you, you will tell Doctor Kindred.'

CHAPTER 21

One of the Kiyol archways that applied the protective body suit was teleported into the Portal Room. Lana was standing in line behind Rachel, while the arch applied the armour material over Rachel's entire body. Lana had been concerned about suffocation, but the machine had prompted Rachel when to hold her breath. And the material did not cover Rachel's mouth, eyes or her nostrils. It followed her jaw and left a comfortable gap for her mouth and cheeks.

Lana opted to have the armour applied to her as well. Using her reactive armour was like flexing a muscle and keeping it flexed. She had found it difficult to maintain continuously during her fight against the Sabre Company intruders. And Rachel had often told her, *You won't be able to armour yourself in time every time. You can be hit by a bullet from afar before you hear the shot.* Lana stepped up into the arch with her legs apart like Rachel had, and blue laser sensors swept over her body, scanning her dimensions. Lana held her breath upon the machine's monotone instruction, and the armour material jetted all over her body. Two seconds later, a tone sounded completion. Lana's suit expanded and held its close-fitting form.

Lana found that the alien armour weighed very little. The minor thickness that it had expanded around her body defined her muscles. She raised her knees and threw some air punches. She was impressed by how much mobility the suit afforded her.

Rachel looked at her reflection in a mirror. 'We look like superheroes.'

Her eyes were covered by black armoured plates that matched her eye size. She didn't know how, but her vision wasn't affected at all. She pushed her fingers through her blue hair and found where the suit material met her hairline. The material was elastic, allowing her to lift it from her skin and feel the inside. Rachel also loved how the pearlescent sheen of the black suit matched her hair. But her excitement waned when she saw Sam in the reflection of the mirror. She was up in the Control Room, hunched forward, her eyes fixed on the monitors displaying the camera feed to the SC camp.

'Lana,' Rachel said. 'Time to gear up.'

Sam hadn't moved an inch for hours, hardly blinking, afraid to miss any sign of her father being moved from the camp. Lex brought her a mug of coffee.

'Anything?' she said. When Sam didn't reply, Lex rested a hand on her shoulder. 'Sam, you should eat something.'

Sam ignored her advice, silently remaining focused.

Rachel strapped a handgun to her right thigh and a set of two spare magazines for her assault rifle to her left thigh. 'Extraction team ready?' she called to Lana and the AM units standing by.

Lana and the team of thirty soldiers shouted, 'Hoorah!' in unison.

'Hold up,' Sam called down to them. 'There's a patrol heading into the forest. Better wait till they complete their route.'

Captain Lincoln was standing on the other side of the portal room. He caught Lana's eye and smiled.

Lana smiled back. She knew AMs could act like humans, but she always wondered if they were able to truly feel emotion.

She asked Rachel this question while the two of them clipped on their gear—utility belts and thigh holsters.

'Not sure,' said Rachel. 'Pete said their design is based on Alan Turing's "Imitation Game". I don't really understand it, but I'm pretty sure they can't stray outside of their programmed parameters.'

Lana watched the Autonomous man's blank facial expression. 'I learnt about Hutch Branner's work,' she said. 'The Sabre Company soldiers were built to match the designs the Corporation stole. But they had to be modified so they would serve Sabre Company. They had to be fitted with an inhibitor chip, to enable them to commit acts that went against their original programming.'

'A-hole chip, more like,' Rachel commented. 'Every one of them are built to be bastards. Especially the Captains. Watch out for those.'

'Captains?'

'You'll know 'em when you see 'em.'

'Hey,' Lana leaned back, considering something about Rachel she had never thought to ask. 'Do you have a military rank?'

'I'm a Major, but—'

'Wow! You out rank Henry Drake?' Lana exclaimed; Rachel quickly hushed her.

'Nobody calls me Major,' said Rachel. 'I don't work for the UC Security Division anymore. I work for Pete.'

I'd like to be a Captain someday, Lana mused to herself. But she didn't know her own last name. How would that work?

Rowan stepped out of the elevator. He spoke to Fiona through his comm link before he arrived at the Control Deck.

'I've gotta go. Rachel's about to head in. Be careful.' Stopping at the monitors beside Lex, Rowan pulled on a headset to assist Sam with communications.

'Everything all right?' asked Sam, overhearing the concern in Rowan's voice.

'We're all under a lot of pressure right now,' he answered.

Sam saw a small flash, like something had exploded. It happened at the holding cell area. 'I think Dad just blew the lock off his cell door.'

Lex peered over Sam's shoulder and saw the cell door swing open. 'Must have been waiting for the guard detail to change shifts.'

'Rache,' Sam called down to the portal room, 'get in there before he does something stupid.' Then she programmed the Shifter on the Control Deck console to open a portal to the Forest Realm.

≡ Forest Realm ≡

Despite the dense humidity, the air felt much cooler than inside the cell. Instead of making a run for the forest, Pete crept towards Luke Palmer's tent. He was halfway there when he saw the distinct bright flash of portal light in the corner of his eye. *Williams must have left,* he thought. He noticed he was wearing a tricorne hat and thought, *he must be based somewhere in the Frontier Realm.*

Once inside Luke's tent, Pete searched for a Shifter device, lifting data tablets and printed maps with his wrists still bound. He spotted the rectangular console poking out of the pocket of a grey jacket. He retrieved it and dialled home.

'Professor O'Conner to Genesis Lab, come in.'

Sam's voice came through the Shifter comm. 'Dad, get out of there. Our extraction team are on their way. Make your way south into the forest.'

'Copy that, Sam. Leaving now.'

Sam drew a sharp breath. 'Wait, Dad, somebody's approaching your position. Hide!'

Lana moved through the trees like a predator. When she reached the clearing, she focused on Luke. She turned and signalled to Rachel that she had spotted their target.

The enemy patrol Sam had warned them about suddenly appeared, walking towards the holding cell area.

Rachel spoke into her comms. 'Execute flank formation. Secure camp perimeter. Do not engage hostiles until perimeter is sealed. Move out.'

Five soldiers spread to create a line of defence across the outer forest. The remaining units split into two groups, heading either side of the SC barracks. The entire tent formation was eventually surrounded. Lana and Rachel entered the dirt clearing.

Two AM soldiers reached the cell blocks and found Professor O'Conner's door open. Lana engaged them before they could report it in, shooting one soldier in the head with her sidearm. Though Lana had equipped her handgun with a suppressor, the other soldier had heard the sound and took cover. Rachel circled the cells, arrived behind the female soldier and shot her.

Lana heard whispering and looked in through the bars of a large cell in front of her.

'Please, help us.'

Lana saw five people in the one cell: a woman, a man, two young children and a teenage boy. She guessed that they were a family of forest dwellers. She aimed her pistol and shot at the lock. Once the cell was open, she instructed them to return to the forest.

Shiah pulled the two children behind her, while Anook and Chahtu took the lead. Shiah thanked Lana and hurried away with the children.

'Perimeter units, be advised: civilians heading your way. Let them through,' Lana ordered.

Pete ducked behind Luke's desk when he heard the tent flaps swish open. Luke walked in and sat down heavily on his bunk bed. He took a bottle of pills from his jacket pocket and popped two into his mouth. Running his fingers through his short red hair, he froze.

'Who's there?'

While searching the footlocker at the end of the bunk, Pete had found a handgun. He stood up, aiming it at Luke. 'Don't move.'

'Professor O'Conner.' Luke was unarmed. He stole a glance at the gun in his leather jacket draped over the pair of jeans beside Pete. 'How do you plan on getting out of here alive?'

'Kind of making it up as I go along.'

'There's nowhere for you to go, old man.' Luke slowly rose from the bunk and moved closer.

'I said, don't move.' Out of the corner of his eye, Pete saw a knife blade stab through the wall of the tent behind Luke. It swiftly sliced a line down to the ground.

Luke flinched when gunfire started around the camp outside. Soldiers yelled and alarm flares shot into the sky.

Rachel slipped in through the opening of the tent that she had cut. Red light beamed through the canvas. She aimed her pistol and fired a tranquiliser dart in the back of Luke's neck. He lurched forward, dropped to his knees and sank to the floor.

After checking Luke's slowing pulse, Rachel applied binders to his wrists and ankles. She stepped over him to free Pete's hands. 'Good to see you're alive, Boss. Can you run?'

'I can manage, thanks Rachel. I… wasn't sure if I could pull the trigger.'

'Good thing you didn't. We need him to find the General.' Rachel spoke into her comms.

'Requesting two units for prisoner evac.'

'Their Colonel was here. He's gone to the Frontier Realm.' Pete showed her Luke's Shifter device. 'This should have his coordinates.'

'Good. We'll check it out.' Rachel was watching Luke, as he lay unconscious on the floor.

Lana and two UC units stepped in through the tent flaps. 'Professor, are you all right?' She saw his hand pressing against his abdomen and spoke into her comms. 'Jolie, Pete is injured.'

'On my way,' Jolie replied.

'I'm fine,' said Pete. He took a bottle of pills from Luke's bunk bed. 'I think I know how they've been keeping his mind subdued.'

'Drugs from Doctor Kindred?' Rachel asked.

'Most likely.'

In the forest, Shiah and the children halted alongside Anook and Chahtu. 'Why have you stopped?'

'I smell blood,' said Chahtu.

Shiah scanned the dense black of the forest. She heard rapid footfalls approaching.

'Run!' Shiah yelled.

She pushed the children, urging them on through the trees. Anook saw someone collide into Chahtu. A second later, he was knocked down as well. They were both being pinned to the ground by dark, painted figures, who yelled and shrieked in crazed excitement.

Shiah couldn't see, but she felt the rough fibre of rope being tied around her. The children were screaming. She punched, kicked and clawed. 'Run children! Run!'

The boy, Tinba, pulled at the young girl's arm and they did as Shiah told them, running as fast as their short legs would allow. Fern leaves whipped at the boy's arms as he ploughed through the forest with Mehra in tow.

Mehra resisted, begging to turn back. 'Mummy!'

Her brother's hand closed over her mouth, muffling her cry before she could put them in greater danger.

'Quiet!' Tinba carried her across a stream to hide their tracks. 'Hold on to me.' Gripping a hanging vine, he swung over a steep slope to the safety of high trees. 'Wait here. I must find the dark woman who freed us.'

'Don't leave me!' Mehra cried.

'I must,' said Tinba. 'She will help us. Don't worry, you are safe up here.'

Mehra nodded, trembling. Tinba hugged her close before climbing down the vine-covered tree.

Rachel and Jolie flanked Pete on their way to the camp perimeter, while their UC team provided covering fire.

On the other side of the camp, Lincoln returned fire on a group of enemy troops. Moving quickly along the tent rows, he spotted Rachel and the Professor. The next step was almost his last; he only just raised his rifle in time to deflect a machete strike. His view was blocked by a broad- chested AM unit that could only be a Sabre Company Captain.

The Captain's name was Heller. He was larger and more muscular than regular AM troops. Heller advanced, swinging his blade at head height. Lincoln ducked and stepped in to punch the Captain's stomach. He tried to take hold of Heller's weapon, only to receive the unit's elbow hard in his face. As Lincoln staggered backwards, he noticed a child running through the camp's centre square. He spat synthetic blood and called through his comms. 'Child civilian sighted! All units check your fire!'

Tinba ran through the flickering yellow lines of gunfire. A fragmentation grenade exploded next to a petrol tank on the back of a truck. Flames spewed out and reached high into the air. UC soldiers taking cover saw the boy running into the impending blast zone, unable to reach him.

'Somebody grab him!' one shouted.

Lincoln ducked and weaved to avoid Heller's onslaught of combination punches. He landed a right hook across the Captain's jaw and broke away to get a line of sight on the running child. Heller followed and rammed Lincoln with his shoulder. The impact threw Lincoln onto the roll cage of a military dune buggy.

Heller brought his blade down hard. Lincoln pulled his head sideways and yelled out when his left ear was sliced off. Red battery fluid dribbled down his neck and shoulder. He rolled off the buggy onto the ground. Heller kicked Lincoln in his ribs and slammed him into the bull bar of the vehicle. Lincoln caught Heller's next boot kick and shoved the Captain back.

'Does anybody see the boy?' Lincoln shouted. His eyes darted between muzzle flashes. 'Report! Where's the boy?'

Lana spotted Tinba and ran out into the fray to intercept him. An SC soldier stepped into her path and fired his pistol at her head. Lana weaved left, jerking her head as the bullet flew through her swinging hair. Spinning her whole body around clockwise, she threw her extended leg. The back of her heel hit the soldier's right temple. Fluid spilled from the concave side of his skull as his body flew sideways. The momentum rotated his body and the fluid streamed out in an arch. Lana regained her balance and broke into a sprint before the trooper hit the ground. She leapt up onto a fallen utility crate and gripped the far edge. She landed in a frog-leap position and she projected herself forward, covering the two-metre gap to reach Tinba.

The steel hull of the tanker burst. Twisted metal flew in all directions. The radial blast wave thrust everyone within ten metres to the ground. Lana snatched up the running boy from mid-air and wrapped her arms and legs around him. The wall of fire swept over them both and spread across the ground, eating up the air like a starving flame beast. Vehicles rolled and toppled over, consumed by the intense fire. Rubber tires burned and wounded soldiers screamed, while they were engulfed inside the orange and black cloud.

Lincoln picked himself up from the dirt. Heller rose, wincing at the pain in his bleeding arm. Jagged pieces of shrapnel protruded from his bicep. He lurched over to Lincoln, still carrying his machete.

Lincoln slowly circled the SC Captain. He assessed his opponent's injury and took in the surrounding battle field, transformed by the explosion. The assault rifle he had dropped lay three feet away.

Rachel lifted herself off the Professor and patted down a flame burning his sleeve. She coughed, trying to yell Lana's name. She accessed her comms. 'Fan out! Secure the area!'

The wind blew cool through the grassy field. Rachel could feel it on her naked back. Her suit had extinguished the flames that had burned over her.

'All units call in. Lana, can you hear me?' Rachel made her way through the burning wreckage and debris towards the source of the explosion. Her squad members replied, stating conditions of injury. She counted nine soldiers ready for orders.

'Lincoln, where are you?' Rachel called through her comms. 'Do you have eyes on Lana?'

Heller advanced, slicing his machete at Lincoln. Lincoln dropped to the ground and swung his leg across the dirt, tripping the SC Captain. Heller landed heavily on his injured arm.

Lincoln retrieved his rifle, stood over Heller and aimed at his forehead. He could see now the dark surrounding Heller's sunken eyes. The Captain would not live another month. Like all of the other Sabre Company soldiers, their deviant programming would cause their bodies to shut down.

Heller reached for his blade, despite his defeated position. 'By the time we're done with your world, you're gonna wish—'

Lincoln fired a round through the Captain's head. He stood, staring down at him, until Jolie appeared at his side.

Jolie saw that Lincoln was missing his left ear and the comms device that had been imbedded in it. She prepared adhesive padding.

'Just a scratch,' said Lincoln distractedly, his eyes searching through the smoke for Lana and the boy. 'Is the Professor safe?'

'Yes, but we can't find Lana.' Jolie leaned in to assess the head wound more closely. 'Hold still. You're no use to any of us if you fall apart.'

'Rachel, it's Sam. Are you all right? We've lost the feed.'

'Your dad's safe,' said Rachel. 'I can't see Lana.'

She spotted lights bobbing up and down at the north end of the field and took a magnifying scope from her utility belt to scan the horizon. The lights were flaming torches held over the heads of half-naked men and women. They were running towards the camp. Rachel counted over thirty of them. Bones dangled from their necklaces and shrivelled human hands bounced at their sides.

'What the f—' Rachel hit her comms and spoke rapidly. 'All units retreat to evac position. I repeat: all units pull out!' She raced towards the forest, gaining on the Professor and his escort.

'Sam, open the portal.' Stopping at the edge of the clearing, Rachel turned back to scan the burning barracks for any sign of Lana. Flames wavered and licked at blackened bodies on the ground.

Tears welled in Rachel's eyes and her hands began to shake as she activated her direct comms link to Lana's. 'Lana, if you can hear me, I'm sorry.'

The cries of the Blood Demons rose into a frenzy when they reached the charred bodies of the Sabre Company soldiers.

'We're coming back with reinforcements. Please, just stay alive.'

CHAPTER 22

≡ Frontier Realm ≡
Bear Ranch

Colonel Jericho Williams rode up the hillside to a coastal ranch. He was followed by a group of six armed men that he'd hired from the nearest town. Orange light crept over the morning horizon. The wind blew chilled air through the tall grass and along the rolling hills of the coast.

Williams ordered two of the men armed to peel off and circle the property. He ordered two more to take position outside of the perimeter fence line. The remaining pair stayed with him. They all dismounted when they reached the veranda of Bear Ranch House.

'The Royal Army require your land,' Williams called. 'Surrender it to us now and you will not be harmed.'

Riana threw off her blanket and jumped out of the single bed. Spying men outside through the bedroom window, she quickly pulled on a skirt and long boots. After tying her corset over a long sleeve shirt, she clipped on her belt, equipped with a pistol and knife.

Yanking on the handle, Riana swung the front door open and strode out, aiming her pistol directly at Williams. 'Get off of our property!'

Williams raised his hands. He looked to the house and to the servant's quarters. 'I take it your brothers are on escort duty. No men to protect—'

Riana clicked the gun hammer into firing position. 'I should kill you right now and put an end to the injustice and suffering you have brought to this land.' Her bottom lip trembled as the men slowly approached her. 'Cowards!'

Williams signalled the riflemen beyond the fence line to open fire. The window behind Riana shattered and she dashed back into the house.

'Come and get me, you sons of bitches!' she shouted. Glass raining across the floor and splintered wood flew from the walls, while the remaining men opened fire.

Williams whistled for all the gunmen to enter the property. He pointed to those closest to him.

'You two, with me.'

They mounted their horses and Williams spoke to those remaining. 'I'll be back with the Royal Cavalry.' He glared menacingly to the old weathered house. 'Do what you want with her. If the brothers show up, kill them.'

'Aye, sir,' said a man called Bryan.

Williams looked down at Bryan, recognising him immediately. Williams had been operating in the Frontier Realm for almost two years. He had hired a lot of different men. All of them had done as he had ordered in exchange for gold pieces, save this man.

'Do not think your insubordination went unnoticed,' he said to Bryan. 'I trust you will not disappoint me this time.'

Bryan met Williams' gaze and held it. 'I don't kill children.'

Williams assumed a thinker's pose, his gloved fingers propping his chin. 'Perhaps the welfare of your own two darling children would be proper motivation for you to behave more like a man and do as you are ordered.'

Knowing what Williams was really capable of, Bryan gave

into fear and reluctantly saluted his leader. 'We'll have the Bear family detained by dawn, sir.'

Home Realm
Aqua Sierra Otami Palace

'Copy that, Sam,' said Hank. 'Glad to hear your old man is safe. Any sign of Lana yet?'

'Thanks, Hank. No sign yet.'

'I've seen what she can do. She'll be all right.' Hank nodded to Brad when he entered the main comms station to the compound. 'Brad and Renee are heading through to the coordinates Pete gave us.'

Sam had arranged for Luke Palmer to be teleported to Hank at Otami Palace. 'You have Luke?'

'We do. We're about to start working on him,' said Hank.

Jin Otami pushed a trolley of equipment along the corridor, carrying instruments designed to detect deception. He reached Luke's cell and nodded to the AM guards to let him through.

'How are you feeling?' Jin asked Luke politely.

Luke sat in the centre of the interrogation room, strapped to a steel chair. 'Screw you, commie bastard.' The single overhead light shone down bright, making it hard for him to identify his soon to be interrogator. Jin stepped closer, preparing a set of syringes. Luke saw that he was of Asian descent, muscular, with a wavy backwards fringe. 'You're wasting your time. I've never met the General.'

'Progress.' Jin opened a black case and took out a cerebral scanning headset. 'And we haven't even started.'

Hank entered the room and looked from Luke to Jin. 'I want everything he knows.'

Jin set about fitting the headset to Luke's temples. 'So, you're some kind of hero?' Jin asked Luke. Once everything was in place, he raised the eye scanner to align with Luke's.

'Was,' said Hank. 'Pete said somebody called Kindred messed with his head. He'll see what he can do to reverse it, once we're done here.'

≡ Frontier Realm ≡

Brad and Renee emerged from the rippling portal sphere and stumbled when their feet met with a steep hillside. They slid down maple leaves and arrived at level ground.

'We're in,' Brad reported.

'Hi guys, Chesh here. Cap's busy beatin' it out of Rachel's old squeeze. I'll be the sexy voice in your head this morning.' Chesh got a laugh out of Renee before continuing. 'So, readings from the drone indicated multiple heat signatures about a kilometre from your position. What do you see out there?'

Renee looked around, brushing wet leaves from her behind. 'We're in a forest.' She glanced at Brad. 'You hear that?'

He nodded. 'Cannon fire.'

Chesh's voice returned. 'Sounds exciting. Let me know if you need backup.'

Renee took out her palm console and checked the topographical report from the drone that had been sent ahead of them. 'This way. There are buildings ahead. We should be able to get close enough to replicate whatever the people are wearing, find out if they've seen anybody fitting Williams' description.'

After spotting some of the townsfolk in the settlement, Brad and Renee replaced their military uniforms with cotton shirts, slacks and boots.

'This could be a problem,' said Renee, looking Brad up and down.

'What?' He looked himself over, his dark brown skin juxtaposed the white cotton.

'These people might not be very socially evolved.' Renee shrugged. 'We'll see how we go.'

Brad still wasn't following Renee's thinking. In Home Realm, race was a made-up concept, like gender or religion. In the past, there had been hatred between people with different skin colour. It was called racism. Brad and Renee were both thirty years old and belonged to a generation that had moved beyond that ignorance. Neither of them had ever experienced racial prejudice.

Brad and Renee made their way into a tavern and approached the barman.

The barman's brow was furrowed. He opened his mouth to tell them to get out but then his eyes swept approvingly over Renee. He liked her smooth black hair and full lips.

'Good morning, we…' Renee paused. 'Is something wrong, sir?'

'My apologies, madam.' The barman moved his gaze and began wiping his bench. 'We don't get many of your kind in here. You're both obviously free people.' He gestured to the local clientele seated hunched over their drinks at the tables. 'I suppose your money is as good as any of these drunks'. My name's Burt. What can I get for you?'

'Our kind?' Brad asked, confused. 'What—'

'I see,' said Renee, having guessed right that the people in the Frontier Realm would regard dark-skinned people as less than equal. She glanced about the room. The men were indeed drunk and hadn't even noticed Brad or Renee.

'We're looking for a man,' Renee said to Burt. 'He's tall, no hair, has a scar. Have you seen anybody of that description?'

'Jericho Williams,' Burt said with disdain. 'What does a fine-looking woman like yourself want with a dirty rat like him?'

'He's a criminal. We're the law.'

Brad heard another explosion in the distance. 'Burt, what's happening out there?'

The barman looked at them both, puzzled. 'Not from around here, huh?'

Leaning on the bar, Burt told them of the situation surrounding the coastal settlement. He said an invading army from across the sea was acquiring land to build forts and station troops. Everyone living along the coast was required, by 'The King's Law', to surrender their homes to the Royal Army and seek residence elsewhere.

'Damned Red Coats. Jericho Williams is a very powerful and wealthy man. Nobody really knows where he came from. It's plain the bastard is all about capitalising on the war.' Burt spoke softly, so as not to be overheard. 'Has his own band of armed men. Word is, he offered his assistance to the commanding officer of The Royal Army, promising the "peaceful" surrender of any requisitioned property and land at the King's request. Word from The House of Royalty, back in their land, says the invasion is unpopular, so of course the Reds agreed. I suppose they saw it as a cost-effective tactic.' Burt shook his head in disgust before continuing. 'Williams has been given access to the army's finest weaponry. And he's been promised over a month of shipments.'

'Shipments of what?' Renee asked.

'Steel, rare metals, all mined abroad and brought here,' said Burt. 'Each week, Williams and his men remove families from their homes. The Red Coats in turn move forward and establish a stronghold in the newly acquired area.'

Burt looked to Brad and Renee, concern spreading across his face. 'So happens, the most sought after and strategically advantageous area is here, our coastal settlement, in particular, Bear Ranch. If you're looking for Jericho Williams, you should start there.'

CHAPTER 23

Tinba scooped water from the stream using a large leaf, folded into the shape of a boat. He listened to the early-morning cries of birds and monkey-like animals he knew as piraps. It was another humid day in the forest. A thirsty deer lapped at the edge of the stream, cautiously watching the boy.

A group of adolescent piraps threw pebbles down at Tinba, trying to provoke him into play. One of the pebbles skittled across the surface of an iron girder. The boy ignored the piraps and walked by the ruins of a warehouse building on his way back to Lana and Mehra.

Lana had teleported herself and Tinba into the forest when the explosion had burned the Sabre Company camp. Part of the blast wave had travelled with them. Lana had been thrown into a tree and knocked unconscious. Her body suit had reacted to the flames and burst into particles that took away the air around her.

Tinba wasn't able to wake her. He had dragged Lana as far away from the light of the fires as he could and he left her to find his sister.

Mehra waited with Lana now. She trusted Lana, because the strangely dressed woman had released her family from the metal cage. Mehra was crouched beside Lana, watching her sleep.

Tinba returned, carrying the water. At the sound of his footsteps Lana snapped awake, coughing and gasping. Mehra leapt on top of her and pressed her tiny hand over Lana's mouth.

'Please be quiet,' she whispered. 'The demons will hear us!'

Lana checked herself over for injuries. She could feel minor abrasions along her back. Her body suit had done its job. The blast had reduced it to a slim leotard but she had no burns at all. She did have a cut lip though and a nasty bruise on her forehead.

Tinba approached and handed the water-filled leaf to his sister.

'Where are we?' Lana said.

'I don't know,' said Mehra. After sipping the water, she passed the leaf to Lana.

Lana saw that the ragged animal skin clothes Tinba wore were singed, but he wasn't hurt. She drank deeply and glanced around the forest, before returning the leaf to Mehra. 'I freed you. Why did you come back? Where is your family?'

'Taken,' said Tinba.

Mehra's eyes watered. 'The Blood Demons have them. Anook as well.' She buried her face in Lana's chest and clung to her waist. 'Please help us find them. Please!'

Lana hugged the little girl. 'I don't know where to look.' Tinba jumped up and pointed in the direction of the city.

'That way,' he said, 'in the city.'

Lana raised herself to her feet. The jagged roofs and spires of what was once a city were visible through the trees.

'I'd better contact my people. They'll be looking for —'

Her comms device was gone, along with her thigh holstered sidearm. Lana looked from one worried child to the other.

'I need you both to walk back to the camp where I freed you. Stay out of sight when you get there. My people will be looking for me. Wait until they arrive. Tell them where I went. I'll look for your parents.'

Mehra took Lana's hand and squeezed with her tiny fingers. 'Please hurry, Lana.'

'I will,' Lana assured her. 'Now go.'

Lana walked in the direction Tinba had indicated, making her way through the forest until it was clear enough to start a running pace. Curious pirap monkeys followed her along the treetops above, gliding through the air, their long arms outstretched to catch the next tree branch.

≡ Frontier Realm ≡

Michael, Nathaniel and Riana Bear had inherited their Irish father and Native mother's land. As well as the family ranch, a tavern lodge had been left to them. It was run by their old friend, Burt.

The currency which had been feeding the community for five years now was whisky. The Royal Army invasion brought dangerous, opportunistic sorts to the coastal lands. Some were desperate, others were driven by greed. They all took advantage of the turmoil of war. And hostile Native tribes roamed along the coast, hunting invaders, killing all people with pale skin.

As their whisky caravan fell under constant threat, the Bear brothers served as an escort, accompanied by a few hired men.

Nathaniel stepped silently through the plumes of smoke. He kept a safe distance from the burning wagons, wary of the kegs of gun powder. The sound of musket and cannon fire drummed in the distance. Calling again to his brother, Michael, he spun around at the sound of rustling leaves. He raised his rifle, pulling the hammer until it clicked into firing position.

Michael came staggering out from the forest edge, struggling to catch his breath.

'There you are.' Nathaniel sighed with relief. 'I told you to meet me at the clearing.'

'I was delayed.'

Nathaniel looked to where his brother had come from. 'Our men?'

'Dead. A war party took the caravan before I could reach it.'

'How many?'

Michael shook his head, uncertain. 'They turned south. Our concern now is the twenty or so Red Coats heading our way. I watched a troop marching along the north ridge.' Michael crouched to brush away the leaves covering the dead body of a young man.

Nathaniel watched his brother take a pistol and a knife from the body. 'There's no future for us here, Michael.' He wiped sweat from his brow. 'We should go home, pack up and leave as soon as possible.'

'Agreed. We can move west. Grandmother will take us in.' Michael slid the knife under his waist belt and tossed the pistol to his brother. 'Let's move.'

Bright morning sunlight shone through the bullet-riddled walls of Bear Ranch House.

Bryan signalled for one man to enter, and a brown bearded man stepped up onto the front porch. After a few quick paces he heaved himself at the door, his meaty shoulder splitting the old wood down the middle.

Bryan heard a scuffle ensue after the man disappeared into the dark interior. A moment later, the man staggered backwards onto the porch, clutching his throat. Blood oozed between his fingers. His eyes rolled back and he fell from the steps to the dusty earth.

Bryan swore, stroking his thick black moustache. He gripped his rifle and ran towards the house, drawing a briquet sabre from the scabbard at his side. 'Hamish, Barthol, in through the windows!' he yelled to the two remaining men.

Riana wiped the bloodied blade of her hunting knife on her cotton skirt and returned it to her belt. A large boot smashed through the window, two paces away from her. She raced across the room to the staircase, only to meet with Hamish, busting through the hallway window.

Hamish was short and stocky. His momentum sent him rolling across the glass-covered floor and onto his feet. He rose with a sinister grin, blocking Riana's path.

Riana took out her pistol but Hamish struck her wrist with his rifle. The pistol fell to the floor and he kicked it into the kitchen. Riana thrust her knee-high leather boot into Hamish's stomach. He fell backwards through the doorway, colliding into the kitchen table. By the time he struggled to his feet, Riana was on top of him, trying to pry away his rifle.

Hamish swung Riana away from him and her hip struck the table, hard. Riana refused to let go of the rifle, tugging with both hands, her muscles rope-hard under her cotton shirt. Hamish hurtled her across the room, the rifle slipping from her grip. She flew into the bookcase on the opposite wall of the kitchen and dropped to the floor. Books toppled over her.

Back at the tavern, Renee had spied the open money drawer behind the bar. While Brad distracted Burt with conversation, she had used her Shifter console to replicate and then produce enough money to buy weapons and horses.

Now, Brad and Renee were cantering up a steep hillside, when they spotted a lone rider.

'Judging by his uniform,' said Brad, 'this guy might be with the invading army.' Renee turned her horse and urged it into a gallop to block the Red Coat's path.

The man was Sergeant Sebastian Germaine of the Royal Army. He called to Renee before reaching her. 'Who goes there?'

'My name is Renee Riley. We're looking for Jericho Williams. Do you know where we can find him?'

Germaine's hand dropped on to his sidearm and he slowed his horse as he approached. 'Why do you wish to find him?'

'Take your hand off your weapon,' said Brad when he reached Renee.

'Answer the question and we'll be on our way,' Renee advised, glancing at the archaic looking rifle in Brad's steady hands.

'Williams is clearing Bear Ranch. I'm headed there now.'

'Good,' said Renee. 'Lead the way.' She noticed Germaine stare past her at two men riding out of the nearby forest.

Nathaniel leaned back in his saddle as he and Michael rode down a grassy slope. 'This war will pass,' he said. 'We may be able to return in a few years.'

Michael glanced over his shoulder to see three riders approaching from the west. 'The Militia will drive them out,' he agreed.

'Don't feel guilty for refusing to join, Michael. We have to take care of our sister. Nothing else matters.' Nathaniel looked at his brother. 'Are you listening to me?'

'We have company.' Michael pulled his rifle from its saddle holster. 'Red Coat.' They stopped and Nathaniel squinted. 'Are you sure?'

'Eagle eyes, brother.' Michael pointed two fingers to the riders in the distance. 'I can see his golden lion-crested buttons from here. He appears to have two slaves with him.'

Nathaniel turned his horse and leaned forward in the saddle. 'That Red Coat looks familiar.'

'He won't be looking familiar to anyone in a minute.' Michael raised the light weight, long- range rifle. He became very still, closing one eye while he lined the sights to the lead rider.

'Wait.' Nathaniel reached over and pushed Michael's gun barrel down. 'It's Germaine.'

'Who?'

'He tried to help us, remember? I discussed a bargain with him to give up the ranch in exchange for enough payment to set us up elsewhere.' Nathaniel waved to Germaine. 'He took care of the papers, but his superiors found out and he was reprimanded. He lost his station pleading our case.'

Michael rested his weapon in his lap and gestured to the hill before them. 'How do you know a dozen more of them are not behind that rise, waiting for his command to collect us?'

'We're not that important.' Nathaniel urged his horse into a canter to meet Germaine.

'Mr Bear!' Germaine called.

Nathaniel noticed a hint of anxiety in Germaine's eyes. 'What's happened?'

'Williams and his mercenaries have taken your property.' Germaine turned to look back the way he'd come. 'I fear your sister may be in danger.'

'I have a little trouble trusting a man wearing a red uniform,' Michael said, keeping an eye on the hill crest. 'And why do you have slaves?'

Anger simmered inside Renee.

'Enough!' Nathaniel yelled. 'Come or don't!' He wheeled his horse and sped off in the direction of home.

Germaine followed, gaining easily with his superior horse. Michael gave chase, riding alongside Renee. '*You* are law enforcers?' he asked her, sceptically.

'We are agents of a secret service,' she called over the drumming of hooves. 'Jericho Williams is a wanted criminal where we come from. My partner and I are here to capture and take him to our courts for judgment.'

Barthol pulled himself through a side window and into the house. Glass crunched beneath his heavy leather boots.

Straightening to his full seven-foot height, he unsheathed a machete from his belt.

Bryan entered through the doorway. 'Where's the girl?' he asked Barthol.

Barthol nodded in the direction of the kitchen. Bryan returned his sword to its scabbard. 'Bring her out, Hamish—alive!'

'She's a wild one, sir!' Hamish called back.

Riana groaned, clutching her injured torso. Using the lower bookshelves as support, she painfully pulled herself to her feet.

Hamish stood over her, waiting.

'My, my, you are a strong girl.' He brought down the butt of his rifle. It smashed into Riana's left brow. Dazed, she slid back to the floor. Riana moved to her knees after a few seconds and crawled towards the pistol lying beneath the kitchen table.

'I admire your strength, little lady.' Hamish set his rifle down and grabbed the back of Riana's corset. 'A blow like that would knock a mule stone dead.'

Riana's fingers were just touching the wooden handle of the gun.

'Come on now.' Hamish pulled Riana up from the floor, tearing the floral material.

Riana snatched up the pistol, twisted her upper body to face Hamish and aimed the barrel to his head.

Barthol and Bryan heard the micro-second hiss of sparked gun powder before the gun shot. A moment later there was a dull thud against the floor.

There were two entrances from the dining room to the kitchen, one on either side of the staircase leading to the second floor. Bryan and Barthol were between them, preparing to take one door each.

'Hamish, you idiot,' Bryan muttered to himself. 'You had better be dead.' Bryan raised three fingers for Barthol to see, then two to indicate a countdown to enter the kitchen simultaneously.

Barthol froze, raising a hand at Bryan. He pointed to the dusty road outside. Five riders were approaching the house at speed.

'The brothers are here and they've brought some friends.' Bryan glanced over at Barthol. The big man's grip had tightened around the handle of his barbaric-looking chopping knife. Bryan unbuckled his belt with its scabbard and pistol. 'We're done Barthol.' He held out his free hand.

'Give it here.'

Barthol looked nervously from Bryan to the party of riders.

'I said we're done.'

Germaine and the two brothers reached the house and dismounted. Renee checked the body before the porch.

Barthol hesitated. 'But Mr Williams said—'

'Williams is a gutless murderer. Barthol, you saw what he had the men do to that family last night. They were good, honest people.' Bryan moved closer to the big man. 'This is not what we do—not for any man, not for any sum of money.'

Barthol hung his head and handed over his knife. Bryan threw it to the floor with his own weapons. The two mercenaries knelt down and raised their hands high just as Nathaniel's silhouette appeared at the door.

Bryan jerked his head to the kitchen. 'Your sister is in there.' Michael and Germaine followed Nathaniel into the room.

'Michael,' Nathaniel said, pointing to the left door. Then he looked at Sergeant Germaine.

'Watch these two.'

With Nathaniel taking the door on the right, the brothers entered the kitchen. Michael ducked under a swinging blow from Riana, narrowly avoiding a heavy saucepan.

'Riana, it's me!'

Riana dropped the cooking pot and hugged her brothers.

'The caravan, is it safe?'

Nathaniel shook his head.

'Lost. They were attacked by a war party a mile or so before our meeting point.' He pushed a lock of dark hair away from Riana's face. 'We shouldn't have left you alone.'

Bryan began to plead when Michael and Nathaniel returned to the dining room. 'I have children, a family of my own. We needed the gold. You have to understand. I agreed only to convince landowners of this settlement to leave, before the Royal Army—'

A distant explosion from the north echoed out across the hills, followed by the unmistakable sound of cannon fire.

Germaine looked to the road outside and addressed Renee, who stood by the door. 'Wait here if you still want Williams.' He turned back to Michael and Nathaniel. 'The army will be here by morning. We must leave.'

'We go west,' said Nathaniel.

'What's in the west?' Brad asked.

'Our grandmother. She'll take us in.'

'Do you have a wagon?' asked Bryan. 'Barthol and I will help you pack supplies. We can follow you inland until you're clear.'

'You cannot trust these men,' Germaine warned with a glare at Bryan. 'I was there last night, when your posse burned that cabin. The women and children were still inside! Did you not hear them scream?'

Bryan lurched toward Germaine and stopped himself, fists clenched. 'I heard! And what did you do?' His voice turned hoarse. 'Nothing!'

Germaine did not offer any rebuke. He knew he was just as guilty of inaction. He could see now that Bryan's eyes were bloodshot from lack of sleep.

Bryan spoke in a low, resigned voice. 'We are both of us, cowards.'

Germaine took off his tricorne hat and gazed at the floor. 'You speak true,' he conceded.

'Nathaniel, I knew your father,' Bryan said to him. 'He and your mother helped my family in times of need and we yours. Allow me to help you all on your way.'

'The wagon is out back,' said Michael. 'Bring it and the horses to the front. I'll start moving supplies to the porch.' He set his rifle down and strode away to gather food.

Riana watched Brad and Renee walk back to the porch to speak with one another privately.

'Who are they?' she asked.

'They say they work for a secret service,' said Nathaniel. He noticed that his sister's hands were shaking. 'Riana—'

'I'm not hurt, brother.' Riana walked to the bathroom with her head held high. 'It'll take a lot more than a few louts to bring me down.'

Renee watched flashes of cannon fire light the trees along the horizon. She accessed her comms and asked Chesh to put her through to Hank.

'Renee,' Hank answered. 'Have you found him?'

'Not yet, Captain. We're going to survey the area. We expect Williams to return to this position soon.' Renee tapped at her console menu screen. 'Sending link to terrain scan now.'

'Copy that, Renee. Good work. We'll be ready to move in on your command.'

CHAPTER 24

Lana splashed through a shallow stream and climbed onto the leaf-covered ground. After running along the forest floor for another fifteen minutes, she found herself inside what was once a two- storey horseshoe of flats, looking into a courtyard. She slowed her pace to inspect the dilapidated fountain and the statue atop of it—a woman wearing a loose toga, pouring a jug of water.

The walls free of vines and shrubbery were pocked by shell fire and shrapnel damage. Patterned brickwork rose and fell over tree roots that stretched across the courtyard floor. A deep, blackened crater lay below the corner, by the entrance. Lana climbed over a collapsed balcony and made her way up stairs to an exposed room. Sunlight beaming through the open ceiling created a light orange hue.

The floor was covered in leaves, beneath which lay old books strewn about the carpet. Shell casings rolled and clinked together when Lana's stepping disturbed the uneven floor. She looked up to find her pirap monkey companions climbing along the top of the surviving walls. Their relaxed nature suggested the area was safe from predators.

Lana entered an adjoining room, where there was only partial flooring and no walls. On the small platform of space was a high-backed armchair, striped green and brown. She gasped at the sight of a skeleton slouched to one side. It wore a military uniform belonging to a nation Lana didn't recognise. Tangled strings of long grey hair hung about its shoulders. The head of the chair was stained dark by the exit wound at the top-rear of its exposed skull.

Lana saw a Colt pistol below the bone hand hanging from the padded arm rest. There was also a hatchet by the soldier's side. Lana was about to reach for it when one of the piraps screeched a warning. She turned and looked up at the monkey. There was charcoal writing on the wall above the door she had entered. The pirap's tail was hanging down between the first letters.

This, the war we wage against ourselves
The war to end all wars
Is the end of us all.

A dark figure appeared in the doorway—a woman painted red. She bared her sharp brown teeth. Lana raised her hands and was about to utter peaceful words. But with a sharp intake of breath, the woman advanced at speed.

The armchair rocked as Lana was pinned against it. She armoured her skin, caught the woman's wrist and elbowed her across the face. After a feral shriek, the woman raked her fingernails down Lana's neck, across her chest, slicing four lines through her suit.

Lana felt for the axe handle. Her eyes widened when the crazed woman latched her jaws over Lana's neck, applying over one-hundred-and-sixty pounds of sharp pressure. She took a firm hold of the axe, swung it around the woman's shoulder and buried the blade in the back of her skull.

Lana had to pry the woman's jaw open to get her off. She braced her knee against the limp body and pulled the hatchet free. The monkeys had been screeching wildly during the fight. They fell silent, watching on while Lana sank to her knees. She breathed heavily, holding her sore neck. The wind blew cool into the exposed room.

≡ Frontier Realm ≡

Riana lit a candle and set it into the lantern cage. Lowering her aching arms, she looked herself over in the mirror. Her fingers trembled when she wiped her hand across her brow, wincing as the swelling on her forehead stung.

She untied her corset and dropped it to the floor. The effort of lifting her ruined shirt over her head sent fire up her spine. Shuddering, she clenched her jaw and thumped her fist down on the wooden dresser before her. After taking a moment to breathe through the pain, she took a swig from a whisky bottle.

Staring into the mirror through her tangled hair, Riana used her shirt to dab at the cuts and grazes around her ribs, under her arms and lower back, turning the bowl of water red as she rinsed and squeezed it. There was a dull rumble, followed by an explosion in the distance. The room shook and the lantern swayed.

Germaine hefted a wooden box onto the growing stack of supplies. He wiped his clammy hair away from his face and sat down to catch his breath. 'That sounded close.'

Nathaniel was leaning with his boot on a thick log by the fireplace.

'Will you return to your home country?' he asked.

Germaine straightened his back and let out a heavy sigh. 'There's nothing for me back there.'

Michael returned from the kitchen, carrying a sack of potatoes over each shoulder. 'You should come with us.'

Germaine let out a laugh. 'Desertion. Why not?'

The door to the bathroom opened and Riana strode out, tying her dark wavy hair back into a ponytail.

'Miss Bear.' Germaine rose, concern in his voice. 'Are you all right?'

'Fine, thank you, Sergeant.' Riana gave him a sideways glance. She set a bottle of whisky on the dining table and smiled at his gentlemanly manner. Behind Germaine was her father's portrait. It was hanging askew on the wall.

Nathaniel watched his sister standing, silent and solemn. 'Riana?'

'We can't leave,' she said. 'This place has been in our family for three generations. How can we let them take it from us?'

'We don't stand a chance against the Royal Army.'

'Your brother is right, Miss Bear,' Germaine said softly. 'We must leave.'

Michael was carrying a bag of wheat across the room. He stopped and let it fall to the floor.

'The mine.'

'What mine?' Germaine asked.

Nathaniel turned, immediately catching on to his brother's realisation. 'There's an abandoned mine not far from here,' he explained to Germaine.

Pacing, Michael began to formulate a plan. 'The access tunnel is at the bottom of the hill by the quarry. The shaft leads right up to the edge of the ranch boundary.'

Riana's hopes rose with her brothers'. 'We must reach the resistance. Their Militia can use the mine to ambush the Red Coats at night.'

'First, we must hide the entrance.' Nathaniel made for the door to call Barthol and Bryan. 'You two, with me!'

Michael picked up his coat and rifle. 'We'll take the wagon to the road and leave the horses for the three of you to catch up.'

Royal Army Officers Camp

'Mr Williams, of course we appreciate your assistance, but I'm afraid we cannot spare the resources you need,' said the Commander of the Royal Army. 'Your payment will be gold.'

Jericho Williams sat before the table of high-ranking officers. He rotated a black, four-by-four- centimetre cube in his fingers. The scar running through his damaged eyebrow twitched and he set the cube down to rest on the arm of the red oak chair. He glared at the Royal Army commanding officer seated before him. 'We had an agreement, Commander. Six weeks of shipments.'

The large candle-lit cabin room was silent. Over a dozen other RA officers were in attendance. The muffled shouting of orders could be heard outside. The evening meeting was held to discuss the advancement of forces across the coastal settlements. Williams had arrived to advise them of the hilltop property, Bear Ranch.

'I suggest you take what the King can offer.' The smug, greying sixty-year-old Commander took a white quill and dipped it in ink. He returned to the documents on the table before him. 'That will be all.'

Glancing about the room, Williams stood and straightened his trench coat. 'Very well, gentlemen.'

The Commander watched Williams leave the cabin hall with his two men. He noticed the small cube on the arm of the oak chair. 'Your… toy, sir.' The other officers laughed in unison.

Williams and his men rode across the open field, to the top of the hill overlooking the Royal Army camp. He pressed a button on his wrist console. When the two-storey building exploded, the ground shook and the horses reared in fright. The neighbouring tents were flattened, troops and the lines of artillery cannons disappeared into a flash of light. Williams' horse staggered sideways as the shockwave travelled across the field and up the hill, lifting dirt and shaking trees. A forty-metre-high mushroom cloud rose into the darkening sky.

At Bear Ranch, Brad and Renee returned from the outskirts of the property and made their way over to Nathaniel. 'What's all the commotion?'

'We're going to leave the property as bait,' Sebastian told them 'Then return with the Militia through a mine shaft which leads to the edge of the ranch.'

'Very good.'

Brad turned with the others in the direction of a deep rumble in the distance. A strong wind blew through them and they saw the haunting fire-lit silhouette of a dark grey cloud on the horizon. By the time the sound of the explosion had reached the hilltop, the cloud had already risen to form its shape.

Renee stared in horror and disbelief. Only in holo-videos had she seen the devastating result of such a weapon. Though the cloud was miniature compared to what had been used on Earth, it was no less frightening.

'Williams,' she said. 'He must have access to plutonium.'

Brad moved to the horses. 'His men will collect the remaining supplies they need and he'll be gone.'

Renee followed. 'We can still track him.'

She pulled herself up onto her horse. Typing a quick message into her comms, she informed Hank of the development.

Nathaniel walked alongside Brad's horse to say goodbye. 'I hope you catch Williams.' Brad reached down and shook Nathaniel's hand.

'The forces that are on their way to you now may be the last of the Royals here. You all have a fighting chance.' He kicked his horse into a canter and called over his shoulder. 'Good luck.'

CHAPTER 25

Screeching and screaming calls of warning, Lana's company of pirap monkeys refused to follow her into the city. A body of water lay between her and the ruins of office buildings. It was an impact crater full of rainwater, two hundred metres in diameter. Lana's eyes followed the trickling streams flowing down the deep crevasse. An exposed sewer tunnel on the other side seemed to lead under the city buildings.

Tinba and Mehra's parents were somewhere inside. Lana tightened the strip of vine she had tied around her waist to secure her hatchet.

Stepping tentatively towards the very edge of the crater, she stood with both feet together and raised her arms. She bent her knees, let her body fall forward, then launched herself into a swan dive. Lana bladed her hands one over the other and slipped into the cold, murky water.

Lana climbed out of the dirty pool and up into the tunnel. There were symbols painted in red inside it. Lana guessed they were made by the savages, like the one who had attacked her. She stepped cautiously into the dark underground. The tunnel went on and on. Lana had to feel her way along the wall. Years of water flow had cleared out all of the human waste that had coursed through to the ocean outlet.

Lana saw light and the tunnel soon came to a small ledge overlooking the floor of a large, fire-lit cave. It looked like it had been dug out over the years by many workers.

Flaming torches protruded from the walls, illuminating sleeping bodies on animal skins spread across the uneven floor. On the opposite wall, beside rock steps leading into another tunnel, were several raised cages. Three of which were occupied by the people Lana had freed from the Sabre Company holding cells: Mehra's parents and a teenage boy.

Although she had entered silently, Lana saw three, then five, of the sleeping savages wake and sniff the air. They communicated shrieking barks at one another, searching for the origin of the foreign scent.

In seconds, all of them were awake and shouting. Lana recognised the dark-red crust covering their skin as dried blood. Having emerged from stormwater, her body was emitting its natural odour. Lana looked up to steel rods protruding down from beneath the building supports above the cave. She backed into the tunnel behind her. Dashing five metres, she leapt off the ledge.

Reaching the first steel bar, she caught it and swung onto another further along.

Still unable to place their intruder, the Blood Demons left through the other tunnel openings.

The room soon became quiet. But Lana saw one remaining cave dweller, so she continued to hang from the ceiling.

The Blood Demon was of average build, pale under the dried blood, with a single long plait of dark hair hanging from the top of his otherwise shaven head. He waited for the others to leave before unlocking the cage in which Shiah was being held. Sniggering, he grabbed Shiah's hair and hauled her out. Chahtu yelled threats at the man, while he watched her fall to the rock floor.

Shiah scrambled to her feet, her wrists bound, trying to pull away from the man.

A young woman appeared at the top of the rock stairs, leading to the dark tunnel. Her long, knotted hair hung down to her hips, covering most of her blood-crusted body. She shouted a shrill command, calling the pale man Ganev.

Lana's shoulders began to ache as her body weight took its toll on her muscles. She couldn't understand what the naked woman was saying, puzzled also by her rasping voice, despite her youthful appearance.

Ganev left Shiah to release Anook from his cage, as ordered. He addressed the woman submissively as Queen Galai and brought the boy to her. With surprising strength, Galai dragged Anook into the tunnel from which she had come.

Ganev returned to Shiah and hauled her to a confined space at the edge of the cave.

Lana climbed down the bars to the cages, signalling for Chahtu to be quiet. She unlocked his cage and thumbed over her shoulder at Shiah. Lana then pointed to the ledge of the tunnel she had come from to indicate the way out.

Chahtu nodded and advanced on the pale one called Ganev.

Lana hurried up the rocky steps leading to the tunnel which Queen Galai had dragged Anook into. As she made her way through the darkness, the sound of chanting voices rose from ahead.

Lana searched the dry rock walls. Her feet slipped through puddles of rank-smelling grime. The chanting grew louder and orange light appeared at the end of the tunnel, opening up to another dug-out cave. Dozens of men and women, painted red, stood in a wide circle. Lana's stomach turned when she saw the light of flaming torches flicker across a reflective surface in the middle.

The chanting people stood in a knee-deep pool, crimson with blood. Stretching fifteen metres across, dismembered bodies floated in it between them.

Queen Galai stood in the centre, up to her belly in blood. She held a long bone that had been carved into a sharp dagger.

Lana spotted Anook, tied down to a freeway exit sign. She assumed he was to be sacrificed to whatever evil these savages served.

The room was small. The single torch in the doorway threw Ganev's shadow against the cave wall. Shiah kicked and screamed while the cannibal leaned over her, clawing away her animal skin clothes. He paused, sniffed the air and turned around. Chahtu was standing behind him. Ganev shrieked and snatched a wooden club from the floor.

Chahtu stood motionless. His muscles twitched along his clenched jaw. His eyes left Shiah's to glare at the pale man crouched between her legs. Chahtu assessed Ganev's weapon briefly before returning his gaze to the savage's crazed, shifting eyes. He raised his empty hand and curled his fingers twice, gesturing for the fight to commence.

Ganev advanced and swung his club at Chahtu's head. Chahtu weaved left, stepped into Ganev's path and dropped his dense bicep into his opponent's chest.

Rolling backwards across the floor, Ganev wheezed, winded. He dropped the club and launched himself into Chahtu.

Ganev avoided Chahtu's punch, climbed over the giant man's shoulder and onto his back, then dug his teeth into flesh and muscle.

Chahtu bellowed at the excruciating pain. He thumped Ganev's head but the cannibal's jaw proved difficult to shake. Swinging his body, Chahtu slammed Ganev against the jagged rock wall.

Shiah struck Ganev's head with the club, until he dropped to the floor. Ganev screamed, retreating on all fours. Chahtu caught his ankle and the cannibal yelped as he was dragged back.

Chahtu looked up at the jagged steel protruding through the ceiling. Taking Ganev by his plated hair, Chahtu lifted the man's body by his groin with his other hand. Chahtu hefted the screaming flesh-eater up over his head.

Ganev barrel-rolled up into the ceiling and cried out. Skewered through his lungs and back, he gurgled blood. Limp as a ragdoll, he slid down and hit the rock floor in a twisted heap.

Lana crept over to Anook and untied him while Queen Galai's worshippers were occupied with their pre-ritual chanting. She and Anook made it back into the tunnel, but they stopped when the chanting fell to an abrupt silence. Lana turned back to the blood pool. The circle of men and women were facing her, but none moved. Queen Galai's head was turned like a curious animal. Lana could see the glint of the woman's eyes through her tangled hair.

'Come to me, child,' Galai's voice croaked in English, echoing through the cave. 'You have found your fear. Face me.'

Lana returned to the pool, gazing out at the naked figure surrounded by red ooze.

'I am you.' Galai pushed away her tangled hair and raised the tip of the bone dagger to her chest.

'Inside you.' A fresh line of red appeared as the bone tip ran down between her breasts. 'All that you fear.'

Anook steadied himself against the tunnel wall, urging Lana to follow.

'Go without me,' said Lana. 'Chahtu and Shiah will be waiting for you.'

As soon as Lana stepped into the pool, the circle of people began a rising chant. The pool deepened, as Lana waded towards Galai.

Galai's lips spread into a welcoming smile, revealing sharp, black teeth. The two women circled each other, their increasing pace causing the blood to swirl.

Lana drew her hatchet.

Galai raised her hand and the chanting stopped. She dropped into a crouch and sprang towards Lana, screaming.

Lana sidestepped and caught Galai's wrists, barely avoiding the bone dagger tip. Galai's teeth gnashed an inch from her jugular. Lana struck her fist across the Blood Queen's jaw and brought her arm back to strike again with the back of her elbow. She swung her axe, but Galai threw herself sideways, into the pool.

The men at the pool's edge parted when Lana backed close to them, watching the blood pool for Galai to resurface. The rank, metallic stench filled her nostrils and settled in her throat. Anook's escape echoed along the tunnel behind her. She could hear whispered chanting coming from those closest to her. Lana froze, widening her stance when she felt a disturbance below.

Galai's arms shot up and struck away Lana's weapon. Her slippery hands latched onto her throat in an instant. The Queen lifted her prey from the pool. Lana's legs kicked and splashed the surface, before she was pulled back down into the blood.

Struggling under Galai's immense strength, Lana held her breath. Bones lying on the bottom of the pool jabbed and scraped her back. Visions of torture and suffering forced their way inside her head: an assault of agony and terror.

For the first time in her short life, Lana felt absolute fear. Buried in darkness, her pulse—her life rhythm—was dying.

Lana's muscles began to relax, her limbs limp, her body still, weightless in the dark. When she opened her eyes, she could see stars. The stars multiplied as Lana drew closer to them. She felt nothing. She drifted purely as an observer. The stars flew by her and Lana saw constellations, systems, planets.

Her feet touched the ground and Lana found herself among men, women and children, plants and animals as well. The Milky

Way stretched across the night sky and vines surged over the ground beneath her feet. The vines were pulsing and glowing with energy. People and animals alike lay down and relaxed.

Lana received subtle gestures of acknowledgement from those close by. Others were arriving. Some looked as confused as she felt. Others set off, as though searching for someone.

All of this seemed like a dream. But usually when she dreamed, Lana had some influence, some drive or purpose. *Maybe I'm in somebody else's dream,* Lana thought. She looked around her. *Maybe I'm in a lot of people's dreams.*

Lana didn't know any of these people and she began to feel very alone, detached. Her throat began to hurt and she could taste blood.

Lana dropped to her knees, struggling to breathe. She fell onto her side, her head lolling against her arm. Chest heaving, eyes glazing over, Lana thought she had reached her end. But then, she felt warmth beneath her. She had fallen across a pulsating vine. Her heart began to beat in sync with the pulse pumping through the vines. Lana heard murmurs approaching, hands gently lifting her back onto her feet. When she looked around her, Lana was stunned to see that several people and animals had come to her aid.

'Hodge!' Lana breathed. She barely recognised the man standing closest to her, his hand on her shoulder, comforting her. He looked twenty years younger, but she could see sadness in his eyes—regret. 'I'll tell them, Hodge. I'll tell your family you love them.'

Hodge smiled. Other people, strangers, reached their hands to Lana's chest, back and shoulders. The person behind Lana's support had placed a hand on whoever was in front. Behind them were people doing the same until Lana couldn't see how many there were. Their shared energy glowed at each pulse: through the ground, through the vines, through them and through Lana.

Lana expressed her thanks and closed her eyes.

Galai removed the bone dagger from the back of her knotted hair. She reached down to pull Lana's body up from the bottom of the pool. She wanted to cut herself off a new trophy. 'Your soul is mine.' Then she paused, grasping at nothing but red.

Lana's head rose silently from the surface behind Galai. She stood slowly, blood dribbling from her chin, down her chest, her hair hanging heavy on her shoulders. Thin rivulets of red travelled over the curves and down the shallows of her body.

The Blood Queen turned and Lana struck away the bone dagger, sending it clattering across the cave floor. She brought her arms under Galai's armpits, one hand gripping the back of her head, the other holding her jaw. Lana snapped Galai's neck and let the woman's body slip down into the crimson pool.

The blood worshippers' chanting began to rise again, while Lana stood dripping. The chorus rose louder and echoed through the cave.

One of the cannibals emerged from the shadows, a man with an athletic build. He drew a long knife from his side and sloshed through the pool towards Lana.

She assumed that he was Galai's mate and retribution was in order. She took a step forward and stood on the handle of her axe. When the man reached her, he turned his shoulders to swing his knife across Lana's throat. She dropped, took her hatchet, rolled left and rose with a sweep of her arm. Blood travelled from the head of her axe, slipping from the blade into a long stream of red. Lana buried her hatchet in the man's spine. He cried out and dropped to his knees.

Lana freed her weapon and left the pool. The chanting continued, echoing after her, while she entered the tunnel and walked back the way she came.

She exited the tunnel and soon entered the area where all of the Blood Demons had been sleeping earlier. She gazed down from the steps across dozens of hungry faces. They all gazed upon her blood-soaked body. Those closest to her sniffed at her legs, stepped back and uttered words from the chanting Lana had heard before. These words rippled among the other cannibals and they parted, allowing Lana to pass by the cages to the stairs leading up to the exit tunnel.

'Someone is coming,' Anook whispered over his shoulder to Chahtu and Shiah. Lana approached and they all stared in shock.

Shiah saw that the blood covering Lana's body was not her own. 'The children. Where are they?'

Lana didn't reply. Her mind was still adjusting, after all she had just experienced. But she heard a voice shout inside her head. *Please, my children! Where are they?* The voice was Shiah's. But Lana was standing right in front of her and Shiah's mouth hadn't opened.

'They're safe,' Lana assured her.

She ushered Shiah and the others through the tunnel. Walking through the dark seemed to take forever. She could hear Anook, Chahtu and Shiah all reliving what they had experienced during their captivity. The cannibals had eaten people from another village. Anook said that he, Shiah and Chahtu would have been next, were it not for Lana.

They soon emerged into the light of day, above the crater pool. Lana saw soldiers in Kiyol armour circling the edge. They spoke through their comms upon sighting her.

Captain Lincoln rappelled down the building above them and landed next to the exposed stormwater tunnel. He fired a stabiliser hook into the concrete, attaching the ladder that was being fed down beside him from the ledge above. Lincoln called up for the feed to stop.

'Ma'am, are you injured?' he asked Lana, looking her up and down.

Lana helped Shiah onto the ladder. 'I'm fine. How did you find us?'

'Two child civilians tracked you here. They advised us to follow.'

'Good work. Ouch, man what happened to you?' Lana gestured to Lincoln's missing ear.

'An SC Captain caught me off guard. Won't happen again.'

'I'm sure it won't.' Lana climbed the ladder after Anook. 'These people will need food and clothing.'

'Yes, ma'am.' Lincoln spoke into his comms. 'Chief Jolie, we'll need supply packs for a civilian party of five.'

'Copy that, Captain.'

Once Lana reached the top of the crater edge, she was happy to see Shiah cradling Mehra in her arms. Tinba watched Jolie tend to Chahtu's neck wound. Anook sat alone, still shaken from the ordeal.

Lana turned back and stood at the edge of the crater, watching pensively as the wind blew ripples across the water surface.

The murky brown darkened and Lana thought she could hear chanting.

Lana felt her heartbeat quicken and her pores perspire. The rippling surface had become still, and red clouds of blood were pluming like something or someone had been gutted below.

The chanting rose dramatically, growing louder.

A sanguine hand reached up through the centre of the red glaze.

'Are you okay?'

Lana spun around and saw that Jolie was about to touch her shoulder.

'I was calling you.' Jolie withdrew her hand and her brow was furrowed with concern. 'We're done here. Let's go home.'

Lana realised the sun was going down and that only Jolie and one other AM unit were on top of the building with her. Everyone else was gone.

Lana glanced back down at the crater. The water was brown, the surface rippled by nothing save the wind.

CHAPTER 26

Brad and Renee dismounted from their horses when they reached the high timber walls of the Royal Army barracks. The sound of gunfire had led them to the gate, where they found the guards lying face down in the mud by the entrance.

There was no longer any need to blend in, so Renee had armed herself with dual automatic pistols and changed into a carbon armour vest and cargo pants.

She ran to the barracks' gate and pressed her back against the timber. Peering around the hinge, she counted the Royal Army and SC soldiers. The RA troopers were outnumbered. Jericho Williams had called in an entire platoon of AM units to take the barracks.

Brad spotted Williams walking confidently towards a two-storey building, followed by a four- soldier escort. He wore a dark grey, high collar military uniform, with a Mauser HSC pistol holstered at his side.

'He's here, Captain, obliterating the local army,' Brad reported over comms to Hank. 'Building on the west side of the barracks. Sending sonar terrain and structure layout.' He looked around the clearing outside of the walled barracks. 'Setting beacon to safe entry point. Back-up would be appreciated.'

'Copy that Brad,' said Hank. 'They're coming in now.'

A moment later, a portal opened ten metres from the entrance. A Kiyol warrior, Jihna, and two Kiyolo, stepped into the clearing, followed by fifteen UC AM units. The Kiyolo separated, flanking the perimeter of the barracks, while Jihna sprinted through the gates, leading the AM soldiers into the fray. Brad and Renee followed, parting from the group to pursue Jericho Williams.

Jihna struck down two SC troops with a swing of her staff. Stepping into a forward kick, she sent another flying backwards into a group taking cover, knocking them all to the ground. The RA troops froze in fear, as they watched the purple alien beat down enemy after enemy.

The timber walls at the east and west perimeter fence exploded into splinters. The two Kiyolo appeared through the blue residual mist from their staff fire. They aimed and fired rapid energy blasts. The haunting growl of their war cry shook the RA soldiers to their bones.

Bullets bounced off of Jihna's armour, her glowing jade eyes fixed on the commanding RA officer of the barracks. The man dropped his sword and called for retreat, ducking underneath a building on raised timber stumps. Jihna flinched when she heard Renee's voice through the human comms attachment to her long narrow ears.

'Cover the entry point at my location!'

Renee kicked open the door of the building Williams had entered. Brad followed her up a staircase leading to an observation deck. One of Williams' guards appeared and opened fire. Renee rolled as splinters of wood flew up from the floor. Brad aimed his Magnum revolver and sent two rounds into the soldier's chest. The AM unit staggered backwards and tumbled over the handrail.

Another guard descended, firing AK47 rounds. Renee shot from the other side of the stairs, hitting the man's legs. He fell forward, hitting every third or fourth step heavily. There was a moment of silence after the trooper landed on the floor.

'Eat this!' one of the remaining guards called from the level above.

A fragmentation grenade bounced from the top of the staircase. Renee ran forward to intercept it. She pushed off from the first step into a backflip and clipped the grenade with the heel of her boot. Aiming her pistols in mid-air, she fired as her feet met the floor. Bullets flew rapidly on either side of the grenade, as it made its return journey to the SC soldier.

Williams watched his guard stagger backwards, riddled with bullets. His eyes widened when the grenade struck the top of the stair railing and flew towards him. The blast threw Williams through the window. Shards of glass pelted a stack of wooden crates below, the boxes shattering under the weight of Williams' body.

Williams coughed and spluttered, pulling off his shredded uniform to work off the straps of his bulletproof vest. Splinters of wood protruded from his legs. Williams took a Shifter from his side pocket, issuing an order while programming a portal.

'This is Colonel Williams. All units retreat to HQ. Await further—'

Something gripped Williams' forearm so tightly that it instantly snapped his bones. He screamed in agony as Jihna pulled him from the broken crates.

Slowly removing a kukri-shaped knife from the sash around her waist, Jihna drew the man close, so she could look into his eyes. She pressed a button on the handle with her thumb and her blade heated to white hot in seconds.

Williams screamed again as Jihna raised his arm, lifting him off the ground.

'For the Kiyol you killed on our trade station,' she said.

She sliced below Williams' elbow, the heat of the blade cauterised the wound. Williams fell to the ground, holding the stub of his arm.

'Wow, hey, hold it!' Brad stepped between Jihna and Williams. 'We need him alive.'

'He lives, for now.' Jihna loosened a leather strip from her waist belt and tied Williams' arm, letting it hang at her side.

'That's disturbing,' Brad said, glancing at Jihna's dangling trophy. 'Really disturbing.'

Home Realm
Aqua Sierra Otami Palace

Jericho Williams was taken to the infirmary, where Jolie treated his wounds. Pete, Sam, Charlie and Lex had evacuated the Genesis Lab. They met everyone else in the Palace Dome Room.

The Dome Room was an open space near the command station levels. It was lit by sun rays shining down through the ocean surface. The windows along the curved ceiling sparkled with the rippling light.

'Excellent work, guys.' Rachel pulled Renee into an embrace. She then approached Jihna, who hesitated for a moment before allowing Rachel to hug her as well.

'So…' Rachel shot a finger at Jihna's trophy. She saw the Kiyola's proud expression and nodded. 'That's Williams' arm. You mess with the bull, you get the horns, huh?'

It took a moment for Jihna to understand the metaphor, but then she smiled with a nod.

Professor O'Conner shook Hank's hand. 'Good to see you, Hank.'

'Glad you're safe, old man.' Hank slapped Pete on the back. 'So, everybody else is en route to San Francisco.'

'Everybody is clear of the Parabola,' Pete confirmed. He glanced in the direction of the holding cells. 'Think you can get Williams to give us the General?'

'Definitely. Jin has ways of making people talk. Williams will give up his own mother by the time we're done with him.' He paused and added with an impressed tone. 'I met Lana by the way. Very impressive girl.'

'We're all very proud.'

'Just curious though, why armour her skin but not dull her nerves?'

'Everyone needs to know when they're hurting.' Pete's fingers wandered over his wedding ring, rubbing the silver. 'We need pain.'

Rachel hadn't joined the team searching for Lana. She had been debriefing Pete after pulling him out of the Forest Realm. She couldn't find Lana in the Dome Room and she was getting worried.

Hank saw the concern in Rachel's eyes and he took her aside.

'Rache, Lana came back with Jolie,' he said. 'Jolie told me that Lana is showing signs of post trauma. Whatever happened, it was bad.'

Rachel felt so heavy with guilt she thought her heart would break.

'Where is she?' she said, throat tight.

Silica
Liberty Building

Fiona sifted through the folders on her data pad to bring up a confirmation document. 'The Mariner communities on Boson are running low on housing materials,' she said, addressing her fellow Council members in the meeting room. 'I've spoken with those in charge of shipping logistics and they're awaiting official confirmation.'

The Council all agreed to sign the digital document displayed on the consoles before them, except one. Council member

Christian McCain raised a query.

'Doesn't a depletion of materials suggest there are too many people living on the new colonies?'

The others looked up in surprise.

'With all due respect, Mr McCain,' Fiona said, 'no. It means they're thriving. They're almost independent. Also, the people who travelled to Boson are those who agreed to be among the very first Migration Party. Their bravery deserves our support.'

Senior Council member Henin, a sixty-year-old woman, who had left Earth behind to live on a new colony, spoke. 'Humanity itself owes those people a debt of gratitude for uprooting their families in order to help reduce Earth's population.'

McCain didn't show any understanding of the sentiment Henin or Fiona imparted. 'The people on the outer colonies are living on planets that contain raw materials,' he said. 'Surely they can dig up and process the materials they need.'

This shocked the other members into silence. Fiona had always viewed Christian McCain's role on the Council to be more managerial than contributory, in terms of serving the people. This was the first time that McCain had shown any interest, let alone spoken out against aid for a community in need.

'Mr McCain,' Fiona said, keeping her tone formal, 'self-sufficiency is, of course, the ultimate goal. But they can't mine quickly enough to meet building demands. And the reason Boson and the other new colonies continue to grow is because family members who were left behind are now following those who migrated.'

McCain's blank expression moved from Fiona to his data pad. 'For the record, I am merely stressing caution. These are, after all, precious resources we're dishing out.' He signed the document and the screen confirmed that all signatures were accounted for. 'Someone has to be the antagonist.'

Henin opened her mouth to speak words that would both patiently acknowledge McCain's sentiment, as well as rebuke his suggestion that the council were distributing resources without deliberation. But the doors to the meeting room opened and Commander Greer entered.

'My apologies for the intrusion, Council members. The Sabre Company Colonel, Jericho Williams, has been captured. Parker, if you could please excuse us for moment—'

Fiona ignored Greer's dismissal. Concern for her colleagues took priority.

'They should be on high alert,' she said. 'Sabre Company will attempt extraction.' Fiona accessed her comms to call Rowan.

'Miss Parker, this is classified,' said Greer. 'Only senior members of the Council—'

'Commander,' Henin interrupted, 'Fiona served in the Silica Underground. She has earned her place and she deserves to hear everything there is to know.'

'My apologies,' Greer conceded.

Fiona noticed the Commander's brief eye contact with Christian McCain when he said this.

'Williams is being held at Aqua Sierra,' Greer continued. 'Captain Drake will give you the details now.'

He moved to a vacant console, standing side-on to Fiona while he brought up the holo-display comms link. Hank appeared and greeted the members of the Council.

'Captain,' Council member Henin said. 'We are aware that the threat is not over. However, allow me to express my congratulations on behalf of all of us here. This is a great step towards achieving the justice that the people of Silica deserve.'

'I couldn't agree more. I'm confident we will find Dennis Conroy as well.'

'And, ah, when will you commence interrogation?' Christian McCain asked.

Fiona's ears pricked at McCain's atypical hesitation. She watched Tony Greer carefully. He maintained a square-shouldered stance, chin raised, projecting pride. Fiona watched his hands swing and she leaned subtly to see them clasp behind his back. His thumb rubbed his other hand: self-reassurance.

'Immediately,' Hank confirmed. 'Jin Otami has extensive experience in the area of coercion.'

Fiona's eyes flicked to McCain in time to catch him flinch for a micro second, then back to Greer to see a confident smile spread across his face.

Hank glanced over his shoulder. Chesh's voice could be heard in the background. 'Please excuse me, Council members.' He nodded to Commander Greer. 'Don't break out the champagne yet, Tony. We still have a way to go.'

'Oh, quite a way,' Greer replied under his breath, before applying a more jovial tone. 'Well done, Hank. Keep us posted.'

CHAPTER 27

Aqua Sierra
Otami Palace

Rachel eventually found Lana alone in the shower room. The walls were wet and the steam hung like fog.

'Are you okay?' Rachel asked, watching Lana closely.

Lana turned her head slowly, but she didn't look at Rachel. She was standing under a hot jet of water, scrubbing vigorously under her arms and around her neck. Lana pushed her fingers through her hair, catching flecks of dried blood under her nails.

'Lana, what happened?'

Lana was mesmerised by the foam bubbles being swept along the shower drain trench.

'People were in trouble,' she murmured. 'I helped them.'

She continued to rub soap over her skin. Rachel stepped in front of Lana and turned off the water. Her heart broke under a wave of guilt. She should never have left Lana alone in the Forest Realm.

'Lana, it's me,' she said, the weight of failure crippling her. 'Please, tell me what happened.'

She took Lana's hand. Lana hung her head, tears rolling down her cheeks. Rachel drew her close.

'I'm so sorry,' she said. 'It's my fault.'

Lana buried her face in Rachel's collar and wept. After a while she pulled back from Rachel, without letting go.

'Don't blame yourself, Rache. You had to get Pete out. You had no choice.'

'Hank said when they found you—'

Lana saw the image of herself, wet and dazed. She tried to push it out of her mind. But when she did, it was projected into Rachel's.

Rachel's head jerked back and her eyes widened. She saw the pool of blood, the woman standing in it. She could hear the chanting surrounding her. The scene left her mind as quickly as Lana had inadvertently put it in.

'I saw,' Rachel breathed. 'Lana, how…?'

'I'm sorry. I can't control it.'

Rachel swayed. 'I need to sit down.'

Lana helped her to a bench and she dressed without drying herself. 'I'll go and get Jolie.'

'I'm fine,' Rachel stopped her. 'Lana, how did you…?'

Lana shrugged. 'Pete said I might develop new abilities.'

'No,' said Rachel. 'I mean, how did you get out of there? I saw a dozen of those freaks where you were.'

'They let me leave after I killed their queen.'

'Shit Lana…' Rachel looked at her with deep concern. Jolie had said that she observed signs of post-traumatic stress in Lana. Now Rachel knew why. 'That must have been… absolute horror.'

Having felt the pain and the guilt Rachel had been holding on to, Lana couldn't bring herself to mention that she had died and come back to life.

'It was no worse than what you found in the COG motor pool,' said Lana.

'You saw my memory.'

Lana shrugged. 'Apparently I can read minds… and project my thoughts.' She placed her hand on Rachel's shoulder. 'I didn't mean for you to see that.'

'Have you told Pete what you can do?' Rachel stood with Lana's help and they left the shower room.

'With all that's happened.' Lana shook her head. 'Any progress with Williams?'

'No. Jin's on it. In the meantime, let's grab Sam and get some sun together top side.'

Jin looked up when Hank and Professor O'Conner entered the interrogation room. He shook his head.

'No dice,' he said, gesturing to the unconscious Colonel lying on the raised medical bed. 'Williams' defences are better than I expected. Taking it to the next level might kill him.'

Hank stared down at the bald man's face. 'Do it.'

'Hank…'

'There's too much at stake.'

Pete stepped in. 'There's another way.'

Hank's eyes left Williams to give Pete his full attention. 'I'm listening.'

'We can enter Williams' subconscious and unlock his memories. Charlie has already hooked Luke into the Garwyn program to try and bring him back to who he was. Garwyn can't get what we need from Williams, but he can open the door. All we need is somebody who can walk through it.'

'Mind invasion?' Jin shook his head. 'With all due respect, Professor, there's too much we don't know about the human subconscious to go screwing around like that. Whoever goes in could fall into a coma.'

Pete selected a file from his remote console to search for a program. 'I understand the risks, Jin, but there's a way to do it safely.'

'I'm not following.' Hank looked from Jin, back to Pete. 'Somebody has to go inside this asshole's head?'

'Rachel,' said Pete. 'She can go in and access Williams' memory.'

'Why her?' Jin couldn't help his defensive tone. Pete's idea was dangerous.

'When Rachel dreams, she enters a space inside memories which belong to her relatives, always the women of her blood line. There isn't a lot of literature on it, but psychologists who have encountered it call it Mitochondrial Memory.'

Hank turned to Jin and raised his eyebrows, clearly lost.

'Charlie and I designed a simulation program for Rachel to use,' Pete explained, 'to help her develop tools and give her more control over her dreams. Some of the memories she experiences are frightening. Many of her ancestors experienced war. It takes a lot of energy for her to escape the memories. The simulation we designed has given her mechanisms to help her dream normally. Apart from the occasional episode, she has been doing quite well.'

'Rachel may be compatible with an entry program, but she would have to fight Williams' defences alone,' said Jin. He moved around the bed to check the Colonel's pulse. 'The risk is, if Rachel is injured in the program, her body will respond as though it is actually happening to her in the real world.'

Hank was aware of a growing tension in the room. He respected Jin's point of view, but he could see no other way of extracting the necessary information.

'Explain it to me again,' he said to Pete. Pete's hands became animated.

'Most of Lana's cognitive development training is conducted through the simulation program, Garwyn. Lana entered it while she slept, so she was able to learn while her body developed.'

Pete glanced down at Williams. 'What I can do is connect both Williams and Rachel to a modified version of the program, which will essentially be a point of entry. Rachel should be able to enter his subconscious and access the information we need from there.'

'Pete, I've seen this movie before.' Jin tried to stress the worst-case scenario. 'What if she gets trapped in there? That can happen, right? Rachel could be lost to us.'

The Professor nodded. 'I'll program an exit mechanism in case Williams tries to lock Rachel in. And she'll need to learn how to manifest defensive support. Garwyn will help prepare her.' Pete looked from Jin to Hank. 'I'll go and talk to Rachel, see if she's up for it.'

'You really understand all of what Pete just said?' Hank asked Jin after Pete left.

'Enough to know the risks.'

Hank watched Jericho Williams pensively.

'Oh, hey,' he said to Jin, 'your wife told me you two are expecting.'

'I didn't get a chance to bring it up.' A smile spread across Jin's face.

'Good for you, man.' Hank slapped Jin's muscly shoulder. 'Congratulations.'

'Thanks.' Jin glanced down at Williams on the bed. 'I just hope the world will be safer by the time we bring Otami Junior into the world.' He was silent for a moment, busying himself with the medical monitoring equipment. 'It could work. If Rachel has enough support going in. I mean, think about it,' he said and nodded to Williams. 'The location of every hidden Sabre Company base, their plans, everything is in that man's head.'

Lex made her way up the steps to the command deck carrying the components for the last inhibitor node. 'How's the leg?' she asked Charlie.

Charlie sat at the main computer console, running diagnostics. 'Okay, thanks.'

Setting an armful of electrical equipment down on the floor, Lex began assembling the node. She gazed over at her nerdy looking ex-boyfriend, while tightening a casing screw.

An unexpected wave of affection came over her: memories of being together, making plans for the future—before it all fell apart.

'You should let Pete take a look,' she said. 'He could work on armouring your skin or something. You'd never take a bullet again.'

'I was thinking of going bionic.' Charlie laughed and turned away from the computer. 'Last node?'

Lex didn't answer while she unsheathed wires and connected them to complete the circuit. She sniffed and turned away, wiping her eyes. 'Just about done.'

Charlie pushed away from the computer console and rolled over to her. 'What's wrong?'

'You could have been killed, Charlie.' Lex stopped what she was doing, reached up and wrapped her arms around him.

'Hey, hey.' Charlie held her, gently stroking her silver hair. 'I'm okay now. We're safe.' He looked down, bringing his face close to hers. He was taken by the unexpected warmth of Lex's concern. 'I didn't think you cared anymore.'

Lex squeezed him. 'I care, Charlie. I've always cared.'

Pete came up the stairs and stopped when he saw the two of them in an embrace. 'Sorry guys, have you seen Rachel?'

Lana, Rachel and Sam were in their swimwear, reclining on beach chairs. The warm sea wind blew in from the vast ocean.

Sam stretched and arched her back. 'Ow-yeah… this is the life.' The others giggled, enjoying their time of absolute warmth and comfort.

The cage elevator arrived on the platform and Lana turned in her chair.

'Professor, come join us. It's beautiful out here.'

'Thanks, but I forgot my bathers.' Pete crouched down beside Rachel. 'We need you down at holding.'

'What's up? Is Williams talking?'

'Not yet. Sorry girls,' he apologised to the others. 'I need to borrow Rachel.'

With a sigh, Rachel clambered to her feet and followed the Professor back to the elevator.

'Enjoy the water for me,' she called, as the elevator door rattled shut.

Sam pushed herself up from the chair and quick-stepped across the hot metal platform to the edge. She beckoned for Lana to join her. Lana leapt from her chair, dashed forward and dove into the water.

CHAPTER 28

'You want me to do what?' Rachel crossed her arms over her chest. Pete's idea did not appeal at all.

Pete raised his hands and kept his voice calm. 'It's the Garwyn program. He'll give you everything you need. You go into Williams' head only when you're ready.'

Jin's comms console beeped and he checked the screen. 'Sorry guys, I've gotta take this.' He stopped in front of Rachel on his way out. 'You don't have to do this. We'll find Conroy and the rest of Sabre Company eventually.'

Rachel appreciated Jin's concern, but the plan seemed more and more imperative. Conroy had to be found and stopped before the SC attacked the Council.

Hank looked from Williams to Rachel. 'Jin's right. If you don't want to do this, we'll try something else.' He glared at Pete. 'Right, Pete?'

'Of course.' Pete rested his hand on Rachel's shoulder. 'Take your time to think about it. Whatever you decide—'

'I'll do it.' Rachel stared at Williams' placid, scarred face. Her knuckles turned white as her hands made fists.

'Rachel…' Hank felt uncertain and protective.

'I said I'll do it.'

Pete watched Rachel's face, hoping to read some confidence in her cold, blank expression. Her eyes met his. 'Tell me what to do.'

Jin and his wife, Mel, stepped out of the cage elevator onto the base level of their compound.

'We have to expect that Sabre Company will retaliate,' said Jin. 'When that happens, I want you to be with the Professor's team. They'll have plenty of UC protection.'

They reached the airlock chamber on the far side of the corridor. Jin keyed in a password on the panel, then turned the wheel at the centre of the door until the seal was open.

'We're going to be all right.' Mel nuzzled under Jin's jaw. The familiar warmth from her light brown skin abated her husband's concern.

'Go,' she said. 'Don't keep the Laicians waiting.'

Jin kissed her before she left. He leaned against the wheel, pushing the heavy steel door open. Once inside, Jin closed and locked the door behind him and the air compression sequence commenced automatically. He opened a tall cylindrical cabinet and took a deep-sea exploration suit from a hook.

The air chamber comms beeped. 'They're on their way to the perimeter now.'

'Thanks, Mel.' Jin pulled his shirt off, dropped his trousers and stepped into the diving suit.

Vents on the exterior door opened and water flooded across the steel floor. Jin waited until the room was completely full before opening the door to exit the compound basement. Hand over hand, he pulled himself along one hundred metres of beacon-lit cable line, to the meeting point. As Jin made his way along the ocean floor, the sand puffed up into slow forming clouds with each step. Spotting the Laicians, he stopped and connected his waist belt to a hook on the cable line.

The leader of the Laician party of three—Prince Ohkwai Chillo—opened his arms in greeting.

'How are you, my friend?'

Like many male Laicians, the Prince was athletically built, with a humanoid upper body and the lower body of a fish. After the first time he had met Chillo, Jin had realised that drawings from old sailor stories portrayed mermaids with a prominent fin that would swing up and down. All fish however have a fin that swings side to side. Chillo's was the same. With each breath he took, gills fluttered either side of his neck. His skin was pale blue, while his fins, including those running from his forehead to the back of his skull, were orange. Chillo's large, webbed hands moved constantly, steadying his position against the subtle push and pull of the underwater current. His lower body was a beautiful pattern of aqua, pale orange and light green scales. The broad wings of his luminescent tail swished through the water with ease, allowing him to float tall and erect.

'Hey, Chillo, just fine,' Jin said, offering his hand. 'How's your boy?'

'Very well, thank you.' Ohkwai Chillo gripped Jin's inside forearm and pulled him into a manly hug. 'And your wife?'

'Good, today. Been north and south with the mood swings.' Jin shrugged. 'To be expected I guess.'

'Dude,' Chillo pronounced the new human word he had learnt from Jin with perfect lethargy. 'I couldn't go near my woman during her waiting. Seriously, she could take a brother's head off.'

Jin laughed. 'Thanks for remembering to wear the comms link I gave you.'

Chillo touched a webbed finger to the waterproof microphone earpiece. 'I hear you perfectly now.'

'So, what's this?' Jin nodded to the other two Laicians. 'Cruising with body guards now?'

'Ergh.' The Prince glanced at the pair floating behind him. 'My mother insists.'

The two guards nodded to Jin and he noted the rods strapped at their waists, guessing them to be their long-range weapons. The female of the two wore savage-looking spiked gauntlets, which covered her hands and forearms. She watched Jin, her lower eyelids blinking upwards over deep blue eyes.

'I wanted to meet with you today because I'd like to offer my assistance,' said Chillo.

'You know about the conflict?'

'Word has reached the deep,' said Chillo, nodding seriously. He reached into a pouch hanging from his elegantly plaited belt and removed an oval stone. 'This is a beacon stone.' The prince handed it to Jin. 'If you need our help, all you need to do is speak into it.'

For a moment, Jin was speechless. It was an honour to receive the offer of royal aid by the Prince of all Aqua Sierra clans.

'Thank you,' he said. He glanced at Chillo's guards. 'Does your wife know about this?'

Pretending not to have heard, the Prince bowed to Jin. 'It will be a privilege to defend these seas with you, Jin Otami.' He and his personal guard flicked their tails and disappeared into the deep.

Rachel pulled the collar of her coat up around her neck as she walked along a row of clothing stores. Everything looked real inside Charlie's Garwyn program. Rachel's skin responded to the cold air. She even caught the scent of perfume when a woman walked by.

Through the yellow illumination of the streetlights, she could make out a solitary figure thirty meters ahead. The man stood in the shadows, wearing a long coat and a dark brown fedora. The hat was tilted down, hiding his face. Weaving between the crowd of late-night shoppers, Rachel watched the man raise his head, only a pair of gleaming eyes visible in the darkness.

A voice Rachel knew could only be his, spoke inside her head. *Walk with me,* he said. The man turned and disappeared into a dark alley.

Rachel walked through clouds of steam pluming from the heat vents on the rear buildings. She reached the man and offered her hand. 'Garwyn?'

'Pleasure to meet you, Miss Navara.' Garwyn removed his hat, bowed slightly and gently shook Rachel's hand. 'Welcome to my program. I will be your guide.'

Rachel noted the man's accent, possibly German. Garwyn gestured for them to walk and she followed.

The exit at the opposite end of the alley brought them to a brightly lit street. Nineteen-thirties style cars rumbled along the road, as Garwyn led her to the entrance of an expensive hotel. The doorman greeted them in French on their way into the lobby.

Gazing up at the thousand-piece crystal chandelier, Rachel spoke to her strange companion.

'Wow. Charlie went to town on the detail.' Looking over to him in the light, she saw now that Garwyn was about sixty years of age.

He took off his hat, revealing a smooth bald crown, ringed with short grey hair. Garwyn's thick moustache rose at the sides when he smiled. His eyes were a pale blue, kind and intelligent. He emphasised each word he spoke with a hint of excitement.

'Many people require a somewhat familiar setting, to understand how their subconscious works,' he said.

'Pete said I would have protection,' Rachel said, her tone urgent. 'When do I get my weapons?'

Garwyn looked around at the people making their way to and from the elevator, check-in counters and stairways. 'Time is very slow here compared to conscious reality. You will need to learn how to manifest weapons. I will show you how.' Garwyn gestured for her to sit down on a crimson couch. He removed his coat and rested it on the beautiful red material.

'Before we begin, I would like you to know that you may trust me.'

'Charlie made you, so yes, I trust you,' Rachel replied, still wanting to get on with what needed to be done, regardless of slow time.

'This is true,' said Garwyn, unoffended. 'I exist from my author's programming, information comprised of the collected teachings of the most notable emotionally intelligent people in human history. So, there is little reason not to trust me. And therefore, you should not be alarmed to know that this—' Garwyn looked about the room as though he was surrounded by butterflies. 'All of this is, in fact, my creation. Charlie has programmed me to be not only a guide, but the architect of this world as well.'

Garwyn leaned close to Rachel and spoke softly. 'I want you to close your eyes and relax. Empty your thoughts.' Rachel glanced around her surroundings for a moment before closing her eyes.

Her chest gradually began to move more slowly as she controlled her breathing.

Garwyn reached his arm behind her and she allowed him to remove her coat. 'Very good. Now open your eyes and follow me.'

Rachel opened her eyes. All of the people were gone and the elevators had disappeared. There were now two large staircases to the left and right sides, facing the entrance of the hotel. The stairs rose up and around to a second floor. Garwyn was already making his way up the left stairs. He motioned for her to follow.

Elevator doors opened when they reached the second floor. Rachel's guide ushered her inside and the doors closed.

Rachel heard 'Rum & Coca Cola' playing from a hidden speaker. 'Huh!'

'Yes.' The old man smiled. 'This music resides in your memory. While you are linked to this space, you have the opportunity to re-experience what you remember.' A standard panel of floor buttons was on the right of the patterned doors. 'This is your point of navigation. The buttons indicate spaces in your mind. Times, places, deep emotion, past experiences.' He pointed to one.

'This will take us to the doors of Jericho Williams' mind. There, you will learn to manifest what you need.'

Rachel leaned closer to the panel, looking quizzically. 'Uh-huh...'

'Your subconscious is surprisingly ordered,' Garwyn commented. 'The minds of others can be fragmented, some even inaccessible.'

'Garwyn, I'm here to infiltrate the mind of a militant criminal,' said Rachel. 'I'd like to get it over with, if you don't mind.'

'Of course, I am merely offering you the opportunity to use this space.'

'With respect, maybe some other time.'

'I understand you once knew Luke Palmer,' Garwyn said, tentatively.

'I did.'

'Charlie and Sam have assigned me the task of restoring his memory. The post-hypnotic barriers that Sabre Company's Dr Kindred put in place are challenging, but they were built upon fear, so they are crumbling quickly. Had he used love and nurture—the more powerful method of teaching, development or conditioning— restoring his mind would have been almost impossible.'

'You're helping him right now?'

'Yes. My operating systems can manage many different tasks simultaneously.' Garwyn's expression turned solemn. 'Emotional restoration and personal respite will be a practice that Luke will have to maintain for the rest of his life. Any person who has suffered even one day of fear-motivated trauma is a damaged person. One does not simply repair such damage. One lives with it.'

'Please do everything you can.'

Garwyn bowed slightly. 'I will do my very best.' He pressed the button that would take Rachel to the mind of Jericho Williams. The doors opened to a hangar, similar to the one on Glacier II.

A squad formation of a dozen UC uniformed soldiers marched in at Rachel's approach and stood at attention.

Rachel inspected the front line of machine men and women.

'You three,' she said, pointing.

Garwyn nodded to the others and they disappeared. A large square frame appeared vertically in the centre of the hangar.

'You will proceed through this door,' said Garwyn. Double doors opened to a pitch-black void.

'Somewhere inside, you will find Williams' memory centre. It will be the place he is currently using all of his energy to protect. Access could be difficult, but remember, Jin has Williams heavily medicated, so he will be weak. You, on the other hand, are operating at full mental capacity. You have the ability to manifest whatever you need to defeat him. To manifest something, all you need to do is visualise it.'

Concentrating, Rachel looked down at her right outer thigh and saw a holstered handgun shimmer into crisp reality. She opened her hands and created an M16 rifle. Rachel then turned to her three soldiers and equipped them with the same.

Garwyn moved towards the black doorway.

'Once you have created something, your memory will maintain it in this reality. Now, I must warn you,' he said with a measured tone. 'Once inside the Colonel's mind, you must approach everything that takes place as though it is actually happening. You can be injured… and you can be killed.' Garwyn gestured for her to enter. 'Good luck, Ms Navara.'

'Piece o' cake,' Rachel said, swallowing her fear as she stared into the void. 'Piece o' crumb cake.' She nodded to her team and they followed her to the doorway.

'Call me when you have what you need and I will pull you

out,' said Garwyn. Rachel led the soldiers into the black abyss and the doors closed behind them.

Luke Palmer was seated in an armchair, by a dustbin. Flames rose from burning wood and paper. The room he was in was the lounge of a dilapidated house in Liberty. Garwyn watched Luke, hunched over his knees, staring into the flames.

'Your sister was taken a year ago,' said Garwyn. 'Now you are here.' He looked about the dusty bookshelves and broken windows. 'Your family home. But you cannot stay. Why?'

'Because Sabre Company are looking for the leader of the freedom fighters. They're looking for me.' Luke heard the front door open and two of his scouts entered the lounge. 'Were you followed?' he blurted out, and stood as though his memory had taken possession of his body.

'Nobody's out there,' one of them said. 'But we should leave. Air drones are sweeping the area.'

Luke wore a tattered police uniform he had found in an abandoned station. He had stitched on more pockets to hold ammunition.

'Let's move,' he said. Then he kicked the dust bin onto its side and the embers lit the old fraying carpet.

Garwyn stepped through the flames and followed the three men out of the house.

'Why did you burn your home?' he asked.

'Home?' Luke turned to watch the flaming house. The furniture inside was black. Smoke plumed from the roof and up into the night sky. 'A home is where you live, not where you hide.' He looked to the other houses in the street. Most were abandoned; others contained squatters. 'None of us lived in Silica. We survived. We fought for food, for water. That's not living. That's not home.'

The burning house faded when Garwyn took them to a different place in Luke's memory. Wet grass appeared beneath their feet. The sky turned from night to an overcast afternoon and rain drizzled down.

The passive visit Garwyn had prepared was designed to bring forth oppressed emotion.

'Can you tell me where we are now?' he asked Luke.

Luke watched the memory version of himself issuing orders before a squad of Sabre Company AM soldiers.

'After receiving treatment from Dr Kindred, I was assigned to lead a resource procurement team,' Luke said. 'Williams didn't have me serve until after the liberation of Silica. I didn't see any action until he sent word for me to go after Rachel.'

'Why do you think they did this to you?'

'I was a threat.'

'From what I understand, Dennis Conroy possesses a very intelligent and unstable mind,' said Garwyn. 'His punishment for you was not death but to become the one you hate.' Garwyn thought for a moment, accessing words of wisdom from his library of brilliant minds. 'Death is not the greatest loss in life. The greatest loss is what dies inside us while we live.'

Luke's eyes grew hot. The anger that had been present since Garwyn had helped him remember who he was—and what had been done to him—increased. With it came frustration at having been too weak to shake himself out of it. So many times, he had the opportunity to kill Jericho Williams. He'd spent so much of his life spent serving the criminals responsible for the enslavement of Silica's people—and for taking his sister.

'You are not responsible for what has happened,' Garwyn said. He watched Luke wipe tears from his face and look away. 'Soon you will have the opportunity to bring these criminals to justice. For now, you must allow your strength to return.'

CHAPTER 29

Lana and Sam gazed at the serene ocean expanse. Days were short on Aqua Sierra. Late afternoon bade goodbye to the sun, as it descended below the horizon. Light sparkled across the waves and the warm wind began to cool.

Thinking aloud, Lana changed the subject from Sabre Company's clandestine activities to the UC AM units. She had remembered how human-like Lincoln's expressions had seemed, back on Glacier II.

'The AM soldier series has been designed to match us so closely.' Lana rubbed a beach towel into her hair and let it hang over her shoulder. 'It's spooky to think we can just manufacture ourselves.'

Elastic snapped against Sam's skin as she adjusted her swimming briefs.

'There's a lot more to them than people realise. I saw an interview with Hutch Branner once, the guy who made them, explaining how he was able to create machines to help humans, without giving them enough intelligence to turn evil and wipe us all out. Branner said that he created what he calls a Digital Nursery that allows complex brain activity to function, but within pre- determined parameters. Hutch devised algorithm-based directives that could flow as digital cells through a system and could react to outside stimulus like love and fear, good, bad and everything in-between.

'Branner found that the cells could maintain brain activity, but only in a state of flow.' Sam lay back on the platform and stared up at the wisps of clouds, painted like brush strokes across the blue sky.

'When Sabre Company tried to replicate his work, they broke Branner's original algorithmic flow. Their AMs have cells that are designed to react according to directives given by their superiors, in this case, militants suffering from acute moral insanity.

'As a result, Sabre Company soldiers have a maximum life span of five years. Without flow, the body is polluted and the body dies.'

'How long do UC soldiers like Lincoln and Jolie live?' Lana asked.

'Lincoln, Jolie, all UC AM units, can operate indefinitely, as long as they receive proper servicing for wear and tear.' Sam rolled onto her side and held her head, wet locks of blonde hair draped over her bent elbow. 'So what's this I hear about you reading and projecting thoughts?'

Lana remembered her experience in the Forest Realm, hearing, feeling and seeing what Anook had experienced when he was captured by the Blood Demons. 'I think I can send and receive electrical signals...'

'In the form of thought?' Sam prompted. 'Like images?' Lana shrugged. 'I'm not sure I can explain it.'

'Try,' said Sam. 'Sing it if you have to.'

Lana chuckled. 'I'm not going to sing.' Watching the rippling surface of the ocean, Lana felt the steel of the platform beneath her thighs and realised how to convey her new understanding.

'Okay. Think of a number between one and a billion.'

'Between one and a billion... okay, got it.' She watched Lana plant her hand down onto the steel platform.

Sam jumped when she heard Lana's voice inside her head. Thirty-five thousand was her number, and Lana had just said it. Sam sat up, staring at her friend. 'Lana, was that you? You just spoke inside my head.'

'Was that your number?'

'Well, yeah.' Sam was not wearing a comms device and she couldn't understand how she was able to hear Lana, when she obviously hadn't used her vocal cords. 'How did you do that?'

Inspecting her open palm, Lana looked from the metal platform to Sam. 'Conductivity.'

'Huh.' Sam's eyes lit up at the potential applications of Lana's ability. 'If you can do it that way, theoretically you could get some conductivity through air alone.'

Lana's posture straightened. She hadn't thought of that. If that was the case, the potential was limitless.

Explosions and gunfire echoed through the narrow canyon. Red dust and rock flew from the walls and ground, while tracer rounds pelted Rachel's position.

A grenade attachment appeared on the underside of Rachel's M16 when she visualised the loaded chamber. She created a belt of six more shells to hang across her chest.

'Turret sighted!' a female UC soldier called from behind a rock boulder, taking cover from the enemy mounted machine gun.

'Copy. Ready—' Rachel coughed and wiped her eyes when the red sand showered down on her, from the .50 calibre bullets ripping up the rock wall beside her. 'Ready anti-tank.'

She considered the option of manifesting an airstrike, but she didn't want to take the chance. Although none of this was real, Jericho Williams had chosen this setting to be the battle ground inside his mind. Air bombs would most likely cause the narrow passageway to cave in as realistically as it would in the real world.

'Fire on my command,' Rachel called back to the female trooper. Pointing to the clearing ahead, she yelled to the soldier taking cover behind her, 'Smoke, there!'

The soldier threw a smoke grenade and Rachel fired a shell high into the canyon wall above the enemy gun turret. The dark grey cloud plumed from the ground and the shards of rock from Rachel's shell fire. The sunlight shining in from the opposite end of the gully was blocked out.

'Fire.'

The UC soldier stepped away from her cover and dropped to one knee. 'Firing on target.'

The rocket-propelled grenade left the chamber and shot across the clearing and into the gun turret. Fire and shrapnel flew into the air, pelting the canyon walls. The echoing clap of the initial blast travelled down the deep rock chasm.

Rachel led her team through the smoke and burning rubble to a tall steel door. 'Cover the area. You, torch us through.'

The trooper pulled a welding mask over her face and began working on the door with a blowtorch, while Rachel and the others watched for the next wave of enemy soldiers.

Scanning the ridge above, Rachel spotted three figures setting rifles down on bipods. 'Snipers up top. Take 'em out.'

One enemy sniper fell within the first burst of gunfire. The other two took cover. A low rumble echoed through the passageway. Rachel scanned both entrances, listening to what sounded like caterpillar tyre tread grinding on rock.

'Tanks.' She swore under her breath. *How is Williams doing this?* Rachel thought. *He's supposed to be medicated.*

The demolitions soldier dropped to one knee to reload the M72 LAW rocket launcher.

'We need that door down now, soldier!' Rachel yelled back at the trooper working on the door.

'Almost through, ma'am.'

An Anaconda attack helicopter appeared over the ridge

above, swirling dust around Rachel and her team. Its machine guns powered up and blared. Bullets flew down, ripping up the ground at their feet. The soldier aiming the LAW took bullets across his back. He fired and the rocket hit the left treads of the tank. More fire from the helicopter hit him and battery fluid splashed across the side of Rachel's face.

'Door ready!' Dropping the mask and torch to the ground, the soldier side kicked the centre of the oval shape she had burned and it fell into the corridor inside.

Rachel followed into the dark interior.

As her eyes adjusted, Rachel saw a wooden chest beneath a spotlight about ten metres ahead.

'There it is.'

Rachel stopped and shone a flashlight to the ground.

'Hold,' she ordered, slowly scanning the way ahead of them. She manifested a basketball in her hands and commanded her two surviving team members to back up. She threw the ball. It bounced once. On the second bounce it set off a distinct mechanism click. And the three of them staggered back when a land mine exploded.

'This could take a while.'

CHAPTER 30

Silica
Liberty building

Fiona Parker put her data tablet in her shoulder bag. She was about to leave for Boson.

Council member Henin approached, looking apprehensive. Nervous tension had been rising in the Liberty building since security had been upgraded in response to a very possible Sabre Company attack.

'We would all feel a lot safer if you stayed,' said Henin.

'You're in good hands,' Fiona assured her with a smile. 'If there's an attack, Captain Drake and his team will teleport straight in.' She waved as she left the room and headed to the elevators.

Christian McCain received a text transmission to his comms. After glancing at it, he collected his data pad and stood to leave.

Henin paused before lowering herself into her seat at the Council panel. 'We still have a lot of community reports to cover, Mr McCain. We could use your help with—'

The secretary to the Council knocked on the door and entered. 'There are some people here to see you, Mr McCain.'

'Have they been screened by security?' Henin asked.

'They're fine,' McCain interrupted. 'Excuse me.'

He followed the secretary down the hallway to the stairs.

The doors opened and Fiona stepped into the elevator, as McCain and the secretary walked by. She stepped back out and followed McCain, pushing her shirt sleeve back to look over the building layout map on her wrist console. The visual zeroed in on McCain's heat signature and a pulse beacon blinked to indicate a transmission in progress. Fiona input a high-level security hack code she had been given by Rowan and she listened.

'Transport ready?' came McCain's voice.

'Yes, sir. Platform B.'

'Good. Sending UC AM factory coordinates now.' A brief pause followed while McCain sent through a data link.

'Received. Aqua Sierra team are ready to deploy.'

'Send the elites as well. You have clearance to strike the Council, Aqua Sierra and the Branner Factory. Engage all three targets once units are in place. Confirm Operation Reclamation—go for launch.'

'Confirmed. Operation Reclamation—go for launch.'

Fiona ran back along the hallway as quickly as her business skirt and high heels would allow her and pressed the elevator button. She opened her comms link to call Rowan.

'Pick up, pick up,' she muttered. The elevator doors opened and she accessed the recording she had made to send it through to him.

'Fiona,' Rowan answered. 'I was about to call.'

'Ro, they're—'

A hand reached in and the door re-opened. Commander Tony Greer entered. He gave Fiona a nod. 'Parker.'

'Commander.' She watched him without appearing to, keeping the man's hands within her peripheral vision.

Greer hit a button for the roof. 'So, you're heading out to the Boson colonies.' He said the name of the new communities like it was home to rats.

The compartment was brightly lit. Warm evening light streamed in through the floor-to-ceiling glass wall.

'I am.' Fiona put a hand to her wrist to mute the call link with Rowan, grateful Greer hadn't heard her speaking to her partner. While Greer looked away, she quickly turned up the audio-in volume on her wrist console, so that Rowan could hear the two of them speak. In a cutting tone, she said, 'They'll be happy to receive the essentials that we take for granted.'

'Of course,' Commander Greer said, barely disguising his sarcasm. 'We wouldn't want them to miss out, would we?'

The lift rose at speed.

'You've been working hard, Parker,' Greer continued. 'If you decide not come back, I'll be happy to tell the Council you're on leave—' He hit the stop elevator button, turned to Fiona and pulled a suppressed pistol from his uniform jacket. 'Permanently.'

Fiona's hand shot out to grip Greer's wrist. She stepped out of the line of fire before a bullet flew through the glass wall. Greer turned and twisted out of Fiona's hold. She ducked when he threw a punch at her, but failed to avoid the butt of the gun when he brought it down hard upon her head.

'I had a feeling you might be on to us.' Greer padded Fiona down with his free hand, checking for a weapon.

Dazed, she sank to the floor, holding her head. 'So, you and McCain.' Fiona felt blood at the back of her scalp, and winced. 'You've served the Universal Community for over fifteen years. What made you decide that buddying up with the criminally insane was a good idea?' Encumbered by her skirt, Fiona struggled to her knees.

'I was doing all right.' Greer unbuttoned the top of his shirt and pulled at the collar. 'Had half a dozen muscle cars, a yacht, private plane. Then the WSRI started. My wife wanted to contribute forty per cent of our joint account—two million dollars. I said no. She said she'd leave me. Take the kids.'

Fiona shifted, preparing herself for an opportunity to attack.

'She didn't die in an accident,' she realised. 'You murdered her.'

'No,' Greer shook his head vigorously, swinging drops of sweat from his drooping cheek skin. 'Well, I guess paying somebody else to is as good as—'

'You're insane. You value money more than your wife's life, your children's mother?'

Commander Greer was only half listening. The pupils of his eyes were dilating with arousal, as they wandered over her body. He reached down and grabbed a fistful of Fiona's light brown hair.

'We're going to take back what's ours,' he said, 'and all of the spoils. And I think…' Greer unzipped his trousers and pulled out his member. 'It's time to teach you a lesson.'

Greer pressed the end of the handgun suppressor against Fiona's head.

Fiona bladed her left hand, chopped upward at the side of the gun and twisted her upper body, giving full momentum to a swinging punch. Her right fist cracked into the side of Greer's kneecap, dislodging it from the joint. He screamed and fell, rolling backwards across the compartment floor.

Fiona found the line of stitching at the bottom of her skirt, and tore it up to her hip to free movement to her legs. She kicked off her high heel shoes and approached Greer. He raised the gun just as Fiona flicked a sideways kick, sending it into the doors.

Pulling himself up against the compartment handrail, Greer chuckled. 'You think you can take me, Parker?' He hopped to one side to avoid Fiona's next forward kick and punched her in the mouth, splitting her bottom lip. With a heaving push from the wall, he threw his arm around her neck and pulled her back against his body.

When Greer applied increasing pressure against her throat, Fiona felt her trachea constrict. His upper body adjusted against her, as he prepared to snap her neck. Spreading her legs to position one foot behind Greer's good leg, Fiona gripped the man's arm and dropped herself to the floor. He let out a painful groan, as she heaved him over her right shoulder and threw him against the glass wall.

Splintering cracks shot across the transparent wall from the point of impact. Greer flinched when Fiona assumed a martial stance, quick-stepping back to the elevator doors. With a glance over his shoulder, understanding dawned on him.

'No, wait!' he cried.

But Fiona didn't oblige. She leapt and spun her body in mid-air before stretching out her left leg. Her heel slammed into Greer's chest and he flew through the glass, into the warm air of Liberty. Fiona landed and balanced herself at the edge of the compartment, watching the Commander's body fall. She listened to him scream until he hit the entrance portico.

Fiona wiped the blood from her mouth, hit the resume elevation button and retrieved the gun from the floor. When the doors opened Fiona saw Christian McCain waiting on landing platform B. He was accompanied by four UC AM security soldiers. McCain spoke to them and nodded in her direction. She remained calm as they approached, holding AK47 rifles.

'Drop your weapon,' a soldier said, glancing into the broken compartment before the elevator doors closed. 'Where is Commander Greer?'

'It's not what it looks like.' Fiona let the pistol drop out of her hand and held both palms forward, away from her body. 'Okay, it's exactly what it looks like.' She nodded towards Christian McCain. 'He's the Sabre Company mole. He and Greer were—'

Fiona saw a tattoo on the side of the AM unit's neck—a sword crossed over a hammer.

CHAPTER 31

Inside the mind of Jericho Williams, Rachel and her team had successfully destroyed the mines in the corridor leading to the chest. They reached the wooden container and one of the soldiers spotted eight thin wires inserted into the hinges.

'Rigged to blow,' the unit reported.

Rachel concentrated and manifested full-body bomb protection suits for her team. 'See what you can do.'

She stepped behind a transparent blast screen once it materialised on her command and watched the door to the corridor. It was quiet outside. The helicopter had gone and no ground forces had attempted to enter. *Williams may finally have expended his energy,* thought Rachel.

'Ma'am, some more light would help,' a soldier requested.

Rachel made the corridor bright and looked back to the door. Her eyebrows rose and she squared her shoulders towards an intruder. *No way,* she thought.

'Defuse the bomb,' she called over her shoulder. 'I've got this.'

Luther Saint, brought back to life in Jericho Williams' mind, stood twelve metres from Rachel. He was wearing a grey, high collar military uniform. His custom-made silver revolver was holstered at his side. Rachel watched the man's hand. She watched his eyes narrow. In half a second, Luther drew, aimed and fired his revolver. The bullet spiralled through the air. Gold gleamed from its rotating curve and a subtle white line trailed behind it.

With her assault rifle raised, Rachel advanced, manifesting a bulletproof shield attachment at her gun's midsection. It opened like a fan, locking carbon panels into position. Luther's bullet bounced off and Rachel fired. She lowered her aim when her target dropped to the ground, the shower of metal flying over his head. She heard his gun hammer and quickly crouched behind the shield to deflect the shot. Rachel fired blind, sweeping to track the sound of Luther's footfalls, but he was too fast. Her gun was knocked out of her hands. Rachel barely had time to react before Luther produced a knife. She side-stepped and turned, sucking in her stomach to avoid a jab, and struck the man's wrist before he could execute a backhand slash. Her strike sent the blade clattering against the blast screen. The soldiers looked up momentarily before returning to their task.

Rachel saw Luther's hand go for the silver revolver he'd holstered, and drew her sidearm. He attempted to dodge the first shot, but took it in his left shoulder. He pulled his gun and Rachel fired at the bullet he sent. Their rounds collided and fell, fused together.

The sound of two more shots echoed off the concrete walls, both from Rachel's handgun. Luther Saint staggered backwards with second and third bullet wounds.

Rachel stood over him when he dropped to his knees. She delivered the final round and Luther's head jerked back. His body swayed and he sunk to the floor.

One of the AM units reported that they had successfully defused the bomb.

Rachel made her way over to her team and opened the chest. She stared down into its contents: maps, blueprints, security codes.

With a sigh of relief, she spoke to the air above her head, 'Garwyn. I have what we need.'

Rachel blinked, her vision blurred. Professor O'Conner stood beside the bed.

'Rachel, are you okay?'

Rachel sat up and looked at Williams' unconscious body. 'I know where they're hiding. All of them.'

'You were only under for an hour.'

She dropped off the bed and made her way out of the room. 'Come on! We're gonna need a scout drone.'

Chesh suffered from claustrophobia, so she preferred to stay aboard the Black Bird, which was now on the landing platform on top of the palace. All of the doorways in Otami Palace were the same as in seafaring crafts like submarines. The corridors leading to amenities and—more importantly—the mess hall, were narrow and only just above head height. But Chesh was hungry after her workout, and the Black Bird kitchen had run out of her favourite fruit soy bars. She knew Mel Otami was a vegetarian and would have that sort of thing, so she ventured below to raid the galley.

A text transmission came from the Black Bird receiver, just as Chesh was returning. Munching on her second soy bar, she walked on to the crew quarters. When she arrived at Hank's quarters, she found him asleep on his bunk.

'Cap.' Chesh saw no response, so she leaned over him. 'Captain!' Hank jumped to the edge of the bed and rubbed his eyes.

'Sorry, were you sleeping?' Chesh asked with feigned concern.

'Go ahead, Chesh. What's up?'

'We've received a message from the Kiyol Ambassador.' Chesh picked up a white tank top draped over the back of a chair and tossed it to her Captain. 'I've given her an update on the successful capture. She wants to speak with you.' The comms in Hank's room beeped.

'Hank,' Rowan spoke quickly. 'Listen to this.'

He played the recording that Fiona had made of Christian McCain issuing the order for Operation Reclamation. Chesh and the Captain listened:

You have clearance to strike the Council, Aqua Sierra and the Branner Factory. Engage all three targets once units are in place. Confirm Operation Reclamation—go for launch.

'Who is that?' Chesh thought she recognised the voice, but couldn't place it.

'McCain. He's a Senior Council member.' Hank paused to let the ramifications of what he had just heard sink in.

Rowan was preparing his tactical armour and weapons on the Black Bird. His voice echoed in the hangar. 'Fiona recorded that ten minutes ago. Hank, Tony Greer is their informant. He has been for the last five years. I heard him and Fiona fight. She's in trouble.'

'No way.' Chesh swore under her breath in disbelief. 'The Commander?'

'I've already tried teleporting in,' said Rowan. 'Greer must have added our signatures to the inhibitor node matrix set up at the Palmer Building. We need to fly there now.'

'We're on our way,' said Hank. 'Did Fiona get anything on Dennis Conroy?'

Rowan's voice came in loud and clear when he moved closer to the comms receiver. 'McCain is Conroy. He must have had some kind of facial reconstruction surgery since Silica.'

'Posing as a Council member this whole time.' Hank pulled his shirt down over his hairy chest.

'Chesh, ready the ship.' He set the comms to all receivers inside Otami Palace. 'Attention all units. Emergency assembly at the armoury—on the double. Compound security personnel, remain at your stations.'

The comms beeped again and Pete's voice came through. 'Hank, Rachel is awake. I'll put her on.'

'I know where they're hiding,' said Rachel. 'They're on planet Hades, Kurai System, Outer Rim. No colonies were ever set up there. Pete will have a drone ready within the hour.'

'Excellent work, Rachel. Are you all right?' Hank set the comms receiver to his mobile console and walked with Chesh down the hall towards the elevator.

'I'm fine. What's the situation?'

'Fiona is in trouble. We're heading out to Silica. We believe Senior Council member—'

'McCain,' Rachel confirmed. 'He's Dennis Conroy.'

'Then you'll also know that we need to cover the Palmer Building, the Branner Factory, and our own asses, here.'

'They want us to spread our forces thin.' Rachel had been in the elevator when she spoke to Hank. Now, it arrived at the top of Otami Palace and she saw that the hangar door of the Black Bird was down.

Rowan strode to an ammunition box, carrying an M40 sniper rifle over his shoulder. He saw Rachel making her way up the hangar ramp. 'I heard you were diving into Williams' mind. Are you all right? Did it work?'

'We have what we need.' Rachel placed her hand on her brother's shoulder. 'Ro, what's wrong?'

'Fiona…' he said. 'They've taken her.'

'Shit. I'll come with—'

'Jin will need you here.' Rowan took ammunition from the box and loaded the cartridge of his bolt action rifle.

Rachel searched her brother's eyes. He was closing over, like he always did before a serious mission. But this time he was not steeling himself for combat. Rachel knew where Fiona would be sent. She knew Rowan was already there in his mind. She pulled him into a hug, held him for a moment, then hurried from the hangar.

When Lana found Rachel, she was dressed in urban camo pants and a black tank top, with a pistol strapped to her thigh.

'Jin's going to take us through security,' said Lana. She nodded to Sam at the workstation.

'They're working on the drone. Seriously, Sabre Company HQ is on a planet called Hades?'

'I know,' Rachel smirked. 'Conroy thinks he's some kind of supervillain.'

Sam caught her father trying to move a heavy battery to charge the drone. 'Dad, you shouldn't be lifting that.' She rushed over to help him set it down on the work bench among an array of carbon alloy parts. 'You have a cracked rib. Jolie said you have to let it heal.'

'I'm fine. Where are Lex and Charlie? We could use their help.'

Charlie made his way up to the workstation, followed by Lex. 'Sorry, we came as soon as we heard.'

Sam noticed Charlie's untucked shirt and askew tie. 'What have you two been up to?'

'None of your business.' Lex smiled, pushing her hair back into place.

'We have two Quad Rocket SAM launch pads on the east and west sides.' Jin pointed to the four corners of the port platform, explaining the surface defences to Lana and Rachel. 'And there are two .50 calibre machine guns on the north and south.'

Rachel looked at each corner. She observed the large square doors inside the port platform, where the Surface-to-Air Missile launchers would rise from.

'All automated.' Jin walked them to the edge of the platform, where a spiral staircase led into an air compression chamber, which operated as a four-person elevator. 'They'll come at us from above and below.' Once inside the chamber, he initiated the door seal and they descended beneath the water. Jin hit the spotlights and slowed their descent to point out the underwater perimeter defences.

'They'll want to find a weak point to breach. That's where you two come in.' Using a control pad, Jin moved the spotlights over gun turrets on their side of the compound. 'The AM units will be firing these to hold off the main forces. But I'll need you to do a sweep of each deck during the fight, in case they breach the outer doors.' The chamber shook when Jin changed their course to a horizontal slide, heading towards an outer door at the mid-section of the compound.

'I'll show you the armoury,' he said.

CHAPTER 32

The UC Battle Cruiser entered the planet's atmosphere.

'We're approaching the factory now, sir.'

'Very good.' Captain Lincoln reviewed the data on the screen. 'Any sign of Sabre Company?'

'Nothing yet.' The reporting UC pilot gazed out at the industrial complex below. 'Strange to think we were created here, sir. I don't remember any of it.'

'I've been inside,' said Lincoln. 'There's nothing worth remembering, just a whole lot of assembly lines. Take us in. Have all ships assemble a blockade formation.'

'Yes, sir.'

Typing at the comms monitor before him, Lincoln contacted Hank and linked the call to Brad and Renee. 'We've arrived. No sign of Sabre Company forces.'

'Quiet down here,' Brad reported.

'Copy that,' said Hank. 'Stay frosty.'

Renee loaded a mounted four-barrel missile launcher. The comms line closed and she looked at her partner, brow furrowed. 'Hope Fiona is still alive. Can't imagine where Rowan's at right now.'

'If I were him...' Brad turned his gaze from the skies to watch his partner push her hand into a fingerless glove. 'There is absolutely nothing I wouldn't do.'

Renee paused, catching on to Brad's sentiment. She looked at him and smiled lovingly. 'I know, baby.' She walked over to him and kissed him.

Hank and a complement of six AM troops had already set off aboard the Black Bird for Silica. He lifted himself out of the co-pilot chair and nodded to Chesh. 'Let me know when we're approaching Silica.'

'Will do.'

Hank descended a suspended walkway to the hangar. He looked down over the team checking their equipment. 'Anybody seen Ro?'

A female AM unit pulled on a black beret and jerked her head towards the stern of the ship.

'He's in the diner, sir.'

Rowan sat in a booth, staring into a glass of bourbon. The refrigerator in the kitchen hummed. A blues tune played from the jukebox.

Hank walked in and he dropped into the leather seat opposite Rowan. He saw what was sitting between his friend's still hands. 'You don't wanna do that.'

Rowan picked up the bottle of bourbon beside him and inspected the aged, refined drink. He didn't really know what had triggered it. Maybe it was the motor pool under the COG building. Maybe it was witnessing the loss of young lives at the hands of Sabre Company soldiers. Rowan decided that it didn't matter what it was, because he knew that he was ultimately responsible for his own actions.

Fiona had saved Rowan from himself. She would not allow him to be another Sabre Company victim. She told him one word. One word was her motto and his: refuse.

Two years sober.

'She's gonna be all right, Ro,' said Hank. 'She's a strong woman.'

Rowan turned the glass of alcohol in his fingers. He hadn't taken a single sip. He had poured it, and let the woody aroma waft from the glass.

'Fiona told me about the day she came home from Corporate College.' Rowan pushed the glass away from him and watched it from the other end of the table. 'That day, she found her parents lying on the lounge room floor. She'd heard the soldiers upstairs, smelt the gasoline, tried to wake her parents. She said they were already cold. So, she ran.' Rowan wiped away the tears welling in his eyes. 'I don't know why I'm thinking about this. Guess I'm wondering why good people have to suffer.'

Hank knew of no explanation, or if one even existed. 'You and I both know she's no victim. Fiona will fight, for as long as she can.'

Aqua Sierra

Rachel approached the first array of weapons in Jin's armoury. She inspected the modern rifles, handguns, bulletproof jackets and explosives. The next partitioned booth contained heavy weapons, mounted machine guns, grenade and rocket launchers. Rachel stopped at the third booth and gazed over an elegant display of swords belonging to over half a dozen ancient cultures. She lifted a Katana from a rack of three and slipped the blade from its sheath, admiring the craftsmanship.

Lana stood beside her and immediately went for a straight blade ninja sword.

Jin leaned against the partition wall. 'I thought you guys might like this section.'

His comms beeped and Melissa spoke. 'Jin, reports have come in from our trade station. Three unmarked cruisers are heading for Aqua Sierra. Their ETA is around twenty minutes.'

'Copy that. We'll be ready for them.'

Lana and Rachel took the weapons they had selected, then followed Jin to the perimeter guns where the UC soldiers were assembled.

Silica Liberty

Barrelling down in a bowl of flame, the Black Bird entered the upper atmosphere of Silica's night sky.

'Still haven't been able to get through to the Council,' Chesh said to Hank, who was co-piloting.

'Not a good sign.'

The clouds broke as they flew down to the city. Columns of smoke rose from below. Black streaks streamed from flaming windows on each side of the Liberty building.

'Oh shit!' Chesh exclaimed. 'All hands brace for emergency manoeuvres!'

A Sabre Company cruiser had detected the Black Bird's descent and was heading straight for them. It had already fired missiles and Chesh only had a few seconds to react. She cut the engines, pushed the nose of the ship down and dropped two hundred metres, before hitting the thrusters. The Black Bird dipped from a steep descent, then accelerated to level out. The two missiles shot over its tail, narrowly missing their target.

'I'll drop you on the roof, then I'll draw this bastard away,' said Chesh, her muscles hardening as she fought to steer the ship.

Hank jumped out of his seat and spoke into his comms. 'All units, prepare for rope descent. Liberty is under attack.'

The doors opened at the rear of the ship. Rowan and six AM units hooked themselves to rappel lines, before dropping down. Hank followed with another four units, including Jolie.

'Two units hold the roof,' Hank barked over the engines of the Black Bird, while Chesh flew away. 'Two with me. The rest follow—' Hank's eyes searched through the assembling team members. 'Where's Rowan?'

A unit checked her wrist console and saw Rowan's signature speeding down the building's stairwell. 'Gone, Captain.'

Rowan glanced at his wrist map and saw two heat signature readings located in the room he was heading towards. The emergency lights shone a dim yellow. Smoke was circulating through the building's conditioning vents, making the air difficult to breathe. Rowan proceeded along the corridor, his assault rifle trained on each doorway. He dropped to one knee when an SC soldier stepped out of the room, followed by another trooper carrying a large data storage console.

Rowan fired two shots, one at the side of the lead soldier's head and another at the other's right leg. They dropped to the floor and he approached, aiming at the wounded unit. Rowan's map indicated the remaining rooms of the floor he was on were empty, so he took the time to disarm the wounded soldier.

Rowan pulled a combat knife from the sheath at his chest.

'Where is Fiona Parker?' he asked the soldier.

When the unit glared back at him, Rowan stabbed the blade into its left leg, knowing they were programmed to feel pain, so they would seek repair when required.

'I don't know!' he screamed. 'Please, I don't know anything!' Rowan twisted the blade, opening the wound.

'Aaghh! Stop—okay, I'll tell you!'

Hank entered the hallway outside the main Council meeting room. He signalled the four soldiers with him to go to the double doors. Listening to the raised voices inside, he recognised Senior Council member Henin's authoritative tone.

'Killing us won't change anything,' she said. 'The people of the known galaxy are free and there is nothing you can do to take that away from them.'

Hank moved to an open door further down the hallway and peered into the meeting room. He counted one woman and two men, wearing civilian clothes and carrying automatic rifles. Henin and two other council members knelt side by side, their hands bound behind their backs. The man next to Henin had been shot. He was leaning forward, groaning and sweating profusely.

'What you are committing now is an act of terrorism,' Henin continued.

'You're mistaken, Council member.'

Hank stared in angry disbelief. The retort came from the Council secretary. He remembered her name was Amanda, and that she had been born in Liberty and had survived the many years of oppression.

The other armed militants in the room were human. They must have been working undercover in the Liberty building as Sabre Company spies.

Amanda was gazing out of the window at the newest buildings on the east side of Liberty.

'I used to work at the COG building,' she said, with a nod to where it was before it had been razed to the ground and built over. 'I was on assignment. It was an honour and a thrill to make contact with the infamous Luke Palmer. He didn't trust me... but he was desperate. We had his sister.' Amanda took a moment to remember. 'Sweet girl. It took a long time for Kindred to condition her.'

'Amanda...' Henin took on an even tone, wanting to keep the woman talking to buy herself and her fellow Council members some time. 'Amanda, why are you doing this? Surely you can see the world has moved on. We are at peace. We are—'

'My parents were wealthy,' Amanda interrupted. 'The WSRI forced them out here and they had to start again. They strived to regain their former status. When your people invaded—when you tore down our traditional values and our liberal society— you tore my family apart.'

Henin lost her cool. 'Your families did not strive, young lady. They were served, at the very top of a pyramid, by wealth taken from the people below—the commoners you seek to enslave again.' She spat her last words in disgust.

Amanda raised her gun at Henin's head. 'You die first, communist scum.'

'Flash and clear,' Hank commanded the UC soldiers at the opposite end of the hallway.

The double doors opened and a flash grenade rolled across the floor. Amanda and the SC operatives covered their stinging eyes after the room turned white. Hank entered and took down the two men with a sweep of short fire bursts. Dropping to the ground, Amanda avoided the UC soldier's gunfire. Her fellow operatives slumped over the meeting tables, dead.

'Drop the gun.' Hank approached Amanda while she picked herself up from the floor, leaving her rifle at her feet. 'Let me see your hands.'

Amanda raised her arms while stepping closer to Henin. In two moves, she lifted the woman from the floor, and held a knife to her throat. 'Back off, Drake.'

Hank ordered the UC soldiers to lower their weapons and glanced at the wounded man. 'See to him.'

The two units took medical equipment from their waist packs and assessed the man's wound. One of the UC soldiers looked up at Hank. 'Sir, we have to get him to a hospital.'

'Find and reprogram the inhibitor computer,' said Hank. 'Teleport him out of here.'

'Please hurry,' Henin slurred.

She pretended to faint, allowing her legs to buckle. Amanda

was forced to take her weight with her free hand. Henin jumped, jerking her shoulder up underneath her captive's knife wrist. The blade nicked her cheek when she pulled her head back and broke Amanda's nose. Amanda screamed, releasing her human shield.

Hank stepped in and disarmed her. He applied wrist binders and pushed Amanda down into an office chair.

Henin crouched down beside her wounded colleague while the UC soldiers freed her wrists.

'I'm sorry we couldn't come sooner,' Hank apologised to Henin. He glared down at Amanda.

'Luke Palmer's sister. Where is she?'

CHAPTER 33

Rowan stepped out of the mercury portal carrying the data storage console that no doubt contained information stolen from the Council database. He found himself inside what looked like a bunker. Cold air pierced to his skin through the uniform he had taken from the SC soldier. His wrist console detected heat signatures about twenty metres below his position.

'Come in, Hank.'

'Ro,' Hank replied. 'Where are you? We just lost your signature.'

Feeling a draught coming from behind him, Rowan made his way down a narrow corridor. The lights beaming from the ceiling flickered as he followed the breeze. Rowan found a steel door with a circular window. He looked through it and saw ice and snow illuminated by a purple hue.

'No… can't be. Hank, check these coordinates for me.'

There was a brief pause while Hank ran the data he received from Rowan. 'Ro, your coordinates are tagged as a Realm signature. You're on Glacier II but… an alternate version.'

'Looks like the same coring facility. This is how Sabre Company were able to breach the Genesis Lab. They mapped out an alternate version.' Rowan opened the door and stepped into the freezing air. The Parabola Light Band arched across the night sky. 'I took a Shifter from an SC soldier. He said Fiona was being held here.'

'I'm afraid you're on your own,' said Hank. 'I need all of the units I have to secure the Palmer Building.'

'I'll contact you once I have Fiona.' Rowan ended the transmission link and returned through the bunker corridor. He descended a winding stairwell and moved along the hallway. A panel on the wall next to an elevator shaft indicated the same number of floors as the compound inside the Home Realm Genesis Lab.

'What took you so long?'

Rowan froze and turned around slowly to face an SC officer wearing a high-rank uniform. 'Sir?'

The officer glanced at the data storage console Rowan was carrying and jerked his head to the opposite end of the hallway. 'Get that to Intelligence and return to your post.'

'Yes, sir.' Rowan headed in the direction the officer had indicated. He found the door marked *Intel Dept.* and screwed a suppressor onto the end of the SC standard AK47 rifle before knocking and entering.

'About time,' a young man wearing a collared shirt and slacks said to Rowan. He turned from a computer console and nodded to another intel operator across the room. 'Prep the external server. I don't want any UC viruses getting into our system.' Glancing over his shoulder to Rowan, he gestured impatiently to a vacant work table. 'Leave it. We'll take it from here.'

'Where's the security detail on this room?' Rowan asked with an air of authority.

The overweight intel specialist took a can of energy drink from his desk. He pressed the opening between the bloated cheeks that crowded his face and drank deeply. 'Look, until you tin heads kick those hippy bastards out of office, we're stuck down here. So, please get your ass to the front line and start shooting people.'

Raising his gun, Rowan fired a suppressed round into the operator's leg. He brought the gun to his shoulder to aim at the other. 'Walk towards me. Hands up.'

The man did so immediately, staring in fear, while his fellow worker dropped to the floor yelling.

'Look, man, we're just trying to do our part.' The operator approached and flinched when Rowan pulled his arms behind his back to bind his wrists.

'Sit down on the floor and shut up,' Rowan ordered. He turned his attention to the operator clutching his bleeding leg. 'Where is she?'

'Who? I don't know who you—'

Rowan rested his boot on top of the man's leg and leaned heavily onto the wound. They were intelligence. They were privy to every development within Sabre Company.

'Hades!' the man yelled. 'Outer Rim!'

'Give me the coordinates.'

The operator took a small console from his coat pocket, tapped at the menu screen and handed it to Rowan. 'It's our HQ. She's in Kindred's basement.' He gulped loudly. 'Please don't kill me.'

Rowan struck the man unconscious. He accessed his comms and called Rachel.

There was a brief pause before Rachel replied through loud background noise—pounding guns and the dull rumble of impact explosions. 'Ro, have you found Fiona?'

'Not yet. I'm in a Sabre Company bunker. It's located in another version of Glacier II. I'm sending the coordinates to their computer room. Charlie should get in here and hack their system.'

'Copy that.'

Rowan input the coordinates to enter Hades. 'Fiona is on Hades.'

'Shit, that's their HQ. Ro, the drone's not ready. You can't go in blind.'

'I have to.'

A loud explosion interrupted Rachel. 'I have to go. We're under attack. Get in and get out.'

Rachel checked the compound perimeter video feed and saw more armoured aquatic vehicles approaching through the dark, travelling low across the ocean floor.

The UC soldiers seated in the gun turrets opened fire on the SC forces. One turret was assigned to intercept the torpedoes that snaked out from the Sabre Company launchers towards the compound.

An alarm beacon sounded, indicating a lower-level breach. Rachel left Jin to take over command and called out to Lana. 'We're on. Let's go.'

The two women readied their weapons and took the elevator down to the breached level.

'The aerial assault has stopped.' Lana watched the video link of the surface skirmish on her wrist console. SC space carrier ships retreated along the surface of the ocean. One took a missile to its side and plummeted into the sea.

The doors opened and Lana and Rachel stepped into the chill of ankle-deep sea water. Rachel checked her thermal scan. There were no heat signatures.

The lights above blinked on and off. Lana slid the straight sword from the sheath on her back. She sloshed towards the exterior doors and felt the water level rise. 'We need to seal the doors.'

Rachel signalled for Lana to watch her back while she opened the door to the compression chamber. Splashing came from behind. Two SC operatives approached. They wore grey body suits and face masks, scaled with flexible carbon armour. The layered material had enabled them to deceive heat signature scans. As they opened fire, Lana turned the blade of her ninja sword, jutting it to either side of her. She chopped downward, loosening her wrist to bring the blade up again, pulling its weight into rhythmic, forward rotations. Sparks flew and the bullets bounced off of the shining lines and circles of steel while Lana moved her sword faster than the eye could see.

The operatives stopped firing and looked at one another in astonishment. Lana couldn't believe her reaction time either.

The operatives holstered their side arms, took steel rods from their utility belts and flicked them down to their full extensions.

Lana spoke over her shoulder to Rachel before assuming a martial defensive stance. 'Seal the door. I'll take care of them.'

'Be with you in a minute.' Rachel pushed the heavy door open and squeezed in through the gap.

The female operative advanced and struck Lana's blade. Side-stepping around her attacker, Lana deflected the steel rod, slid behind and brought the flat of her sword against the woman's chest. Twisting her upper body, Lana pulled the operative over her hips and threw the woman at the male elite as he approached. Water flicked up and over the woman's scale suit in a circular swirl and she spun horizontally through the air. Her partner grunted when she collided with him.

They quickly rolled to their feet and produced long combat knifes from their belts. One of them threw their weapon and it sailed—end over end—through the flickering light. Lana sheathed her sword and clapped her hands in front of her face, catching the blade between her palms to halt its journey centimetres from her nose. Without hesitating, she took the tip of the knife and threw it back. The blade glinted for a quarter second when the lights above blinked. The operative's head jerked back and his body dropped into the knee-high water, with the knife handle protruding from his forehead.

The surviving operative, the name *Cobra* embossed into her armour, clenched her fist around the handle of her knife. Lana rolled her shoulders and widened her stance.

The walls shook and underwater explosions continued to sound off all around them. Lana raised her hand from her side and beckoned for her adversary to attack.

Cobra waded slowly through the water, skilfully turning her knife in her hand until her thumb rested on the end of the handle, positioned for a powerful stab. Lana matched her opponent's every step, waiting for a sign to advance: the dropping of a shoulder, the turning of hips, the bending of knees.

With quick steps, Cobra weaved sideways and leapt, throwing an arching kick. Lana ducked and rolled through the water. She turned around to find the woman assuming her stepping defensive stance, circling the watery arena. Lana felt the loss of weight on her back and saw that the operative had managed to steal the ninja sword. Lana was impressed.

Cobra advanced, attacking with Lana's sword. The blade glinted in the light as the woman chopped downward, forcing Lana to side-step. Cobra swung sideways and Lana leapt backwards, sucking in her stomach as the tip of the blade sliced through the cotton material of her top.

Swiftly invading her opponent's blindside, Lana launched the full force of a straight punch at Cobra's shoulder.

The operative yelled in fury. Her arm hung limp, dislocated from her shoulder. Cobra splashed backwards through the water and steadied her feet, still in range to strike a desperate blow. Using all of the strength in her functioning arm, she brought the sword down, hoping to cut her opponent in half. Lana stepped forward, raising her forearm against the blade. The razor-sharp steel broke with a loud metallic snap.

Stunned, Cobra watched the slender end of the sword spin, glinting on its way into the water.

'What are you?' she panted, incredulous.

Lana staggered back, feeling slightly rigid. She inspected the superficial flesh wound on her forearm where the blade had hit. Her chest felt tight, as though she were wearing clothing a size too small. And she felt her abdomen, smooth and solid like ceramic.

'I'm… something else,' Lana shrugged.

There was a dull thud and Cobra fell unconscious into the water. Rachel lowered the butt of her rifle and approached Lana, looking over the other body lying in the water. 'Are you okay?'

'I think so.'

Rachel took her friend's arm, inspecting the hard, yet still skin-coloured surface. The damage began to dissipate into Lana's normal skin tissue.

Lana glanced at the water, lapping at the wall from their movement. She realised something, and her eyes snapped to Cobra's unconscious body. She had dislocated the woman's shoulder.

Automated Machine units were able to knock their joints back into place without assistance.

'These soldiers are human,' said Lana. She crouched down to pull Cobra out of the water. Holding the woman's body against her, Lana pulled the mask away from Cobra's head.

'No… it can't be,' Rachel murmured. She leaned down and pushed the long red hair away from Cobra's young, beautiful face. 'Emma?'

Lana gave Rachel a quizzical look.

'This is Emma Palmer,' said Rachel. 'Luke's sister.'

CHAPTER 34

Fluorescent lights lined the ceiling, buzzing and flickering. Rowan covered his nose and mouth at the smell of mercury vapour. The empty cells he walked by were not barred doors, but transparent walls. Rowan stepped around an overturned wheelchair. Inside an open cell, there were signs of a struggle. Bullet holes ran from the top of the wall, along the ceiling and through broken light bulbs, emitting the poisonous vapour still in his nostrils. Inside the other cells were single beds. Some were propped against the walls, others torn apart, pieces scattered across the white tiles.

At the end of the corridor was a door labelled Room 101. Rowan aimed his gun into the well-lit interior, but found only a large, archaic chair and a trolley of surgical tools. The room was surprisingly small. Bottles and syringes gleamed in the light. Leather straps hung from the solid steel arms of the chair and electrical wires fed from a panel at its back. At the head of the chair was a steel skullcap. The leather straps were bloody.

Rowan paused when he saw Fiona's shirt lying in the corner of the room.

'Step out, drop your weapon and put your hands behind your head.'

Rowan recognised the voice despite the flat, empty tone. He backed out of the room and began to turn, but stopped when he heard the click of a gun hammer. 'Fiona…'

'Drop your weapon—'

'Fiona, it's me.' Rowan dropped the rifle behind him and slowly turned around. He shuddered at the sight of her. Her bloodshot eyes were dark and sunken in her pale face. Rings of dry blood circled her wrists. And she wore a grey Sabre Company jumpsuit.

'You are a Community sympathiser,' Fiona said. She raised her pistol and aimed at Rowan's forehead. 'You are the enemy.'

Rowan saw Fiona's eyelids twitch. He could see from the gap in her eyelashes that tape had been used to keep her eyes open.

'Fiona, listen to me. Remember who you are.' Rowan fought back tears, willing himself to reach the woman he loved. 'Please, don't let them do this.'

The gun trembled in Fiona's hands. Her eyes watered, pleading Rowan from her prison within.

'Fiona, don't let them take you. Refuse.' He stepped closer to her, the barrel of the gun level with his throat. 'Remember who you are. You're stronger than them.'

Fiona's body shook and her legs gave way. Rowan caught her and lowered her to the ground. Shaking, she breathed heavily through gritted teeth and let out a guttural scream, gripping Rowan's waist. Tears streamed down her face. Still clutching Rowan, Fiona shuddered as her scream burned out into a low growl.

Fiona sobbed and stared across the room into nothing.

Rowan wiped her matted hair from her eyes and pressed his lips against her forehead. He gently picked her up in his arms.

'Remarkable,' a voice spoke from the doorway to Room 101.

Rowan turned to see a tall, slender man watching on with an amused expression. A hidden compartment in the wall at the back of the room silently shifted back into position. The man wore a formal grey Sabre Company uniform beneath a plastic surgical coat.

Rowan spoke calmly, his heart retreating into itself, cold and heavy. 'You did this.'

The man nodded slowly, large glassy eyes staring behind thick-lensed glasses. He watched Fiona's limp body for a moment before turning his attention to Rowan. His dense, greying eyebrows were slanted in a sinister expression.

'Rowan Navara, I presume?' He spoke slowly, a rasp of excitement beneath every word. 'I am Doctor Kindred. My dear boy, you hold in your arms a rather intriguing specimen.' Kindred watched Rowan set Fiona down against a cell door. She turned and vomited over the floor, her eyes rolling in delirium.

'Miss Parker fought ferociously before giving in,' said Kindred. 'Ultimately, she only surrendered her body. Everything else she buried.'

Rowan took the pistol from his hip holster and shot Kindred's kneecap.

Kindred fell to the floor and crawled back into Room 101, gasping in agony. Reaching for the leg of the steel chair, he tried to pull himself back to the hidden door. Rowan grabbed him under the shoulders, then dropped him into the chair.

'What are you doing?' Kindred fought against the leather straps fastening over his wrists. 'You... you can't do this!'

Rowan pushed the skullcap onto Doctor Kindred's head and pulled the jaw strap tight, so the man could no longer open his mouth. He could hear the doctor's molars grinding against the strain. Kindred spat between his front teeth, his chest heaving in desperation.

'No one will come for you,' said Rowan. 'Before your heart explodes inside your chest, you will feel the pain of every person you have turned.'

Breathing heavily, Kindred watched Rowan's fingers turn the voltage dial.

'Goodbye, Doctor.' Rowan turned on the power to the chair and the hum of electricity began to build.

The doctor's body tensed and started to shake violently. Every muscle strained beneath his pale skin.

Kindred's eyeballs pulled at their optic nerves.

CHAPTER 35

Having lost the Sabre Company craft, Chesh flew the Black Bird to a helipad on a roof. She judged it would give her a good vantage point. She disembarked, hauling a Barrett M82 sniper rifle to the corner of the building. Once she was in place, lying on her chest with the rifle, she lined her sights on the enemy.

Hank let fly dozens of bullets from his minigun. He cut down three Sabre Company soldiers, before the remaining squad members took cover. Hank and his AM units had managed to prevent any more Sabre Company forces from entering the Liberty building, while inhibitor nodes were being deployed along the street to secure the city block.

'Mech units incoming!' Jolie called out.

Two SC troopers wearing mechanical armour suits marched towards the UC stockade. Bullets bounced off of their armour plating as they advanced.

From her elevated sniper position, Chesh shot one Mech unit in the head. The armoured soldier fell heavily to the ground.

Jolie climbed inside a single-pilot Attack Hover Craft that had arrived with the UC reinforcements.

Hank took cover, avoiding a burst of enemy fire from the evacuated street area. He lobbed a grenade and it rolled beneath the solar car protecting the SC soldiers. The explosion obliterated them. 'Captain Lincoln, come in. What's your situation?'

'Our fleet is engaging incoming Sabre Company ships.'

'Copy that. Be prepared to detonate the facility if you're overrun.'

'Not gonna happen.'

Hank looked up when Jolie flew overhead in her AHC, firing machine-gun rounds before launching twin rockets into the SC Mech units below.

Hank's wrist console beeped an incoming call from his daughter. 'Go ahead, Lex.'

'I'm here with Charlie at the other Glacier II Rowan found. We're looking at a tracking database and onscreen schematics for some kind of portal installation in outer space. The rig is huge and there's enough amplification to the Shifter device to open a portal the size of a house. The systems indicate other identical space installations. Their locations register the same coordinates, but with different Realm signatures.'

'Amplified Shifters in outer space.' Hank reloaded his rifle. 'Sounds like they're sending in ships.'

'That's what we thought,' said Lex. 'But the link signatures are all Home Realm locations, scattered over four different systems. All have been installed on a planet's surface. All are populated except one hidden in a mine.'

Professor O'Conner's voice came through the comms link from Aqua Sierra. 'Hank, Lex, I've gone through the data Charlie uploaded from the Sabre Company system,' he spoke urgently. 'We need to destroy them immediately. Every version of Glacier II will be wiped out by the Parabola Light Band.'

Hank pressed a hand against his ear to block out the noise of the battle. 'Say again.'

'The Parabola is made up of high-density energy matter, most likely ejected from an implosion in space. It'll destroy

Glacier II in less than two hours. Sabre Company intends to use the linked portals as a weapon.' Pete raised his voice until it became hoarse. 'If those portals are active when the energy wave passes through the installations, it will effectively travel through the Home Realm portals and wipe out everything within three hundred kilometres of each portal. We need to find and destroy all of the link installations.'

'Copy that.' Hank swore under his breath. 'They've separated and engaged our forces to distract us from the real threat.'

'Captain, SC reinforcements have been sighted,' Jolie reported from up in her craft.

A group of enemy units were creeping along behind burning car wreckages towards Hank. Jolie was about to fire on them when the SC soldiers were pelted with rocks. A Liberty civilian pounced on the remaining trooper, beating him with a baseball bat. Four others appeared in the light of the streetlamps. Seven more followed. A group of fifteen arrived, moving in a tactical formation that indicated some were veterans from the days of oppression.

'Scratch that. SC forces have been subdued,' Jolie reported. 'Area clear.' She looked down to the double lane roads meeting the intersection. Another coordinated group of over thirty people emerged. Each civilian was carrying a makeshift club or bricks—whatever they could find to defend their city.

Aqua Sierra

Sam had returned from the alternate version of Glacier II. She braced herself against her workstation when another explosion outside made the compound shake.

'Are we sure they're not targeting Earth?' Sam asked her father, who was working on the portal signature locations.

'Positive,' he said. 'They want Earth intact.' Pete considered the recording of Christian McCain's commanding words to initiate open war. 'Each planet they've installed amplified portals on will be rendered uninhabitable. The high-level density of radiation from the Parabola would be blown across each planet's surface. Plants, wildlife, people—everything will die if those portals aren't deactivated.'

Sam set the coordinates to the remote Shifter attached to the drone going to Hades. 'All set. What's the plan?'

'To get to each Home Realm portal installation, we'll have to set a timed relay sequence to Hank's Shifter,' Pete said. 'He and his team can enter each location, plant explosives and move on to the next target.'

'They won't need to hit the Glacier II installations,' Sam said. 'They'll all be destroyed by the Parabola. Charlie and I will program a stage-by-stage portal run and send it through to Hank.'

Jin called to the UC soldiers on his side of the compound. 'Prepare to cease fire on my command.'

'Sir?'

'You heard me.' Jin took the white stone Ohkwai Chillo had given him from his trouser pocket. After speaking into it, the stone fluoresced brightly, before fading back to white.

With a flash of light, a mercury portal sphere appeared a few feet from Jin. Hank and Jolie jogged out, followed by a cloud of dust and asphalt debris.

Moving back to the security feed screens to check on Lana and Rachel, Jin saw an open door in the holding cell corridor and no guards outside Jericho Williams' cell.

'Shit! Security to cell block, come in.'

'Jin.' Hank looked to the gun turrets and the soldiers standing by. 'What's your situation?'

'SC forces keeping rolling in, but we're holding.'

The elevator door opened. Lana and Rachel stepped out, carrying an unconscious woman. Two soldiers hurried to relieve them of their prisoner.

'Put her into holding,' Rachel said. Then she turned to Hank. 'It's Luke Palmer's sister, Emma.'

'What?' Hank looked in the direction the woman was taken.

'She's been brainwashed, same as Luke. Sent in as an elite Sabre Company operative.'

'Intense,' Hank said.

Rachel wiped wet hair away from her face.

'Pete gave us the heads-up,' she said, replacing her spent rifle magazine with a fresh one.

'They're smart, I'll give 'em that. We don't have enough units to cover every portal installation, as well as maintain defences.' She breathed heavily, having run several corridors with Lana to weed out SC infiltration operatives from the breach points below. 'How do you wanna do this?'

'Sam has just sent me a relay program which will take us to each installation,' said Hank. 'Looks like we'll have ten minutes per stop to destroy each target.'

'Ten minutes?' Lana blew from her bottom lip and raised her fringe. 'It'll have to do.'

'Sir, the female prisoner is secure,' an AM soldier's voice came through Jin's comm device. 'But the guard detail stationed here is incapacitated. Jericho Williams is gone.'

Jin breathed through frustration.

'Their operatives must have snuck through here as well.' Rachel pulled the strap of her rifle over her head, letting the gun hang against her back. 'How many of those freakin' ninjas do they have?'

Lana inclined her head, listening to what sounded like dungchen Tibetan horns. 'You guys hear that?'

The deep interminable tone grew louder and louder until the walls of the compound began to shake.

'Chillo.' Jin moved to the outside visual feed screens. 'All units cease fire.' Shadows formed along the rear line of the approaching Sabre Company aquatic crafts.

Like ghosts of the deep, Prince Ohkwai Chillo and his personal guard of forty Laician warriors appeared from the darkness, fins flexing, flashing vibrant colours, vibrating vehement energy. A dense cloud moved behind them, as more warriors arrived.

Jin checked the heat signature readings. 'My Laician friend happens to be the son of Queen Sienta. He's brought over a thousand warriors.'

'Excellent timing.' Hank left the console beside Jin and motioned for Rachel and Lana to follow him. 'Now that we have an offensive squad, let's suit up and hit the portal installations one by one.'

Fiona lay on the medical bed while Jolie checked her vitals. 'I'm giving you some oxycodone for the pain.' She watched Fiona's vacant stare with concern. 'Fiona?'

Fiona shook her head and covered her ears against guttural screams—her screams when she was being electrocuted.

Jolie placed her hand on Fiona's arm and squeezed. Fiona flinched.

'Rest and drink plenty of fluids.'

'I... I will. Thanks, Jolie.' Fiona watched her leave and felt Rowan take hold of her hand. He was sitting beside her on the opposite side of the bed. 'I'll be all right, Ro. Mel's coming up to stay with me. Hank needs you.'

Rowan leaned down and kissed her. She was not making eye contact. He read this as regret and offered her consolation.

'Greer's children are old enough to take care of themselves,' he whispered. 'He would have killed you, Fiona. You were defending yourself.'

Fiona nodded slowly, watching Greer's body fall behind her

eyes. It was a memory that would stay with her forever. A deed she would never regret.

It was painful to see her this way. Rowan wanted to stay, but he pulled himself away from Fiona and walked towards the elevators. Sam joined Rowan in the compartment.

'How's she doing?'

'She'll be okay.' Rowan's gaze to the medical room was blocked when the doors closed. Having read the reports on Doctor Kindred and his work, Sam shook her head.

'Luke and Emma Palmer must have gone through that as well,' she said. 'Dad has developed a serum to counteract the drugs Luke was taking. And we've connected Emma to the Garwyn program to begin bringing back her memories. Luke is doing well, so he'll be able to help her.'

Rowan breathed evenly, trying to focus his mind. 'Hank has a team assembled?'

'They're suiting up now.'

The doors opened onto the armoury room and Rachel approached, holstering dual pistols onto her thighs. 'Is Fiona okay? We heard…'

Rowan nodded and let his sister pull him into a hug.

'They'll pay for what they've done,' she said.

Rowan had stayed in the doorway to Room 101. He watched until the smell of Kindred's burning flesh flooded his nostrils.

Rachel pulled back to look up into her brother's blank stare. 'Ro, are you okay?' Kindred's shrill scream through locked teeth stopped.

'I'm fine,' he said.

'Ro,' Hank called from a booth of automatic rifles. 'Suit up. We're moving out in fifteen.'

'I'll head through to Hades. Someone needs to scope out their headquarters to make way for the entry team,' Rowan volunteered.

'McCain won't see us coming,' Rachel said confidently.

'Conroy,' Lana corrected, stepping out from the apparel section. She was dressed in tight black jeans and a blue tank top. She pulled on a pair of fingerless gloves, then clipped on a belt with a holstered Desert Eagle pistol and spare clips. Finally, she took the hatchet she'd found in the Forest Realm, and pushed it into a sheath she had fashioned out of leather.

'I'll go with you,' she said to Rowan.

Rowan tilted his head to look at the unconventional melee weapon sheathed on Lana's hip. He recognised it to be an axe that elite soldiers had used during World War One.

'Thanks,' he said. 'But I'm going alone.'

Hank considered him for a moment. Having trained both Rowan and Rachel, he nodded proudly.

The team assembled on the port platform on top of the compound. A bright orange hue lit the horizon to herald the early morning. Hank inspected the formation of eight soldiers. He nodded to Jolie, who stood at attention towards the back with Lana and Rachel. He was glad to have an experienced medic on the mission.

'Each installation will be heavily defended.' Hank stopped to gaze across their faces. All stared into the rise and fall of the ocean waves. 'Anyone who has a clear line of site on the target, call it in. Destroy it if you can. The sooner we take out each site, the sooner we can move on to the next. Understood?'

The team confirmed loudly in unison and Hank tapped at the Shifter device at his wrist to initiate the portal relay.

The portal opened before them, expanding into a large, rippling ball of mercury. Following the double line leading into the sphere, Lana gazed across the sea to the golden arch rising from the water. She stared at its beauty, soaking in the new sun and tried to control her breathing, the way Rachel had trained her.

A major battle waited on the other side of the portal.

CHAPTER 36

Jolie ran, bending low to use rusted machinery as cover. Explosions shook the walls of the abandoned warehouse. Bullets flew through the air, bouncing off girders. Enemy machine guns pelted old car shells and conveyer belt networks with .50 calibre bullets.

Reaching a wounded trooper, Jolie began assessing the damage.

'My leg's torn up,' he groaned.

'You can still shoot,' said Jolie, applying fast-setting foam to staunch the bleeding. 'Cover me.'

While she was tying a bandage around the unit's leg, she heard heavy footfalls approaching. Her patient raised his handgun and fired at an SC soldier targeting them.

Once again, Hank heard the same phrase being repeated through his comms device. *No visual on target.* He swore, scanning for objects that resembled the installation.

'Four minutes left,' Rachel called through her receiver. 'Our first installation strike and we're almost out of time... This doesn't bode well for the other—'

An attack drone swooped at Rachel and launched a

missile at her. Rachel grabbed hold of the UC trooper taking cover beside her and pulled him to his feet. 'Incoming! Move! Move!'

As they vaulted over a mechanical assembly line and rolled across the ground, the missile detonated against the warehouse floor. Shards of metal flew against the walls, penetrating steel and busting out windows.

Lana climbed an elevated walkway, drew her hatchet, jumped up onto the handrail and dove off.

The drone dipped to one side and dropped a metre under Lana's weight. With her knees gripping the top ridge of the drone's hull, she pulled open the circuit compartment and chopped at the hardware until the drone shut down. It sailed to the floor and Lana threw herself clear before the craft exploded.

Lana landed in a break-fall roll on a rubber conveyer belt. She remembered something she had seen up on the walkway. A five-by-five metre platform was suspended below the ceiling of the warehouse. 'Possible target location on the platform above us. I repeat: possible target location.'

Rachel helped the soldier she had taken cover with to his feet. Hearing Lana's report, she commanded him to hand over the M72 LAW strapped over his shoulder. She extended the weapon lock into firing position, aimed at the suspended platform and squeezed the trigger.

Another nearby UC trooper fired a warhead. The platform was lifted into the ceiling by the double impact explosions. The suspension cables snapped and it came down. The portal installation crashed onto an empty car shell.

'Fire in the hole!' a UC soldier yelled, lobbing a C4 pack into the wreckage. With a deafening roar, it detonated.

'All units, the first installation has been destroyed,' Hank reported. 'Portal to the next location is open. Everybody out.'

Hank stopped to help Jolie carry the wounded soldier, then followed his squad members through the portal.

Planet Darwin
Branner Automated Machines Factory

Brad and Renee fired from mounted grenade launchers, pummelling the port side of a Sabre Company carrier ship that had broken through the UC fleet blockade.

'All units, concentrate fire on the carrier,' Brad ordered, watching a second enemy ship sail through the defence perimeter.

'This is Captain Lincoln. Four more Sabre Company ships have arrived. The blockade can't hold them.'

Renee left the mounted gun and called to Brad. 'Meet you at the jets!'

'Right behind you!' Brad shouted over the firing of artillery shells. Three rounds from the UC ground forces penetrated the hull of the first carrier ship and its port side ruptured with explosions. The propulsion burners keeping it in the sky lost power and the ship leaned into a spiralling descent.

Two SC escape pods sailed over Renee's head from the falling carrier. The impact of the colossal ship burying its nose into the ground threw her to her knees. One of the pods bounced across the landing strip and exploded, hurling chunks of metal and burning bodies against the side of the AM factory. The second pod ploughed into a docked cargo ship. The pod chamber door popped open. Renee took a pistol from her thigh holster and fired on the first enemy soldier to disembark.

Brad sprinted to the two available fighter jets and trained his rifle on the escape pod. 'Got you covered, go!'

Dropping into the cockpit of the craft, Renee started the engine. The ship rose, hovering over the ground. She watched Brad fire on the pod and run for the neighbouring jet. While Renee prepped the weapons systems, the jet craft engaged automatic decompression and life support. Renee steered the nose of the jet to the blockade, pushed the thrust control stick forward. The craft accelerated into a naught to one-hundred-and-sixty-kilometre ascent in just three seconds.

Flying over the UC fleet, Renee loosed twin torpedo rockets at one of the SC ships. The enemy craft shuddered when the explosions ruptured the stern exhausts.

Brad's jet swooped down alongside Renee and he fired a warhead missile into another carrier ship. The impact penetrated the craft's hull and it began to veer off course.

Blue pulse rounds showered down on the approaching enemy ships. An alien fighter craft flew into the fray.

'The Kiyol!' Renee squealed.

'It is I, Renee. We have brought ten cruisers to aid you,' Jihna said, firing her craft's engines to draw next to Brad's jet. She ordered an attack command to her fellow warriors in Kiyol and a swarm of fighter ships flew in, firing on every Sabre Company warship.

Hades

The scout drone exited the mercury sphere and commenced reconnaissance, heading for the area of structures atop of the rocky mountain side. It hovered low to the ground, scanning for a safe zone. Once the scan was complete, it sent the new coordinates back to Aqua Sierra, with a video feed and topographical readout.

Moments later, another portal expanded in the centre of the safe zone. Rowan stepped out of the rippling quicksilver. The drone flew on to the Sabre Company HQ buildings. Taking binoculars from his utility belt, Rowan scanned the rocky hillside of dry shrubbery. Monolithic stones towering over the land. Whirlwinds of red sand danced along the dunes, stretching out to the horizon. His eyes narrowed, settling on the large building complex, high on the mountain ridge.

Inside Sabre Company headquarters, General Dennis Conroy sat in his high-backed command chair, surveying the battle displayed across four large holo-screens. A team of field operators, seated along three rows of computer stations, monitored each battlefield, taking incoming reports from the SC Captains on the ground and in Darwin's airspace above the Branner AM factory.

'General.' An operator transferred the visual feeds from his console dashboard to Conroy's large screen. 'Three of our portal installations have been destroyed and our forces at Aqua Sierra are overwhelmed. Darwin as well, sir. The enemy have received reinforcements.' He brought up several street-view feeds of downtown Liberty. 'And we're sustaining heavy losses on Silica.'

The General's confident composure was shaken by the live footage. He glared menacingly at the scene before him. The people of Liberty—teachers, students, store owners—all marched with the UC soldiers. They were picking up weapons from fallen SC troops. Conroy's soldiers were being backed into a corner of a park square with very little cover and no means of retreat.

His aged skin stretched across his white knuckles as his fists clenched. 'Open all link portals. Issue a full retreat from Darwin and Aqua Sierra.'

An operator's monitor flashed an alert message and he reported it to his General. 'Sir, there are now only two portals remaining.'

CHAPTER 37

Planet Boson
Soumia Island

Sand rose into the air when mortar shells pounded the vast beach. Soldiers on both sides took cover behind dune buggies, trucks and supply crates.

Hank had been told by Council member Henin that the SC operative, Amanda, had let slip vital information. The mariner communities on Boson had requested aid—but not for resources.

Their community had been taken by Sabre Company. Christian McCain, now known to be Dennis Conroy, had kept the operation under wraps. A pilot managed to escape Boson by ship, only to be destroyed by an SC cruiser. But not before she managed to send a radio transmission to the nearest trade station. All communications channels were being jammed by Sabre Company, so the transmission was mostly static. The station passed it on as a request for aid.

Fiona was due to visit Boson. She would have been captured upon arrival.

Crouching beneath the mercury sphere expanding from the enemy portal installation, Hank set a charge timer. Bullets pelted the metal structure. 'Charge set. Two minutes. All units, exit our portal to the final target location.'

Rachel heaved a wounded soldier to her feet and called to Jolie, before offering words of encouragement. 'You're gonna be all right, soldier. We're almost there. One more to go.'

Jolie ducked under the unit's arm, taking her weight. She and Rachel guided the female AM unit to the portal, following Lana and the remaining soldiers as the sphere expanded.

Hank came running from the rear while the last officer disappeared into the rippling silver. He saw a figure appear in his peripheral vision and he dropped into a roll, avoiding a shower of bullets. Rising to his feet, he found the Sabre Company squad Captain blocking his retreat. The unit's arm muscles glistened in the sun. *CPT PACKER* was printed on his chest armour.

A mortar shell landed three metres away from them. Hank took advantage of the wave of sand thrown over Captain Packer and fired a shotgun shell into the soldier's chest.

Packer fell to the ground, rolled to his feet and pulled off his vest. Even a human built as big as Packer would have been winded. Instead, he strode forward, taking a huge knife from the sheath on his back.

Assuming he had incapacitated his target, Hank had headed to the portal. He heard heavy footfalls approaching, raising his rifle just in time to deflect Packer's blade.

Gripping Hank's shotgun with one hand, the soldier launched his boot into his opponent's stomach. The impact flung Hank into the side of a truck, the steel frame jarring his back and shoulders.

Hank threw himself sideways when Packer came down on him with his knife, rupturing the truck's fuel tank. Packer struck Hank across the face and raised his knee into his stomach.

Hank struggled to work the air back into his lungs. Lying on his back, he watched the Captain wrench the knife from the fuel cylinder. Barely aware of the petrol gushing over him, Hank saw the irregularities in the oversized blade and guessed the weapon to be Packer's own handy work.

The heavy-set machine man let out a bellowing laugh. 'What are you doing here, old man? You're not fit to fight.' He waited for Hank to stand, dripping in flammable fluid. The charge timer reached zero and the portal installation exploded. The transparent blast wave threw both Packer and Hank to the ground.

Staggering against the roll cage of a dune buggy, Hank tried to shake his sight back into focus. He quickly pushed away from the vehicle just in time, narrowly evading Packer's sideways slash. He took advantage of his opponent's mistake and punched Packer's face. Hank stepped onto the rear of the vehicle and dove across the SC Captain, bringing his knee into the side of Packer's head. The impact dislocated his jaw. Clutching his face in pain, Packer dropped his weapon.

Hank snatched Packer's knife from the sand before his enemy had the chance to reclaim it. The Captain sprang to his feet and charged. Dropping his shoulder, he slammed into Hank's chest.

Hank rolled across the sand and was lifted up by Packer's strong arms. Hank spat blood into the Captain's face.

Packer smiled through the red dripping over his mouth.

Hank slashed the Captain's arm tendons, broke free and brought his arm around the unit's neck in a strong headlock. Then, Hank dropped into a roll. Packer's body was hurled over Hank's back, falling heavily on the ground with a dull crack. Hank shook his opponent's limp skull, making sure he had snapped the AM unit's spinal column.

'Cap, let's go already! We're getting our asses kicked in here!' Lana called, leaning out of the open portal.

Hank wiped the blood from his mouth and chin. Groaning, he stood.

'Not bad for an old man,' he muttered to himself, as he followed Lana through the portal.

Twenty kilometres below the colony resource sector on a planet called Shale, gunfire echoed against the high walls of the mining quadrangle. Soldiers on both sides took cover behind machinery, carts on rails and piled support beams.

'What happened to you?' Rachel looked over Hank's beaten body, her nose twitching at the smell of petrol.

'SC Captain.' Hank shook sand from his hair, wincing as salt made the cut on his cheek sting. He peered over the giant shovel of the vehicle they were taking cover behind.

Rachel spotted at least four tunnel entrances to the quadrangle. 'We should split up—search each passage.' She pointed to the closest. 'Lana, you take that one. Hank and I will take the next and hopefully intersect with you.'

Lana sprinted into the clearing and took cover inside the first tunnel, before leaning out to fire her P90 on the SC mounted machine guns.

Rachel threw a smoke grenade to obscure her and Hank's path from the enemy. They made a run for their point of entry. As soon as they were inside, Hank pulled Rachel back against the wall of the tunnel. A line of flame shot through the passage, scorching the steel support beams and blackening the stone surface of the opposite wall.

'Thanks,' Rachel breathed, handing a flash grenade to Hank.

He pulled the pin and tossed the grenade hard against the wall to bounce it around the corner.

The SC soldier trained his flamethrower on the passage and watched the grenade roll across the ground at his feet. He staggered backwards when it blew, staring into white before a bullet pierced the top of his forehead. Rachel stepped over the unit's body and into the intersection of the tunnel passageways. She raised her dual pistols to fire on two approaching SC troopers. Hank pressed his back against hers and trained his sidearm on the rear openings.

'Just like old times, huh kid?' he said.

She smiled, listening to the echoing footfalls of approaching enemy units. 'You gonna miss this?'

'No. Not really.'

Lana crept along the rocky passageway towards an SC soldier who was guarding a staircase. Just before she reached him, she launched herself at the wall. Her feet found footholds and she ran up the side of the passage curve. Jumping, she tucked her knees and rotated her body just beneath the ceiling of the tunnel. She landed on top of the unit's shoulders, her knees either side of his ears. Squeezing her thighs together, Lana twisted her hips and snapped the soldier's neck. She rode him to the ground, turning at the sound of heavy footsteps descending the stairs.

The SC Captain of the mine installation reached the passageway. Seeing no sign of the guard assigned to the lower level, he spoke into his radio. No response.

'He took a dirt nap,' said Lana.

By the time the heavy-set Captain could turn around, Lana had leapt and kicked. The dusty sole of her boot was the last thing the Captain saw.

Lana jogged up the stairs and along a passageway, following a set of iron tracks around a bend. A slight breeze blew fine dust across the overhead lamps. Reaching the end of the passage, Lana nodded to Rachel and Hank when they arrived at the opposite end of a large open room.

Rachel peered around the wall of the passage exit to find an eight-foot metal figure standing motionless in the lamp light. The portal installation was active. A large mercury sphere was shining at the back of the room. Rachel returned to Hank's side and nodded confirmation.

'Target spotted,' Hank spoke quietly into his comms. 'All units secure upper-level tunnel at my position.'

'Hold up. Trouble.' Rachel peered back into the room. 'Some kind of mechanical suit. Heavy armour.'

Hank leaned across her to check it out. 'They hit us with Mechs in Liberty. Machine in a machine.'

'Matryoshka,' Rachel commented.

'Huh?' Hank stepped away and ordered an approaching UCAM unit to hand over his LAW rocket launcher.

'Never mind.'

Hank gave Rachel a confused look. He paused when he saw Lana stepping stealthily towards the portal installation.

'Lana,' Rachel hissed. 'What are you doing?'

'Lana, do not engage,' Hank ordered through his comms. He raised the LAW to his shoulder and prepared to fire.

Lana was creeping by the motionless metal suit, when its arm hydraulics churned and latched its steel hand over her shoulder. She struggled against the articulated metal fingers gripping her.

'The name's Hawk. Who might you be, little girl?' The muffled voice came through the helmet's mouth vent.

'Lana,' she groaned, prying at the machine's hand.

'Let me see here.' Hawk held out his free hand as though he were holding a clip board. 'Lana, Lana… nope,' said Hawk. 'Sorry, ma'am, your name isn't on the guest list.'

He lifted her from the ground and swung her back, as if preparing to pitch a baseball. He brought her forward to the point of release and threw Lana back the way she had come. She slammed into the wall and rocks crumbled over her as she fell to the ground.

Hank aligned the rocket to Hawk and was about to fire, when he saw Lana rise from the pile of crushed rock. Stones rolled off her shoulders and dirt-covered back. Her narrowing eyes gleamed in the lamp light.

'Well then,' said Hawk. 'You're made of… something else.' He marched towards her and a machine-gun arm attachment locked into position over his left hand.

Lana stepped out of the rubble and charged at him. She armoured her skin and leapt at the machine man, hurling her body into a corkscrew-spin to deliver two mid-air kicks. The first slammed the centre of Hawk's chest, second to his helmet. Lana landed on one foot, drew her hatchet, spun on her heel and struck Hawk's head with the back of her axe. The helmet came away from the soldier's head in two pieces, red AM fluid streaming from his broken nose. Lana ran to the link portal installation and planted a satchel charge.

'Fifteen seconds,' she called through her comms. 'Open exit portal now!'

Hawk was staggered. 'You wanna play? Let's play.' He lifted his arm, training the machine gun barrel on Lana. He planted his metal boots in the dirt and opened fire.

White-hot tracer rounds cut through the ground, throwing dust and stones into the air. Lana dove behind an empty rail trolley and hugged the dirt, while bullets pelted the steel container.

Hank stepped out of cover, aimed and sent the rocket flying at the Mech soldier. The missile struck Hawk's gun arm, the blast throwing him into the wall behind him. Before he hit the ground, the installation charge exploded and the blast wave pushed him through a support beam. Shrapnel pelted his exposed head.

The dust cleared and Lana approached the fallen soldier as the UC troops arrived, aiming their weapons at Hawk's broken body. The rocket had torn his arm away from his shoulder.

Lana's skin had returned to soft tissue. Her hair and clothing were thick with dust.

'Get to the portal,' she ordered, looking up as the roof supports began to give way. 'We're done here.'

Hawk coughed and spat a mouth full of battery fluid.

'You think you've won?' he said, but in a different voice.

It wasn't a vocal malfunction. Lana had heard that voice in her lessons about the Council. It was Christian McCain.

Despite being pinned down by a heavy support beam and having no motor control over his mechanical suit, Hawk continued to try to work himself free. 'This isn't over.'

It was him, the General of Sabre Company, Dennis Conroy. He was monitoring through the eyes of his soldiers. Somehow, he was able to assume control.

Lana took the Desert Eagle from her hip holster and stared into the soldier's eyes. She aimed the gun at his forehead and fired.

CHAPTER 38

Aqua Sierra

Professor O'Conner sat with Sam, Charlie and Lex, watching the monitor screens on the computer station level. The video feeds of the cameras on Glacier II were still running, so that they could document the Parabola.

Jin arrived from the stairs below. He saw one of the screens showing a pale, purple-lit sky.

'What are we looking at?' he said.

'The Parabola has entered the upper atmosphere,' Lex explained, her eyes fixed on the video feeds.

'Incredible.' Pete watched as the very matter of the mountain formations began to distort, collapse and crumble.

The ice and snow of Glacier II's surface turned to water and the Genesis Lab compound started to sink. Water washed over the lens of each camera. All they could see were ripples of light through steam. Then, the screens went blank.

'That's it,' Charlie said, saving the recording and the readings from the sensor data to his data pad.

'SC forces have retreated.' Jin made his way back down the stairs. 'I want everybody to stay below until I sound the all-clear.' He left them in time to see the elevator cage arrive at the Dome Room. Lana and Rachel disembarked, followed by Hank and Jolie.

'All Home Realm portal installations have been destroyed,' Hank reported.

'Well done, you guys.' Jin gave a sigh of relief. 'You've saved billions of lives.' His comms beeped a text transmission. 'Renee says Darwin is safe. Sabre Company forces retreated, presumably back to Hades HQ. There'll be a lot of heat there.'

Later in the infirmary, Pete reviewed the test results on the counteractive serum he had developed for Luke and Emma. He glanced over his shoulder when Sam returned from the holding cell corridor. 'How are they going?'

'Emma's only had six hours. That's about a week and a half with Garwyn. Luke seems to be all right. I think it's time we brought them together in the real world.' She spoke into her comms.

'Jolie, we're gonna need you at the holding cells.'

Lana had programmed her own spray-on suit and loaded it into the Kiyol machine. She stepped into the arch and it jetted the protective material over her body. Her suit did not cover her head. Instead, it took the form of a black, cropped tank top and black leggings. It also sprayed on fingerless gloves. When the spraying stopped, she stepped down and pulled on military boots.

After equipping her sidearm, Lana pushed the handle of the hatchet into its sheath. With her melee weapon hanging from her belt, she left the armoury and walked by an AM unit who was stocking up on ammunition. A fragmentation grenade and a flash bang grenade were on the armoury table before him. Lana concentrated and tried to enter the soldier's mind. She experimented with some simple instructions. *Choose the frag. Spin it on the table.*

The soldier placed his hand on the flash bang and paused. His hand left it and settled on the frag. After a moment of hesitation, he spun the grenade 360 degrees. He stopped it spinning, blinked twice, then looked over his shoulder self-consciously.

Sam held the door, while her father pushed a still unconscious Emma in a wheelchair into the corridor. The guards unlocked Luke's cell.

Jolie wafted ammonium carbonate on a cotton bud beneath each sibling's nose. Emma woke first. Her nostrils flared and she jerked away from the smelling salt.

'What is this? Where am I?' Emma shook her head. Her hands were strapped to the chair.

Luke woke coughing. He saw his sister wearing a blue medical apron. 'Emma, are you all right?' He strained his arms against the bed straps. 'Why am I tied down?'

'Just a precaution, Mr Palmer,' Pete explained.

'Luke?' Emma became still. Tears began to well in her eyes. 'Is... is this real?'

Pete rested his hand on Sam's shoulder. 'They're back.'

She was uncertain about Emma, but ordered the guards to untie them both.

As soon as they were freed from their restraints, Luke reached over and pulled his sister close. He moved along the bed, defensively pushing Emma behind him, glaring at the guards, Pete, Sam and Jolie. 'Who are you people? What did you do to her?'

Jolie kept her distance and spoke to him calmly. 'We're friends of Rachel and Rowan Navara. You and your sister are safe here. We had you connected to the Garwyn program, to bring back your memories.'

'Fiona Parker is here too,' said Jolie. 'Do you remember her?'

Luke nodded slowly. 'She joined the resistance.'

'She was captured and tortured, like you,' Jolie said. 'I gave both of you a serum that Pete developed, to help you combat what Dr Kindred gave you. Fiona won't need it. As far as I can tell, she went through accelerated psychological manipulation.

Any drugs she was given will be flushed out of her system within a couple of days.'

Jolie gently took Luke's wrist to check his pulse.

'Where are we?' asked Luke. 'Where's Rachel?'

'We're on Aqua Sierra,' said Sam. 'Rachel is prepping. She and the others are going to attack Dennis Conroy's headquarters.'

Jolie shone a small torch into each of Emma's eyes. 'Do you remember your time with Sabre Company? You must have undergone years of combat training to become an infiltration operative.'

'I did,' she said, struggling to put the pieces together. 'I was among others who were taken from their families. We were chosen to excel, because we're human.'

Jolie looked from Emma to Luke. 'It may take several months before you return to more normal, physical and mental states of health. I'll provide treatment, but you'll need to revisit Garwyn from time to time.'

Pete took out his remote console to check a shared update message from Jin. 'SC forces are still retreating to Hades.'

'Take me there.' Luke stood slowly, allowing his balance to return.

'You need to rest.' Sam gestured to Emma, who was still dazed and confused. 'Be with your sister.'

'No,' Emma spoke softly. Her head was beginning to clear. 'I can fight.'

'I really don't think that's a good idea,' Jolie cautioned.

Emma looked at Sam through her long red fringe. She was hurting. But she was angry.

'Okay,' Sam nodded, placing her hands on her hips. 'Let me show you to the armoury.'

'Sam.' Pete took his daughter's arm, surprised by her decision. 'They're in no condition to fight. We didn't cure them just to let them run off and get killed.'

She pulled him aside. 'Jolie will be with them.'

'Sam—'

'Dad, they need this,' Sam insisted. 'They were there. They lost everything. The people of Liberty won their freedom, while Luke and Emma were forced to live on as puppets. They need justice.'

CHAPTER 39

Hades

Two sentry guards on the exterior wall of Sabre Company HQ patrolled the east corner of the complex. Air trapped in the interior courtyard made the sand swirl and dance. SC troops exited portals, returning from their failed assaults on the Branner Factory, Otami Palace and Silica's Liberty building.

Rowan climbed a rope hanging from the concrete wall and heaved himself over the edge. He pulled the rope into a bundle around the grappling hook he had thrown from below. Then he moved silently along the sentry guards' path. When reached them, Rowan aimed his suppressed pistol and fired on one, then the other. Both guards dropped. Rowan moved to the edge of the wall and peered at the area below.

'Hank, I'm looking down on a courtyard of over fifty troops. If your team come up the wall, you'll have the advantage. Conroy has to be somewhere inside the complex.'

'Copy that.'

Taking the sniper rifle from his back, Rowan located another two sentries and lined them up in his crosshairs, before firing suppressed rounds to their heads. He accessed his wrist console and selected a rope ladder. As soon as it shimmered into form, he fastened one end to the wall ledge and unravelled its length over the edge to the ground below. Rowan climbed onto the ledge and descended. The light of a portal flashed beneath him and Rachel stepped out, speaking with Luke and Emma. Jolie followed as well, watching Emma closely.

'It's good to have you back, Luke.' Rachel hugged him.

Emma looked up when Rowan dropped down from the rope ladder. 'Is this your brother?'

Rowan smiled approvingly at their Kiyol spray-on armour.

'Welcome back, Luke,' he said, pulling him into a hug and slapping him on the back.

'Thanks, Ro. Good to see you again. This is my sister, Emma.'

'Pleasure to finally meet you.' He took her hand and nodded to Lana, who had arrived through the portal with Hank. 'I hear you and Lana had a bit of a throwdown.'

Emma rubbed the dull ache in her shoulder. 'I'm thankful that she found me.'

Rowan saw zip ties slotted into Emma's waist belt. He saw that the others had some as well.

'We're planning on taking prisoners?' he asked Hank.

Hank brow furrowed. 'If we can avoid any more bloodshed, we will.'

Rowan held his former Captain's concerned gaze, while he fought back the urge to argue. He nodded and turned back to the ladder to take the lead.

The team made its way up the wall. At the top, Hank signalled for every second soldier to split off along the opposite side. From their perimeter positions, Lana and Rachel trained their rifles on the enemy below.

Rowan, Luke and Emma passed through a door and descended the stairs leading into the compound.

'You're surrounded,' Hank called down to the Sabre Company troops. 'Lay down your arms immediately.'

The clatter of rifles being readied echoed against the walls of the windy courtyard.

Hank signalled for his team not to fire. He called down to the soldiers below again. 'I repeat: lay down your weapons!'

The lead SC Captain among the AM units was named Hiller. The radio clipped on his chest beeped and General Conroy's voice barked through the silence of the courtyard. 'What are you waiting for? Fire on the enemy!'

Hiller quickly turned the radio off, his eyes on the UC soldiers above. His face gleamed with the machine cooling fluid equivalent of human sweat. He had just arrived from Liberty. The scene there haunted him still. Liberty's people had outnumbered his men. Victory had been rendered unachievable. The fight Hiller was assigned to lead was over. Uncertainty for the future—for himself and for his men—interrupted the flow of information inside his machine brain.

'Captain Hiller?' The soldier beside him edged closer. 'Orders, Captain?'

Hot, salty wind blew over the outer walls. Lana watched the SC Captain, his eyes darting from his men to the UC soldiers, with their height advantage. She lowered her P90 and set it down on the concrete wall.

'Lana, what are you—' Rachel said, as her friend opened a portal.

Lana disappeared and reappeared a second later among the SC troops below. Rachel gasped when she heard a soldier fire a round at Lana's chest from point blank range.

'Hold!' Hank shouted. 'Nobody fire.' He called down to Lana, who stood motionless, with her left arm raised, her hardened, closed fist held close to her chest. 'Lana, stand down. Do not engage.'

All guns surrounding her were pointed at her head. The SC troops murmured in surprise and confusion. The unit who had fired on Lana stared, open-mouthed, while Lana walked towards Captain Hiller.

Standing less than a metre from the Sabre Company Captain,

Lana fixed her eyes on his and concentrated.

Hiller aimed his rifle at Lana's heart. The comms speakers above each corner of the courtyard whined before General Conroy's voice returned. 'All units, fire on the enemy! That is an order!'

The Captain's grip tightened around his gun, his trigger finger ready. 'Belay that order! All units hold!'

Lana rolled a bullet in the open palm of her left hand and held it up between finger and thumb. The .762 calibre round she had caught from the SC soldier's AK47 gleamed in the sunlight. Lana spoke to the man through her mind. 'The killing ends now.'

The inhibitor chip inside Hiller's brain was unable to block Lana's signal. He detected network commands coming from his General. Conroy was trying to assume control.

'Order your men to stand down.'

'You're inside my head,' he stuttered. 'How?'

Lana gazed along the top of the courtyard wall and back to Hiller. 'Surrender and we will fix what Conroy has done to you. All of you.'

Hiller could no longer hear his General's voice over the loudspeaker. He couldn't hear the blowing wind—only Lana's voice. 'You'll shut us down. Throw us in a scrap heap.'

'You have my word; you will all live on to serve with us.'

Hiller lowered his rifle. 'All units stand down!'

The SC soldiers were disarmed and prepared for transport. Rachel found Lana alone in a corridor, away from the courtyard. She was leaning against a crate, wiping blood from her nose.

'Lana, how did you—' She saw the blood. 'Are you all right?' Tapping at her comms, she started to call Jolie.

'I'm all right.' Lana tossed the bullet across the ground, watching it clink against the wall of the corridor. 'Just a little dizzy.'

'You were in the soldier's mind. How? You were three feet away from him.'

'Figured he'd start shooting if I tried to touch him.' Lana shrugged. 'I've found I can do it from a distance as well.' She leaned against the crate. 'I remembered from my lessons with the Professor… neutrinos are in the air and they can pass through solid matter.'

'Huh?'

'Neutral energy particles. We can't see them, but they're there. So, I thought maybe—'

'You created a connective pathway through the particles between you and the AM unit.' Rachel nodded while the concept sank in. 'Huh…'

'Conroy can control his soldiers. I had to stop him.' A wave of nausea caused Lana to wobble.

'I'm gonna stick to touching people from now on.' She paused, realising how that sounded.

Rachel heard a report from Luke come through their comms. 'Let's go. They've found the Command Station.'

Rowan, Luke and Emma entered the Sabre Company Command Station. The field operators had evacuated. The screens were blank and the servers had been wiped with a localised electromagnetic pulse. Gears churned and a high-backed chair rotated on an elevated platform in the centre of the room. Dennis Conroy sat holding a Luger pistol. He had given up on trying to regain control of his soldiers. He needed his technical team to reprogram the units, but they had fled.

'It's over Conroy.' Rowan stepped around the computer stations, his sidearm trained on the General. 'Drop the gun.'

Straight-backed and proud, Conroy stepped down from the command podium and walked to the tall windows overlooking the sand dunes.

'You think you've won,' he said. He entered the light beaming through the glass. Dust particles drifted around his grey uniform. 'You haven't.'

'Drop the gun.' Luke approached, while his sister watched the other entry points to the room.

Conroy shrugged his shoulders, deciding to oblige. He set the pistol down on the window ledge. He then raised his arm slowly and pressed the comms button on his wrist console. 'Mr Williams, would you care to join us?'

Emma steadied her aim on the double doors at the other side of the room. They all listened to the hiss of pressure pistons and jolting hydraulics. Heavy, thudding, metallic boots grew closer outside. The sound stopped and the whining of a spinning mini gun barrel rose in volume.

'Down!' Luke yelled.

He pushed Rowan to the floor and Emma rolled behind a concrete pillar. The flash of tracer rounds ripped through the doors.

The firing ceased and red daylight poured in through the swiss-cheesed door. Boots pounded again before the shoulder of a mechanical suit busted through, ripping the wooden doors from the wall.

The machine suit marched into the room, followed by two female elite operatives in grey body suits. A mini gun was attached to the stump of one of its mechanical arms.

Jericho Williams' muffled voice spoke through the metal helmet. 'Why, if it isn't the born-again freedom fighter.' The machine gears whined when he turned to face Emma. 'And who's this?'

Williams' removed his helmet with a gloved hand. He dropped the helmet to the ground and a loud clang echoed off the concrete floor. 'Emma Palmer.'

'Now, if you'll excuse me.' Dennis Conroy retrieved his Luger from the window ledge and tapped at his wrist console. 'I'll let you all become better acquainted.' He saluted Williams and a portal opened behind him.

When Williams returned the salute, Emma saw the trigger mechanism for the mini gun inside his palm.

'Luke, take Conroy!' she shouted, firing at the trigger attachment.

Luke ran along the row of computers towards the portal, as the General entered the sphere. Jericho Williams aimed the mini gun and tried to fire but Emma had successfully severed the trigger switch.

Luke threw himself into the rippling mercury and the portal retracted into thin air. He rolled across a clay surface, slamming into an iron cylinder lying on its side. Searching his immediate surroundings, Luke found no sign of Conroy. But he recognised the suburban houses beyond the miles of desert sand. A crew of bulldozers and machine operated diggers ploughed the dilapidated structures. All around him lay fracking towers, gas mining drills and mounds of foul- smelling clay. Nodding donkeys stood in the distant oil field, abandoned since the liberation of Silica.

Luke gazed across the desert stretching around the outskirts of Liberty. A single-pilot air craft sat by the edge of the drilling site. It was waiting for Dennis Conroy.

CHAPTER 40

Williams released the lock at his elbow and pulled the mini gun attachment from the metal stub connection. Wielding it in one arm, he powered up the weapon and fired on Emma and Rowan. The two took cover behind the command platform as the chair was torn to shreds.

'Too much heat for Hank's team to teleport in,' Rowan shouted over the deafening assault, ducking low behind the circular platform. 'They'll have to rappel in through the windows. I'll distract this asshole, while you take the elite.'

'On three,' Emma confirmed and counted with Rowan.

She spotted the two slender, grey-clad operatives, waited for the count, then dashed from the platform. The female elite duo advanced, unarmed. Emma fired on the first and the operative threw her body into a mid-air barrel roll, narrowly dodging the bullets. She saw the other woman approach in her periphery, having been free to run and reach Emma. The operative leapt into a fly-kick, knocking the assault rifle out of Emma's hands before she could re-aim. Emma pulled her side-arm, aimed, but her shot only grazed her attacker's arm. The partner operative axe- kicked her arm. She ducked the next blow, and dove under a second fly-kick attempt from the wounded one, sliding across the dust-coated floor. She rose into a backwards crescent flip, avoided a sweeping leg and landed into a roll.

Rowan fired burst rounds at Williams' torso while he ran along a row of computer stations. Williams shielded his exposed head with his free arm. He fired blindly, sending tracer rounds through computers, cutting into loadbearing concrete pillars. Rowan slid against the south entrance door, pushed away from it into a sprint and flanked Williams.

The mechanical suit was slow. Williams struggled to reposition his feet fast enough under the weight of the mini gun, so that he could face his opponent.

Slinging his rifle over his shoulder, Rowan unsheathed his combat knife and jumped up onto Williams' back. Williams let go of his weapon and grabbed Rowan's arm. Pistons beneath the armour plating hissed and the mechanical arm threw Rowan across the room. Rowan crashed through computer screens and rolled across the station floor.

Emma took a flick-kick to the stomach, blocked the next high-kick and stepped forward into a straight punch, knocking her opponent off her feet. She leaned forward over her knees, trying not to vomit after the blow she had taken. Turning to check on Rowan, Emma saw him lying motionless on the floor and called out to him.

The partner operative struck Emma across the face, took her into an arm grapple and held her neck. The woman's forearm dug into Emma's throat. Pressed tightly against the woman's chest, Emma struggled to free herself. She threw the back of her elbow across the elite's face and pulled herself free. The other operative approached. Emma jumped sideways, scissor-locked her legs over her stunned opponent's head and swung her inverted body an inch over the concrete floor. Then she released her hold and threw the woman into a mid-air roll.

The partner operative yelled in frustration as her team member's body slammed into her, throwing her backwards across the floor. Turning at the sound of articulating machine hand hydraulics, Emma watched Williams reach for the mini gun.

'Very impressive, Ms Palmer,' Williams remarked, taking hold of the gun. 'We trained you well.' He saw Rowan lift himself from beneath an overturned chair. If he was quick enough, he could cut down both of his opponents before either produced a firearm.

Ropes dropped down the windows outside. Hank, Rachel and Lana rappelled down, each placing explosives in breach position. Shards of glass flew across the room upon detonation, showering the broken computers. The team swung into the station in unison.

Rowan fired a shot at Williams to get his attention.

'Let it go,' he said, as the bullet bounced off Williams' armour.

Williams watched the new arrivals, who were vigilant yet hesitant. He knew they needed him alive. His eyes fell upon Lana.

'So, you're the golden child—O'Conner's secret prize.'

How does he know about me? Lana thought, glaring at Williams, her trigger finger itching to ruin the man's smug face.

Williams pressed a button on the left breast plate of his suit. Rachel looked to Emma. 'Did he just—'

'Get out. Get out now!' Emma yelled, while a canned male voice spoke over the station comms.

'Self-destruct sequence initiated. Ten seconds until detonation.'

Emma ran straight for Williams, who was retrieving the heavy machine gun from the floor. She stepped lightly along the metal arm of his mechanical suit, dropped her knees either side of Williams' head and brought her elbows down into the man's crown, knocking him unconscious. She rode the suit to the floor, as the loss of pilot control caused it to collapse.

'Go!' Lana shouted over the evacuation siren. 'Emma and I will get Williams out.'

Rowan, Hank and Rachel used a portal to teleport back to the courtyard to organise evacuation of both the UC and Sabre Company AM troops.

Silica
Abandoned Fracking Field

Luke edged along the curved steel hulls of containment towers. The towers had been toppled and lay at random angles. The wind blew from the desert and salt lakes, creating eerie noises as it explored the hollows of abandoned equipment and tinkered with loose fencing.

Luke saw the shadow of a figure at his feet. As he turned to face the sun, Conroy jumped down from a container, striking Luke's back with his knee. Luke's rifle clattered across the ground. Rolling onto his side, he pulled a pistol from his hip holster and fired on the General. Conroy raised his arm in time to deflect the bullet with the Shifter on his wrist. Before he could fire back with his Luger pistol, the console screen beeped a malfunction warning and generated a portal in front of him. It expanded and retracted in two seconds, sucking both men into a random teleportation.

Dropping from five feet in mid-air, Luke and Conroy fell onto a stage platform. They immediately covered their ears at the intense volume of drumming, a base guitar and screaming vocals. Conroy staggered to his feet, searching for his gun.

Luke stared out at a crowd of two thousand people, jumping up and down to the band playing heavy metal music. Conroy spear tackled him and he tumbled through a mounted banner. The Shifter activated another portal and the two were pulled from the stage and teleported to the roof of the Palmer Building in Liberty.

Luke tackled Conroy to the ground, tore the device from his wrist and threw it over the edge of the roof. He pressed his boot down on the General's chest, pinning him close to the edge of the roof.

Conroy laughed. 'You'd best kill me, Palmer.'

'Conroy,' Luke puffed, momentarily taken aback by the sight of the City of Liberty, reclaimed by the UC. He barely recognised it. 'Everybody here will know that the man who turned Silica into his own personal empire is nothing but an insane megalomaniac.'

Conroy chuckled. 'It kills you, doesn't it, knowing that your parents just lay down and took it like the rest of them, too afraid to stand up to the Big Bad Corporation.'

Luke used a zip tie to bind Conroy's wrists and pulled him roughly to his feet.

'Once we realised there was nothing we could do to stop the Wealth Sacrifice and Redistribution Initiative, we decided to go dormant,' Conroy said, spitting blood. 'Bide our time while those poxy, tree-hugging morons went about building their "Universal Community".'

The wind blew his thinning grey hair. Sweat gleamed from his brow. He glared down at the ant- like traffic of people returning to the city. Civilians were assisting soldiers and emergency personnel with the clean-up.

'We had it all worked out,' said Conroy. 'Reclamation. Take it all back, restore our world, govern the people.'

Luke's grip on Conroy's arms tightened while he glared at the man he hated most, the man responsible for the deaths of so many.

'Do it, Palmer,' Conroy said, as though reading Luke's mind. He edged closer, the toes of his black leather shoes overlapping the platform ledge. 'Tell them I jumped.' His torn, grey uniform flapped in the wind. The General closed his eyes and waited.

Raising a hand behind the man's back, Luke paused, breathing heavily. He stepped behind him and locked both arms around Conroy's head and neck. Unable to speak, the

General struggled for a moment, his limbs shaking against the strain on his spine.

Luke dropped Conroy's unconscious body onto the roof and took the remote comms device from his pocket.

'Rachel, I have the General.'

CHAPTER 41

Three days later

The sun shone down through the packed streets of Liberty. A cool breeze flowed among the tall buildings. People crowded around the podium before the Liberty building. Brad and Renee urged them to remain behind the barriers. Everybody was eager to see the men who had enslaved them for so many years brought to justice. News crews had arrived and camera operators recorded the scene, while reporters described the growing atmosphere, broadcasting to every television in every home across the populated galaxy.

Meg Green stood by the podium platform. 'We're here at the Palmer Building in Liberty, where just days earlier, UC soldiers fought side-by-side with the people of this city, against an attack staged by the militant group known as Sabre Company.

'Senior Council member Christian McCain will be brought before the people and taken into custody to stand trial before the Universal Community Courts. McCain is now known to be Dennis Conroy, the man responsible for enslaving the people of Silica.' She turned to see a group of six UC soldiers step up to the platform, accompanied by Renee and Brad. A portal appeared and expanded its mercury sphere. 'The crew who risked their lives to apprehend all members of Sabre Company are arriving now.'

Captain Henry Drake stepped out of the portal, followed by a group of four UC soldiers who escorted Dennis Conroy to the edge of the platform. Conroy stared at the thousands of people filling the street intersection. He tried to stand proud, but fear was beginning to take hold. His bottom lip trembled and his eyes watered, unprepared for the sight of so many people. They had fought and won against his soldiers. And now they had come for him.

A man standing at the front raised his right shoe over his head and threw it at Conroy. He raised his left and threw it as well. Conroy managed to avoid the first, but the second landed with its heel against the centre of his chest. The crowd roared triumphantly and the UC soldiers pulled him away.

Meg Green continued to report.

'The taskforce who achieved today's victory were also successful in capturing Dennis Conroy's second-in-command, Jericho Williams.'

Rachel, Lana, Jolie and Lincoln stepped out of the rippling sphere, escorting Williams across the podium.

The crowd's cheer rose into a ground-shaking roar when Luke and Emma Palmer appeared from the mercury, followed by Fiona Parker. The three ex-freedom fighters waved to their people, and the crowd began chanting: *Freedom, Justice and Liberty!*

The man who had lost his arms during the resistance was guided up the steps to the stage by his wife. Rachel held out her hand to him. He squeezed it gently, his bionic arms articulating his every command.

Rachel took a moment to hold her emotion. She had made a promise to these people. She had made a promise to all members of the resistance, to find those who had been taken.

'We found her,' she said, stepping aside to reveal a young woman standing behind her. 'Camilla, come say hello to your aunt and uncle.'

The twenty-year-old approached slowly, tears welling.

'Cam?' The old couple froze, staring at their niece's beautiful green eyes. Camilla rushed over to them, and they held each other and wept.

Fiona introduced Council member Henin, who would address the crowd.

'Fiona, thank you,' Henin said, taking Fiona's hand, 'for your strength and your courage.'

'It was an honour to perform my duty, ma'am,' said Fiona.

Henin approached the microphone. Luke and Emma joined her and they all turned to face Rachel, Lana, Hank and the rest of the team involved in defeating Sabre Company.

'With your undying commitment to uphold our values,' Henin's voice echoed through the streets, 'we have overcome our oppressors yet again. Thank you, all of you.'

The crowd cheered from every corner of the intersection. Children seated on their father's shoulders waved as they gazed across the sea of city dwellers.

While she waited for the crowd to settle, Henin soaked in the atmosphere of love and triumph.

'We, the members of the Council, have served our full term here in your wonderful city,' she continued. 'Tomorrow, we will depart for Earth. There, in the nominated city of Baghdad, we will transfer our duties to the new Council and the next term will begin. But before we leave, please allow us to celebrate with you, on this glorious day.' She paused, giving the crowd time to express their excitement and joy.

'What you have all proved, to yourselves and to every person in the galaxy, is that we, the people, cannot be defeated,' Henin said.

She welcomed Henry Drake to the podium.

A lone figure on top of a building across the street watched the Captain approach the microphone.

'On behalf of the Universal Community,' said Hank. 'I would like to express my gratitude for the aid our allies provided during this conflict. Thank you to the Kiyol and thank you to the Laicians.'

The watcher observed the two representatives from vastly different worlds. Jihna of the Kiyol and Prince Ohkwai Chillo of the Laicians stood side-by-side. Although Chillo was only present in holographic form, his image was projected in high definition.

Hank addressed the two aliens. 'It has been an honour to be your ally, my friends. Together, we will continue to aid one another and learn from one another.'

From her position on the stage, Lana thought she saw a lone silhouette on the rooftop of the building across the street. She brought her hand up to her brow to block the sun. She could see now that it was a man and she became suspicious when he turned abruptly and walk away.

From his position across the street, Sentinel Feen of the alien race, Raekeem, turned his head in the direction of the cheers from the crowd below. Sharp bones protruded from each of his elbows, his bare arms pale against his black uniform.

The small pupils in Feen's white eyes gazed across the desert horizon. When he turned away, his lips parted to reveal sharp teeth. Feen raised his chin and licked the air with a snake-like tongue. He caught the scent of salt, and he didn't like it. Loud cheers rose again and he looked back once more, glaring through the harsh sunlight.

'See you soon, Realm of Three Kingdoms.'

Black cloud tendrils slithered around him, expanding in mass to swallow Feen whole. The clouds rolled inward and the tendrils tightened into a shrinking ball, until it vanished.

To be continued in...

ENTER PORTAL 2:
Attack of the Raekeem

9 781763 787209